LETTERS
CHLOE

LETTERS TO CHLOE

Stefan Gerrard

This book is a work of fiction.
In real life, make sure you practise safe sex.

First published in 1995 by
Nexus
332 Ladbroke Grove
London W10 5AH

Copyright © Stefan Gerrard 1995

Typeset by TW Typesetting, Plymouth, Devon
Printed and bound in Great Britain by
BPC Paperbacks Ltd

ISBN 0 352 330021 X

Contents

Prologue	1
Control	6
Candlelight	13
The Birthday Gift	19
Beginnings	31
Beginnings 2 – Uncle Cedric	44
Beginnings 3 – Swimming Lessons	54
The Interview	62
The House	73
Preparation	85
Amanda	91
Chapter and Verse	103
Fresh Air Is Good for You	109
For Exercise	115
With These Rings	128
Arrangements	139
The Fitting	141
If It Itches . . .	149
Keep Fit	157
Groomed	170
Shopping	179
Camille	189
Punished	203
A Trial Offer	214
Prepared	230
Circles	233

Prologue

The tall windows and Regency façade of Claybourne Mansions overlook a quiet, well-kept square on the north side of London's Brompton Road, in the warren of largely unknown squares, crescents, terraces and quiet mews which lie between that road and Cromwell Road, the main thoroughfare leading westwards out of the great capital, towards Heathrow airport. Not far from Sloane Square, heartland of the wealthy and fashionable, the elegant houses which form Claybourne Mansions and other such properties in the Square and its near neighbours have – after a period of decline into subdivision and occupation by the descendants of those who might once have worked as servants to the original residents themselves – been rejoined, rejuvenated and most of all re-elevated, socially speaking, to the highest ranks of respectability. With refurbishment has come rehabilitation of the most coveted kind.

The Mansions now form a complex of self-contained managed apartments, mostly on short-term lettings to wealthy clients who wish for a comfortable but temporary home in the capital, secure, discreet, anonymous and above all exclusive. Each block shares functional utilities and serviced facilities – such as gymnasium, swimming pool, secure private garden – of the sort found in a top-grade hotel.

Tenants move in, stay for a few months, move out. Some of the apartments are used by their wealthy owners, who themselves have probably never set foot therein, as guest accommodation to be offered, without rent, to friends, business contacts or others to whom such hospitality might be appropriate. Some are occupied by families (although

1

rarely, if ever, with small children) on extended visits to the capital. A few, a very few, because the managing agents for properties such as Claybourne Mansions are particular indeed in ensuring that no whiff of scandal or impropriety might touch the carefully vetted clientele, are occupied by the discreet and usually long-term mistresses of rich, powerful and occasionally famous (but more usually very private) patrons. In at least one instance of suitably modern role reversal, the 'mistress' is not female but male, the patron a wealthy woman of considerable social and some political standing.

And in Claybourne Mansions, the letters which form the core of this book were found. One of the apartments had recently been vacated and, prior to its re-letting, was in the process of redecoration. The letters, in a locked briefcase of maroon leather, the locks secure, well manufactured and of the combination variety, had been left, evidently by accident, with a pile of discarded personal ephemera of the sort that a departing tenant will often leave behind, to be disposed of by whomever the new tenant brings in to clear out and redecorate the rooms.

The case, still locked, was brought by one of her employees to the well-known and fashionable interior designer re-working apartment 16A and she, having failed through the agency which handles the mansions to discover the identity or whereabouts of the departed tenants (absolute discretion is a hallmark of the manner in which the management of Claybourne Mansions, and others of its ilk, is conducted) had little alternative but to force the locks herself, in the hope at the least that the contents might reveal the identity of their rightful owner, and thus be properly returned.

The briefcase contained only letters – these letters – and the letters revealed both much and nothing about either their originator or their recipient, who was, presumably, the out-going tenant. Further discreet enquiries uncovered no further leads, while deeper study of the letters gave no further clues as to the identity of those whom they concerned.

So the letters might have been forgotten, save for their becoming the subject of conversation at a supper party some months after their original discovery. That supper party was attended on the one hand by the interior designer and on the other by an editor of a publishing house.

Hence the present book.

Yet who was – or is – Chloe? And what has become of her? Is she indeed real, and are the letters themselves real? That the reader must judge for herself, and for himself. If indeed the letters and the characters to whom they allude are real, then they describe a regime fantastical by the stretch of any imagination. And if not real, then they are the product of an imagination no less fantastical.

The letters, written with such directness, in the second person and in most cases in the compelling present tense, devoid in the most part of the banalities of day-to-day trivia which pad out so much of personal correspondence, in themselves both describe the remarkable migration of Chloe – whoever she be – from carefree modern woman to powerful enigma, at once controlled on the most intimate and daily basis and yet in evident ultimate control of both her own destiny and that of those immediately around her, and at the same time form a remarkable diary. So remarkable a diary, in fact, that it seems impossible that one person should know so much about another, particularly when the tone and context suggests that Chloe herself does not know, nor want to know (indeed the strong implication is present that she deliberately avoids discovering) the identity of their author. Doubtless Chloe guesses – but when, at what stage? She apparently plays the game to the very end.

Since none of the letters is addressed, and only one – the last – is signed, we have little enough on which to base our detective work.

Chloe we may take to be a woman probably in her mid to late twenties; a successful, self-contained woman with her own business career. It is a career, however, she appears willing either to give up, or at least put on hold, so as to undertake her journey at once of self-discovery and of self-surrender.

Of the author of the letters, it appears simple to say – since his is the signature appended to the final letter – that he is the man Stephen. Yet curiously in such a circumstance Stephen does not appear in the letters – hence in the story – until what we must assume to be several months have passed. None of the letters bears a date, another cloud in the sky of the would-be detective.

So who is this Stephen? And did he write all the letters? If the last, then he must have had an uncanny insight into Chloe's world before she realised she had met him; if not, then who wrote the early letters, and when did Stephen take over, both as author and as puppet-master?

Yet Stephen himself seems too simple an explanation, too pat a solution. There is too much of *The Story of O* about Stephen (his very name, not the least) and his relationship with Chloe, and – on the basis at least of the foregoing theory – of his relationship with Chloe's lover, for him to be truly real. Students of the fictional genre to which *The Story of O* belongs will also recognise within the letters allusions and references to similar if less celebrated works, as if whoever wrote the letters, and orchestrated Chloe's journey, quite intentionally courted parallel, deliberately contrived imitation. It can hardly be coincidence, for example, that the groom Pelham who exercises Chloe's friend Amanda shares a relatively unusual name with another celebrated tutor: that of Thomasina in the book *An English Education*.

The assumption must be that the author and the puppet-master are one and the same person. For the letters to reflect a literal truth, this pupper-master must be both very rich and close to omniscient – a fantasy popular enough to suggest that the letters might not be wholly for real.

One theory, perhaps the most plausible, offered around that supper table was that the letters were at one and the same time both real and imaginary: real letters written for Chloe by a lover, but imaginary in their content, written to titillate, provide a framework for love games perhaps – but on no account to be taken as a literal description of actions and events.

That the letters were written by her lover for a lady is, perhaps, the most plausible explanation of all – and one which prompted one woman present at that supper party to comment, a touch wistfully, one thought: 'In that case, lucky lady.'

Whatever their origin, whatever became of Chloe, and whatever the reality of her situation, the letters to Chloe are here presented for the reader to decide for herself the truth of the enigma.

The letters are arranged, as far as can be judged from their content and context, in chronological order. Such editing as has been necessary to translate them to book form has been kept to the barest minimum, and nothing has been added either within the letters themselves, or by way of footnote or conjunctive speculation. They are simply as Chloe received them.

Control

The telephone rings, you answer. It is your lover.

'Are you alone?'

'Yes.'

'Are you ready?'

'Yes.'

Ready for what? The telephone sits on a low table, a straight-backed chair beside it. Your lover gives you instructions. You obey. You return to the telephone, and place the clothes pegs by the phone.

You speak into the telephone, and listen. Of course, you have already guessed what you are going to be told to do, but you prefer to play the game step by step, as does your lover. You give no thought to what the final instructions will so obviously be, or whether or not you will obey them. To think ahead is to invite decision-making, and decisions are not as intriguing as anticipation. There is no question of obedience, or disobedience: the concepts are not relevant. Your lover has no authority over you so the question of obedience, or disobedience, does not arise.

Again you set the telephone down, carefully, and stand beside the chair. The blouse has seven buttons down the front, and two at each wrist. When they are undone you pull the blouse from the waistband of your skirt and twist it off your shoulders, with an action that causes your breasts to tremble, heavily.

The house is warm, but even so the caress of air on your bare breasts rouses your nipples from their soft unconcern. Half awake, they begin to harden, although not yet fully erect. You hang the blouse over the chair back and sit down, lifting the telephone again.

'I have done that.'

Your lover gazes at you with his mind's eye, and you hold yourself still for his lingering inspection. You are proud of your breasts, of their shape and soft-firm heaviness, which is why you prefer to leave them unsupported. It is one of your lover's earliest recollections of you, of the way your breasts moved under the silk dress you wore. He still enjoys simply watching you move towards him through a crowd, or turn in a restaurant. The movement of your breasts can hold him spellbound. He can never meet you without reaching for and holding your breast, which you will always readily allow.

'Make sure your nipples are stiff. They need to be fully erect.' For what? You know, but do not let yourself know you know. You run your finger tips over your breast, rolling your nipple gently. It has a will of its own, and grows under your fingers, stiff and rubbery. You have never been sure whether you really like your nipples like this, or whether you prefer them more full and rounded, softer, as they are when more relaxed. When your breasts are bare, as they are now, you generally think they look better when the nipples are softer; it gives them a ripeness which completes the sexuality of the bared breast's shape.

Yet when clothed, you always enjoy it when your nipples show through the fabric of blouse or dress. It announces your femininity, emphasises your independence. Sometimes, you deliberately leave the jacket of your suit open when walking in the street so as to allow the fresh air to harden the tips of your breasts. More than once, you have deliberately – although you admit it to yourself only with smiling reluctance – allowed yourself to be taken the few steps to the restaurant by a client without your topcoat or jacket, knowing that by the time you reach the restaurant the cold air will have shaped your nipples flint-hard. They tingle and hurt in the cold, and jut conspicuously through your blouse. The fact that you frequently do not wear a bra to work, despite your boss's express instructions to the contrary, merely enhances the effect.

You squeeze hard with your finger and thumb, and the almost silent intake of breath tells your lover, who knows you so well, exactly what you are doing.

He merely says, 'harder – I shall tell you when to stop.'

How does he know the exact moment when you want to stop? Because he is your lover.

The tip of your breast is hot, tingling and – yes – sore. It feels tender and you can feel that your other breast, untouched, is no less aroused. You know what is coming next, but you groan aloud when he tells you to do it.

You have to put the telephone down, and your hand trembles slightly as you squeeze the arms of the clothes peg and push the open jaws over your nipple. Finger and thumb of your left hand pull the tough, tender flesh fully into the open jaw and you release the arms as gently as possible.

Even so it burns. It hurts. It stabs – yet you live.

Your lover has heard your gasp as you applied the tiny devil to yourself. His mind's eye can see your quickened breathing, see the tightness of your smile, watch the way the rapid rise and fall of your ribcage makes the peg quiver. Like you, he ignores the incongruity of its domestic mundanity, concentrates on its symbolism. You know that, at the other end of the telephone, could you but reach, you would find your lover already aroused at the mere thought of you. It is something you find not at all unpleasing.

You lift the telephone again.

'Yes?'

'Now the other one.'

'No, please. Let me take it off.'

'The other one.'

You perform the same service for your other breast, raising your shoulder slightly as you apply the biting caress. You hold your breasts in your hands, sucking your breath in between your teeth, your head flung back, your white neck curved. Your mouth opens and you breath out noisily. Your torso curves tautly. You are very, very beautiful. Only the sound of your lover's voice, distantly, remotely, brings you back to the instant, to now. You have to pick the telephone up from the table again to hear him properly. As you raise the instrument to your ear your forearm accidentally catches the clothes peg that grips the tip of your left breast, tugging sideways, twisting slightly. The peg springs free from your arm, holding tightly to your flesh. You gasp, aloud.

'Have you done both of them?'

'Yes.' Your lover can hear the breathlessness in your voice. 'I don't like it, I want to take them off –'

'No. Leave them. Just sit there. I'll call you back.'

He has gone. The phone is dead. You put it back in its cradle.

You could of course simply remove them. They hurt. It is a bearable hurt, but only just bearable. It is not a pleasant hurt, the sort you used to give yourself as a child when a tooth was lose, pushing against it to see if you could bear to push it right out. This hurts sharply, and you realise your eyes are watering.

It is too silly to be sitting here, bare to the waist, with a clothes peg attached to each nipple, your breasts heaving. You are even breathing quite noisily now, gasping. Why don't you take them off? You could just squeeze the ends of the pegs, quickly, and lift them off your nipples, away from the twin cones of your proud, out-thrust breasts. The hurt would go away.

Why have you arched your back? It merely makes your breasts thrust forward even more. They jut from your torso without the slightest suggestion of sagging, despite their obvious heaviness.

The best place for your hands is gripping the sides of the chair. It seems to make the hurt bearable, and it stops you touching the pegs. You have been doing it without thinking about it ever since you put the receiver back in its cradle. The telephone rings again.

'Yes?'

'Are they still there?'

'Yes.'

'A moment more. Tell me about it.'

'Please. Its awful. Tell me to take them off. Please. I can't bear it – I don't like it.'

9

'In ten seconds. You can take them off in just a few more seconds. Seven seconds from now. Hold on for a moment more. Think of me . . . think of me. Two more seconds. All right. Take them off.'

You do it gingerly, afraid of causing yourself more hurt. It really is sore, not like it appears in books at all.

'God, I hate you.' With one hand you cup the end of your punished breast, pressing your palm against the crushed nipple. The sharpness of the hurt has already gone, and the ache is almost pleasant – so pleasant that you are tempted for a moment to do the whole thing again, to clamp the peg over the end of your nipple again. It is crazy.

'Does it still hurt?'

'Not so much.'

'Was it bad?'

'Awful. I hate you.'

'You are very brave. I wish I was there to see.'

'I love you too, bastard.'

'Now, now, language. You'll have to be punished.'

'Ummh, yes please.' You both laugh. You talk for a moment or two more, the tension easing and the excitement draining away, replaced by comfort. He will be in London next week, you will meet for a drink. He has his life, you have yours. This is where you meet. You do not want more.

The conversation finishes casually. He has to go back to what he was doing before he thought of calling you, one hundred and fifty miles away and part of a different existence. You put the telephone down. The control you exercise over him gives you a warm glow, a surge of feeling. You cup your still bare breasts in your hands and squeeze gently, smiling.

You have a date yourself, later that afternoon. It is a beautiful day and you meet in the park, your companion waiting for you on a seat by the path, overlooking some grass and a pond with ducks. You have not brought a coat and are pleasantly conscious of the way your bare breasts move under the light summer dress. Your date rises to meet you, trying not to let his eyes linger too long on your breasts.

10

'You look particularly stunning today, Chloe.' His kiss is light on your cheek, his left arm grasping your elbow – but he cannot resist passing the palm of his right hand lightly across the tip of your breast. He does not notice the brief setting of your jaw, nor hear the slight intake of your quickly drawn breath. Only you know that your nipples are still tender, bruised. Every now and again, your hand will rise discreetly to clasp itself over your now soft breasts, one, then the other. Tonight, your date may bend to kiss them, but no matter how greedily his lips may seize upon them – they remind him, he says, of crushed, ripe fruit; he worries constantly at them with rough tongue and thin, hard lips – he will not be able to draw from you so much as a gasp in recognition of the hurt he causes.

You will close your eyes, lean back your head, and bathe in a sweet agony. He will think it passion, you will know it to be self-control.

Once, when you had put the telephone down and sat, bare-breasted and straight-backed, hands at your sides, fighting the need to take the pegs away, waiting for your lover to call again, the telephone had rung. It was not your lover, but someone from your firm, apologising for calling on a Sunday just before lunch but needing to make some arrangements about tomorrow's first meeting of the day, on the way into the office for both of you, hence the need to call you now and not simply wait until tomorrow, Chloe. So sorry.

'That's fine,' you said – and made an instant decision. Could you do it without his knowing? Could you keep your voice even? Could you wear them for that long? You could, you did.

Even when you had to go and fetch your briefcase, bending, breasts swaying, then rising and turning quickly, catching sight of yourself in the mirror, the tiny wooden fingers still clinging to your reddened, swollen nipples, you moved quickly away.

It was a strain to keep your voice even, to pretend that everything was normal. ('I say, Chloe, are you sure I'm not

11

disturbing you? You sound a little stressed.' 'No, no – it's nothing. It's just you've caught me sitting by the phone, stripped to the waist, with a couple of clothes pegs attached to my tits. Nothing out of the ordinary at all; I do it all the time.')

But you did not say that. When your lover got through at last, and you wept and told him yes, you were still wearing them for him, he gave his permission to remove them straight away.

'You must,' he said, 'have amazing control.'

12

Candlelight

It was not so much the candle flame itself that held your fascination. More the melting wax that ran – tried to run – from the deep, dark pool with its surface of molten silver at the root of the flame and down the tapering candle's side. It had built up a raised welt on the satin-smooth surface, each new trickle adding to the height of the scar, extending it slightly, each new drop of wax freezing, ossifying, before it could fall further, thus leaving a new ridge for the next trickle to follow.

There had been a weird bass player once – bass guitar, that is, not a proper bass – in a rock group you had gigged with a couple of times, before respectability and the need to forge a business career had tamed your wilder side. You had been a singer then, and no mean keyboard player, even if your music teacher might have blanched at the sounds you then called music. This bass player: his skin had gleamed, the colour of dark, plain chocolate, his belly had been hard and flat and his chest ridged with parallel chevrons of such welts; tribal scars, he had said, made with a thin razor-cut rubbed with ash when he was thirteen.

Your fingertips, tracing the waxen scar, recalled the feel of the ridged flesh on the smooth, hairless chest. Your lower lips, the lips of your slowly swelling sex which, even as you watched the candle and became lost in recollection, were beginning to tingle with an increasing itch, already liquid from earlier daydreaming, squeezed themselves together at the thought (too many lovers and too long ago for it to be a true memory) of the hard, black rod that had parted them.

Why were your lips already wet, already swollen?

Not, certainly, due to anything your companion of the evening was saying to your wandering brain or doing to your uncoiling emotions. This man had started to bore you weeks ago. Now he was doing it like he had been boring you all your life.

It was the hot sting of a fresh drop of molten wax on your finger that told you, as if you did not already very well know, why your loins were starting to glow with a smouldering that this man (he would have to be changed, and soon) would neither stir into flame nor quench with exploding passion this, or any other, night.

The hot wax pulled your mind back from its fleeting caress with the thought of the bass player and reminded you that it was high time you saw your lover again . . .

. . . Face buried in a pillow, the feel of the rough towelling under your naked thighs scratching at your conscious mind, the sting of the first drop of wax on the bare flesh of your buttock had not hurt as much as you had feared it might. In fact, truth to tell, it had not hurt at all.

It had bitten, but only fleetingly – a tiny nipping bite that wakened nerve ends and started little wheels within your mind. Your sensitive flesh had tingled in the instant afterglow before tickling as it felt the cooling blob of wax contract. Your lover had taken the settling of your face in the pillow and your long, slow sigh – rightly – as your signal that the game was to continue.

And what a weird game it was: in many ways the weirdest yet. The clothes pegs had been more in the way of a trial – a self-test of strength of character and control as much as an ordeal of love imposed by your lover.

The canings now seemed a scientific experiment, an investigation into the real-life truth (or otherwise) of *The Story of O*. You remember the night you wanted to feel what a severe – the severest – stroke felt like? Your lover had refused to tie you, as you had asked, and one had been enough. Never again, you had told yourself. But why then, lately, have you been entertaining pulse-quickening, nipple-stiffening thoughts of enduring at his hands a full, terrible and severe thrashing: tied down, twelve full-force strokes of the cane to your bared flesh; a no-going-back-once-you've-started test of your own fortitude and indeed of his?

But this game? The tingling increased as the drops multiplied. You felt their steady path from the swelling crowns of first one mound, then the other, working its way inwards, towards more sensitive valleys.

When your lover told you what to do next, the tingling spread instantly deeper, rushing ahead of where you dared not think hot wax might fall. The flush of humiliation that spread across your cheeks (and now we *are* discussing your face) matched the heat of lust that instantly lit fires in secret places. That familiar churn of mingled fear and excitement instantly switched on a current of delight that charged the little stem between your lovelips with power, made those selfsame lips – normally, if truth be told, something a little too pale and flat according to conventional sexual wisdom – begin to swell and pout.

Your ankles moved the demanded yard apart, and your hands moved back and round, clasping and pulling.

'Wider,' came the low command.

How you blushed. Could there be any offer more open? Your most intimate, personal and secret place – far more your own than those thickening lips which, with you facing whomever your inspector might be, could be (in the right circumstances) quite blatantly and, yes, proudly revealed and exposed without any sense of shame – totally opened. And as your face burned, buried deeper in the pillow, so spurred on by this burning you pulled even harder, feeling yourself stretch and open. Unbidden, your ankles moved to full stretch too. If he wanted you opened, opened he should have you.

The waxen droplets stung more sharply now, each application moving slowly, inexorably towards the inevitable, until with each splash of hot wax your little gasps grew sharper, higher pitched, each sucked-in breath sucked in more deeply, held a little longer.

You could not see, but your naked lover's throbbing rod, hard as the guttering, dripping candle with which your trial was to be accomplished, twitched involuntarily with each in-drawn gasp, each half-choked cry.

'You know where the next is going,' he said. 'Are you ready?'

You knew, of course. And you hated the thought. You doubted you wanted this, yet you knew you did.

You wanted the burning caress. You wanted it to nip, to sting – but you were truly frightened of the thought of pain. Each drop had stung a little more as each new, more sensitive, area found itself laved with the molten caress. As the craved yet dreaded liquid had advanced towards its goal you had waited, been ready, to call the halt you knew was yours to call. But just as each had seemed to touch the door of unbearability, the wave had receded, become bearable – and then faded, leaving a longing vacuum that had to be re-filled.

But now the wax was to fall on a spot completely virgin to any sort of test. The cane had streaked your bare buttocks, left you some means of measuring this new sensation (spikes which, though comparable perhaps in sharpness, were mercifully more brief in hurt and duration before flowering into warmth). The thongs had flicked into the heavy crevice now so openly laid wide and parted. But nothing had ever nipped at the puckered, tenderest spot now stretched so open. What would it be like? Could it be borne without a scream of genuine agony, which was something you neither wanted nor your lover sought to inflict? A step into the unknown for both of you.

'Oh no, please no,' you said. But your hips rotated, pushing your pelvis up. Your ankles pushed outwards till you felt the muscles of your inner thighs complain in their stretching. Your fingertips dug harder into their fleshy handholds, your hands pulling your flesh wide.

The hot wax bestowed its burning kiss. Your single cry was buried in the pillow, but your hips pumped madly up and down, your muscles contracting and working as if by rapid movement to dissipate the sting. And your hands, your own hands – not those of some cruel torturer, but your own hands, voluntarily applied – kept your flesh pulled wide, inviting the inevitable repetition.

As swiftly as it had come, the hot sting cooled to tingling delight, leaving you triumphant. Its passing left you with real loss.

'Again,' you heard your own voice say. You felt your own hips rise in open invitation, felt your own hands grasp and pull, turning invitation to demand. Your lover, incredulous, offered no mercy.

Again and again the hot silver droplets fell, tracing down to over-puffed lips, riveleting in between. You felt your lover's thumb and finger part the puffy lips, knew what was coming, turned your ankles so that your inner thighs turned too, widening and opening the closed oyster.

Tender inner flesh tingled.

It was your idea, standing, to have your nipples waxed. Those peach-skinned breasts, admired to the point of worship by your lover, glowed with their silver coating. You gasped and arched your back as the heat ate into the pale pink tips.

Your lover's throbbing maleness lay pulsed between them. You bathed it in the running fire; his turn to gasp and endure.

And finally, your ultimate sacrifice. Spread-eagled, your own fingertips pulled your secret lips apart as earlier your grabbing hands had spread your broader channel wide. Your rigid stem lay all exposed, soft red tissues trembling.

You gasped and writhed until the waxen sheath began to harden over the bee-stung, swollen, aching morsel; the process took several applications. Pearl-white teeth clamped tight over bared lips, little sobs fell on deaf ears – yours and his – but not once did your trembling thighs close, not for an instant did those often traitorous fingers release the parted, branded flesh.

Now the waxen river ran, molten, into every nook and cranny. Your breath hissed at every drop – but sensing the approaching end of the ordeal, the quivering muscles strained to hold you open until the rite was complete.

Your lover held the mirror between your still wide open thighs and, laughing through misted eyes, you saw the seal, complete and unbroken, you now so proudly bore. A waxen maidenhead, to be broken afresh.

And as your lover's ram, still silvered and coated from its own ordeal, an iron-flesh rod tempered by heat, broke down the waxen door of the heat-sealed portal, a passion such as you had not known before swept you, lost you in a plundered, rooted taking that filled you more completely than anything before.

'Chloe,' said the bore, 'I'm not sure you've been listening. Look, your finger is covered in that candle wax. You should be careful. You could get burned.'

The Birthday Gift

It was, was it not, the American, Henry James who wrote: 'Summer afternoon, summer afternoon – the two most beautiful words in the English language.'

Despite it being only the month of May, your birthday, this was such an afternoon: hot, and lazy; buzzing with the drone of insects and the taut anticipation of languorous adventure; an afternoon that sent warm tingles of pleasure, light as a lover's touch, up the inside of your thighs, almost as if an unseen hand were gently stroking the smooth, sensitive flesh. Even sitting by the pool, the last sips of wine warming in the glass, the bottle empty in the ice bucket, you could feel that unmistakable tightening of the muscles of your stomach, feel that inimitable warmth grow at the base of your belly; feel, without touching, the lips of your sex thicken, the first half-itch of glistening moisture warming the soft membranes.

The house was Victorian, a warren of rooms on many floors; the long-established, mature garden wherein you could sit, even in spring, amongst heady-scented flower-beds, tall hedges and warm, brick walls. The pool, at the side of which the three of you had just finished lunch, was modern but so cleverly blended with its surroundings that its turquoise terrazzo tiling and pale blue water seemed undisturbed from an age long gone. Your lover had brought you to the house for lunch, saying only that he had a gift he wished to offer you for your birthday, and that there was someone he wanted to show you to.

The expression – not 'someone I want you to meet', nor even 'someone I want to have meet you', but specifically,

19

clearly, 'someone I want to show you to' – had immediately thrown that special switch which only your lover (and sometimes, your own solitary caress) could activate. You had suspected this would be no ordinary luncheon, and when the friend, older by a few years than your lover, had turned out to be called Stephen, suspicion became certainty. Was that his real name, or a contrivance, to help set the mood, help explain what might – what would – happen? It did not, does not, matter. When your lover had said the name, the entire outing hung for a brief age between the possibility of derisive abandonment by you on the one hand, and on the other compliant acceptance by you of all that would inevitably follow.

Your own, 'I am pleased at last to meet you', had been what allowed the game to go on.

At lunch, the talk had been light, amusing and of many things, but throughout, you had sensed this Stephen's appraising gaze. It, along with the languorous disposition of such an afternoon, accounted now for the highly charged state of your own sexual awareness. Naturally, you had dressed for lunch as it pleased your lover to have you dress – which was, let it be clearly understood, also how it pleased you to be dressed, at least for such occasions as these.

Beneath the lightweight, bright yellow-patterned cotton dress, you were naked save for a peach-coloured suspender belt and sheer, flesh-toned stockings without seams. Pale yellow shoes, with modestly high heels, completed your outfit, along with a pale yellow belt drawn tight around your waist. The dress itself buttoned all the way from its discreet décolletage to the hem. To be without a bra was your normal state, but only for your lover did you go without pants also, revelling in the feel of freedom, of daring even, it lent to such outings, enjoying too the occasional touch of the breeze upon the soft flesh of your sex.

As was your wont on such occasions, you had that morning, after your bath and before dressing, feeling warm and powdered, luxuriating in the promise of the day to come, carefully and neatly trimmed your pubic hair. Clipping it to neat shortness on the hump of your mound, you ruthlessly trimmed along the lips of your sex so that, as you pushed your flesh one way, then the other, your thumb more than occasionally pressed hard (and, you could in safety pretend to yourself, accidentally) against the nub of your clitoris. The lips themselves thickened, the thickening heightened by the unmasking as the fine, shorn hairs fell away.

By the time you had finished, tiny beads of silver had gathered, pearl-like, in the crevice of the lower join of your sex lips, to make your inner skin itch and tingle.

Just before you had sat down to lunch, when Stephen was for a moment engaged elsewhere about the house, your lover had kissed you gently on the lips, undoing at the same time the top button of your dress, drawing wider the twin lapels to expose the pale expanse of your throat and flawless shoulders, revealing the first indentation of the deep valley between your firm-soft breasts. Without a bra, no crushed cleavage pushed itself upwards like that of some vulgar barmaid, but the proud firmness of your breasts was nevertheless erotically emphasised. Under Stephen's undisguised appraisal, you knew your erect nipples, their stiffness reinforced by the heat of his burning gaze, could be seen clearly outlined beneath the fabric.

Stephen was talking about the house, its many rooms, though redecorated, still authentically Victorian. There was, he said, in several of the bedrooms, a most remarkable contrivance. 'A yard,' he said, 'used by maids to help lace their mistresses into the corsets. Come, I shall show you.

'And you were of course, entirely correct' – he had turned not to you, but to your lover – 'Chloe should be tightly laced. It enhances more than merely the figure; it gives a lady poise, bestows an inner calm. It is a most excellent discipline.

'It is time,' he said. 'Bring her.'

It had been as simple, as bereft of preamble, as peremptory as that. He had risen and led the way. You and your lover had risen together, and followed, without speaking.

21

The room was large, flooded with the warm light of summer despite the lightly drawn curtains. Heavy rosewood and mahogany furniture lent weight to its impressive authority, the broad bed with its high headboard newly made with freshly laundered linen. Upon the bed lay, in readiness, opened like the hinged halves of a case for some curiously shaped muscial instrument, the primrose-yellow satin corset, its whalebone stiffening uncomfortably apparent, its hooks and eyes glinting in the shafts of sunlight which pushed past the drawn curtains, its broad tapes flung loosely alongside. Beside the corset lay a pair of long velvet gloves of matching colour, and a finely tapering riding crop.

The message, less than subtle, caused the ever quickening butterflies hovering between your navel and the juncture of your thighs to convulse with momentary panic before pulling you, inexorably, forward.

No words were exchanged. You simply moved to the bed, watched closely by your lover, more languidly by this Stephen, and began to unbutton your dress.

Under Stephen's instruction, you kept on your shoes and stockings (how had he known what colour corset to select?), then drew on the gloves. Then, you turned to face the two, your arms, satin-covered now to just above the elbows, you kept simply by your sides, your gaze neither submissively downcast nor defiantly brazen, but merely patient, awaiting the next move.

Stephen's eyes assessed your body with more interest than lust. Since you moved to cover neither your breasts nor the neatly trimmed bush of auburn hair at your lower belly (you were suddenly conscious of the way in which, thanks to your morning's ministrations with the scissors, the lips of your sex and the top of your slit were plainly visible, unshielded by the usual camouflage of hair), he saw, for the moment, all that he might wish to view.

Your lover, meanwhile, had stepped to the wall beside the largest wardrobe and there unwound from a large brass hook a heavy, blue velvet rope that led diagonally toward the ceiling.

22

From the ceiling, and by this rope, was lowered the 'yard': a horizontal bar of polished wood, rather like a circus trapeze, some three feet in length. From each end hung a loop of soft leather, into which you were told to place your wrists.

You did so, and found yourself drawn upwards, your arms slightly spread, until you were stretched onto tiptoe, your belly pulled hollow, your breasts raised and slightly flattened on your stretched chest, your thighs pressed close together not by any desire for modesty on your part, but more by the need to gain maximum length from your legs to keep your feet on the floor.

It was while you were suspended in this position that you were to be relieved of the vulnerability of your near-nakedness by means of your lover fitting the corset. This moment of ritual significance prompted in you a flicker of apprehension. You knew how tightly the garment would be laced.

The corset stopped below the breasts and above the hips. Two crescent-shaped, lace-trimmed cups reached the underside of your flattened breasts, almost holding them tight against the tautened tube of your torso; beneath, the board-hard front of the corset was slightly concave, pressing already into the soft flesh of your hollowed belly, forcing your arching buttocks into prominence and rendering more prominent too the padded bulge of the mound above your sex. The garment's lower edge, curved upwards and likewise lace-trimmed, framed the bulge of your soft-haired mons and its pursed lips.

By the time your lover had pulled tight the laces at your spine, you were gasping for breath from the constriction of your waist and diaphragm – but the grip of the garment was to be rendered even tighter. As Stephen directed your lover to pull again the tapes at the small of your back, he himself moved in front of you. Hanging, breathless as you were, you had let your head fall back to leave you staring, untroubled, at your wrists and the bar to which they were so simply, so immutably, attached. Once or twice you had groaned, half pleasure, half discomfort, as you had felt

23

yourself pulled tighter, but otherwise you had been content to hang there, feet just touching the floor but virtually all your weight on your shoulders and arms, allowing yourself to be ministered to. The sensation was by no means unpleasant, nor unwelcome, the sunlit warmth of the room a caress on your bare flesh.

Thus you sensed, rather than saw, Stephen stand close in front of you.

'Move your feet wide apart, please, Chloe.'

Then, as you complied (it was not easy, stretched thus already) 'A bit further, please. Thank you. Hold them wide apart, right out like that, for a moment.'

Only the toes of your shoes kissed the carpet as you strained, your weight now fully borne by your arms, to hold your thighs wide apart. You felt Stephen's palm cup the bulge of your sex, and – within the limits of movement imposed by your strained position – you eased your mound compliantly into the caress.

Using two fingers of his left hand, he gently stroked the length of your split sex, arousing you more fully, his gentle fingers slipping smoothly, easily, in the silky oil that quickly coated your outer flesh, fed from the warm well within. His strong index finger slid back and forth along your opening sex, the fingers on either side caressing the swollen labia before separating the heavy lips widely, laying fully open the pink stalk of your now swollen clitoris. You were fully relaxed and exposed to his caress, already beginning to moan with pleasure, when with his right hand, without warning, he smacked the pliant leather tip of the riding crop, very hard, full against that most sensitive core of your being. The result was explosive.

Your gasping yell was one as much of surprise as hurt. The yard above your head rattled as your hips bucked wildly away from the lash-tip, arching backwards, your belly sucking even tighter. It was precisely the effect your lover needed to pull tight the tapes of the corset the final notch as Stephen, his face now very close to yours, ran his hand in comfort through your hair, stilling your sudden sobbing.

24

'There' he soothed, 'there, there.' He spoke as if calming a frightened beast, his mare or his bitch. 'Steady down, Chloe. It wasn't as bad as that – and there's just the one. You are fortunate. A hundred years ago a lady might have hung thus, suspended as are you, while the head groom was brought in to assist with winning that last fraction of an inch.'

For some reason, the thought of hanging thus, your waist encircled, cinched tight by your corset, your breasts bared, the bush of your pubis on display, even the long, slick lips of your sex opened, exposed by your wide-legged stance, hanging helplessly while from the stable-yard is brought one of your (imaginary) husband's rough employees, to harness you even tighter, drinking in your vulnerable nakedness, filled you with less horror than it might.

Lowered from the yard, stood firm again on your own feet and with gloved arms again by your sides, you stood patient and still, your clitoris throbbing hotly, while adjustments were made to your appearance. The crescent-shaped half-cups beneath your breasts, you had realised as your arms had been lowered from above your head, had cleverly elasticated sides so that they gave under the weight of your full, firm bosom. Thus they framed and gave gentle support to your breasts without pushing them upwards, or distorting their natural shape in any way.

Your pink nipples with their ripe, full areolas were left wholly uncovered, and now they too burned, hot and erect. Stephen, in adjusting the set of your breasts on the half-cups of the corset, had done so by the simple expedient of grasping, in a cruel grip between his finger and thumb, each nipple in turn, and using it to pull your breast out and upwards, stretching it away from the constriction of the corset until its stretched tautness and your indrawn breath had caused him both to pause and to tighten further his already firm grip, while with his other hand he had flipped down the shelf-like crescent of the half-cup, laying your breast gently on it as one might arrange the display of a delicate flower.

Suspenders at the lower edge of the corset held your stockings taut on your thighs, and instinctively you stood more erect than you had ever known yourself to do before. Relaxing into the corset's firm hold on the middle of your body, you were surprised, pleasantly surprised, to find how comfortable it was to wear. Now that the ordeal of being laced was over, the sensation was entirely agreeable.

Taking your elbow, Stephen led you to stand in front of one of those full-length, free-standing mirrors so beloved of Victorian bedroom designers. You saw yourself, framed in the heavy mahogany surround – and were forced to admit you liked what you saw. Full-frontal, the constriction of your waist emphasised the swell of your hips and of your body above. The upward curve of the lower edge of the corset, from each hip bone to mid-way between navel and pubis, lent length and taper to your thighs, and framed the thatch of your pubic hair, leaving the join of your sex lips just discernible. Between them, the fleshy morsel of your still-throbbing clitoris pulsed visibly.

Above, the half-cups raised and thrust your breasts both forwards and slightly outwards, leaving them more widely separated than would be their natural position, but not in any way misshapen or contrived. Over the pale yellow satin the full tips of your breasts glowed pinkly, the prominent nipples still hard and erect and faintly bruised from Stephen's crushing grip. You were, you decided, very pleased with your gift. One final, Victorian, ritual remained, inevitably.

You had noticed the heavy-framed trestle with its green leather, padded top, as soon as you had entered the room. It came as no surprise when Stephen, his grip firm on your elbow, had guided you to it. He stopped as you stood, facing it – but to your surprise he then stepped back himself. It was your lover who came forward, holding the light leather riding crop that earlier had won from you at such cost the final cinching of your waist, from which your clitoris still tingled, the hurt itself absorbed.

'How do you want me?' you had whispered.

'Bent fully over and wide open,' he had said. 'I want you

26

to show him everything. Put your hips against the padding, feet wide apart, then lean over the trestle and grasp the handles on the other side, at the bottom.'

You moved to stand as directed, your feet moving apart to nudge against the insides of the trestle legs. You placed your hands on the leather padding, holding the top at either end, the outstretch of your arms matching the spread of your splayed thighs. Leaning slightly forward, you arched your back, thrusting forward your breasts above the corset cups. The corset itself did not make bending easy, but helped support your torso. You were only too well aware of the picture you presented from the rear.

It was to your lover you spoke.

'Now I have a special gift to offer you,' you whispered. 'Have Stephen whip me.' And you bent fully forward, your hair cascading as you reached for the lowest rung of the trestle.

Your wide-parted stance hid nothing. Stretched fully over the trestle, your hands grasping the lowest pair of handles, your humped, bare buttocks, the pink anus clearly visible, were pulled apart by the stretch of your parted thighs. The haired lips of your sex, parted as in anticipation, thrust brazenly outward.

Stephen laid the crop lightly across the padded flesh above the join of your thighs.

'Chloe,' he said. 'You'll take the first few strokes here, to warm you up. The third-from-last stroke you'll take here,' and he laid the crop lower, over the tops of your thighs and across the slot of your sex. He pressed the crop deeply into your flesh, and you felt its leather-wrapped length touch the lips themselves.

'The last two strokes I shall give you here,' and he pressed the crop diagonally across first one swelling buttock, then the other, in such a manner that you felt its length lay deep into the crease between buttock and thigh, and along each full-swollen lip of your sex in turn.

You shuddered, and felt yourself thrust perceptibly higher, opening even wider. Stephen withdrew the tip of the lash, drawing it up the length of your parted sex. The lips, and the dark line between them, glistened with the slippery, silver evidence of your arousal.

'But it is for you, Chloe, to say how many strokes there shall be, and of what severity.'

Your voice, husky and muffled by the cascade of your hair, wavered only slightly.

'Twelve. As hard as you can.'

By the time you and your lover had returned to your flat, the marks from the lightweight crop had already faded to thin, pink lines; the searing stiffness across your buttocks and along your sex-lips – which in the immediate aftermath had swollen thickly – had quickly receded to a suffusing warmth which, faintly, was with you still. To the gift of the corset had been added that of a wide-brimmed, low-crowned hat, a perfect match for gloves and shoes, and you had known yourself, seated erect beside your lover on the short train journey home, to be the object of a succession of admiring glances. Not all of them had been from men.

In your bedroom, your hat already carefully laid aside, you kissed your lover hard as he unbuttoned your dress, quickly removing his own clothes to reveal his pole-hard shaft, rising almost to his belly. Your gloved hands stroked his chest and arms before your fingers closed round his pulsing maleness. He closed his eyes, and saw again the effecting of your own gift.

Despite your open-ended invitation, Stephen's whipping had begun lightly, the first few strokes of what he had called 'warming you up' doing just that, stinging but not biting your flesh. Your hips had writhed but you had made no sound, although by the sixth stroke all concession had disappeared from your whipper's full-blooded strokes and you were hard pressed to do no more than gasp. At the seventh stroke you could not restrain a low, keening moan and after the eighth Stephen had paused while you re-adjusted yourself over the padded bar, placing wide again the feet which had involuntarily begun to creep protectively together, re-opening yourself to fully offer to the crop the most secret parts of your body.

When, your whipping drawing to its end, the crop on its tenth stroke had bitten into the crease between buttock and thigh, searing full across the soft and parted sex, the noisy sucking of your breath between clenched teeth was indication in plenty of what this gift was costing you.

But even your stoicism could not resist the cruelty of those two final strokes, biting hard along the length of each tender lip. Your sharp, single cry at each echoed loudly in the still room. After the first you had seen your gloved knuckles clench as you tightened your grip on the bar at the base of the trestle over which your sacrifice was being accomplished; you watched with dread as Stephen, visible only in the form of well-polished tan shoes and neatly pressed slacks, walked with slow deliberation from beside your left hip – whither he had moved to administer the first diagonal – round to your right hip, for the second. You wondered if you could hold out for what you knew must come. Tiny beads of sweat glistened at the base of your spine, between your dipped shoulder blades, between your stretched buttocks and on the backs of your taut legs. Yet despite your fear, you had found yourself not merely trying hard to hold still, but forcing your parted feet hard against the wide-spaced feet of the trestle, dipping your back to push your sex higher and even turning in your toes, to offer yourself as fully open, as wantonly displayed, as possible to that final, searing test.

The shaking of your parted thighs was only just controllable; even the lips of your opened sex, reddened hectically and already swelling to puffy protuberance, trembled. Stephen had judged the severity of your whipping with exactitude.

After the final stroke, your head hanging between your outstretched arms, your eyes brimming with tears, you had waited for long moments, still bent and opened (your lover's phrase was with you still) and had been about to rise when you had felt the nudging of male-hard flesh at your sex. You knew immediately that the flesh was not that of your lover, but of Stephen, and for an instant, your head jerked back to let you stare straight ahead at the wall

29

before you, and you had considered rebellion. Strong hands grasped your hips, holding you firmly down, and you felt your thighs and feet locked against the heavy trestle by the parted thighs of the man close behind you. Stephen's steady voice said simply, quietly:

'No, Chloe. Stay.'

You had allowed your head to drop, relaxed the momentarily locked muscles of your thighs and the unseen maleness, feeling the way before it suddenly open again, had slid into you in one long, deep stroke. This too, you realised, would be part of the ritual.

The solid maleness withdrew, returned, withdrew. Instinctively you knew that you were not expected to respond – were required, indeed, not to respond. Passive, you felt the intruder, iron-hard and long, slide within you, withdraw almost to its tip, then slide within you again, withdraw, slide, withdraw, slide.

When it came, the hot flood deep within you was strangely calming, a balm almost, despite your own lack of passion, and you heard yourself utter a tiny sob as your visitor withdrew for the final time, leaving your bee-stung sex lips gaping. 'Stilled', to use the Victorians' quaint phrase for what had just occurred, you had sagged limply over the whipping-horse, the cascade of your hair veiling your face, your grip on the bar loose.

Your lover, silent, had stepped close beside you to help you rise but for a full minute you had purposely stayed thus, feeling the mingled juices, yours and Stephen's, trickle down the inside of your wide-splayed thighs towards the tops of your stockings. You had wanted your lover fully to savour the totality of your gift to him . . .

Now it was your turn to receive. Your lover lay you gently back on the bed and bent over you, the first of an age of kisses already forming on his lips. You closed your eyes and sighed. This would be the best gift of all.

Beginnings

Until now, you have assumed that these letters are written by your lover, that I am he. Now you are not so sure – your lover puts on a convincing display of non-response when you allude to the letters, but you do not ask directly, or mention them openly. You sense already that to do so will merely destroy their illusion. Let us, then, play our game a little longer.

You have been thinking about how it all began.

It was a visit with your lover to some friends' country house for a lazy weekend. Left alone for a day, you wandered and finished in the deserted stable yard, thence a barn, with hay. It was high summer, and you made love, wildly and roughly, in the hay barn. Encouraged by your provocation, led by your invitation, your lover took you harshly, stretched face down over the hay bales. The hay scratched your bare breasts and belly; you were plundered, exhausted, drained and filled, all at the same time. Sweating, exhilarated, exhausted, you lay panting on the pile of bales, the sharp straw stalks prickling, the hay-dust already beginning to itch where it stuck, damply, to your warm skin. As you almost subconsciously ground your breasts into the rough straw of the bale, relishing the mild, sharp hurt from the prickles, savouring your animal sweat, the sudden recollection came to you of an incident from your schooldays, until that moment long unremembered ...

You were seventeen, still at school, and had gone from your own school to another, playing lacrosse. After the game you had piled, laughing, with the girls of your own

31

and the other team into the changing rooms of the school you were visiting, to shower before tea and the journey home.

The school, Highpark, was one of those minor public schools for which the English educational system is famed – more often, it must be admitted, for the schools for boys than those for girls. Highpark was old, Victorian, revelling in its lack of modernity in either outlook or fabric.

The changing facilities were primitive. Instead of, as at your own school, curtained cubicles and individual shower booths, Highpark had only a large communal changing room, divided into sections by high wire mesh and low wooden benches, with rows of cages underneath for shoes. Your clothes you hung on metal hooks, side by side with the next girl.

After the game, you came in and stripped off your playing things and, giggling with your companions at the primitiveness of Highpark's facilities, trooped naked from the changing rooms along a stone-floored corridor and into a large communal bath-house, complete with large communal bath, filled to brim level with hot, soapy water.

Twenty-two naked sixteen and seventeen-year-olds clambered and jumped, splashing, into the enormous, tiled pit of the bath, laughing and joking. The hot water eased the pleasant ache of honest fatigue in your limbs and you relaxed, washing unconcernedly. Although the facilities in your own school were more modern, affording greater privacy, you had no particular concerns about being naked among your peers, being blessed with a youthful figure as attractive as any and the envy of more than a few.

You had been relaxing thus for perhaps ten, fifteen, minutes, laughing and joking with your friends, when a shrill whistle demanded silence above the babble of girlish voices.

At one corner of the big single room bath-house, opposite the door by which you had entered, by another door, open, stood a Highpark prefect, clad in a grey tracksuit top and bottom, the whistle just blown falling from her lips to hang on a string around her neck.

32

'All right then,' she called in a shrill, drill sergeant's voice. 'Let's be having you then, one at a time. Adamson, you can be first.'

A cheer rose from the girls in the bath, accompanied by not a few wolf whistles and cat-calls, as a girl at the side of the bath furthest from you heaved herself from the water to stand, dripping, near the prefect.

'Oh God, not me first again,' she wailed. 'Why couldn't my parents be called Murphy, or Smith, or Young, or even Ziblatt? Anything but Adamson, right at the top of the alphabet. Couldn't you start with the zeds sometime? It's nearly always me goes first,' she said, laughing.

Adamson was about the same age as yourself: seventeen, perhaps sixteen, no younger certainly and unlikely to be older. She was tall, with a bob of flaming red hair and white, almost translucent skin, high, firm, rounded breasts with tiny nipples – so pale as to be almost invisible on the tips of the white breasts – and a bright bush of red hair at the junction of her long, slim thighs. From your position, watching from your corner of the bath, she was in half-profile toward you as she stood, grinning broadly at the prefect.

'Come on – off you go,' laughed the prefect, 'or I'll tell Pre Watson to make you run the drive instead of the quad.' And the girl Adamson, still naked, disappeared out through the open door.

'What on earth was all that about?' you inquired of your next door neighbour.

'Ah, this is your first visit here, isn't it?' she replied, somewhat rhetorically. 'The famous Highpark Hose-Down. It's their games mistress really – a bit Victorian. Doesn't believe in mollycoddling, as she calls it. Thinks it's unhealthy to get dressed straight after a hot bath. Great believer in cold showers, and all that – only snag is, this place is so old it doesn't have showers. So they have the Hose-Down instead. Through the door there's another pre, with a cold water hose. She hoses you down, back and front, before you're allowed to go and get dressed.'

A few moments, and another name was called by the

prefect by the door, and another girl – cheered on by her friends still in the water – heaved herself from the bath to run, dripping, through the door.

Your own name came fairly quickly.

'Go for it, Chloe,' yelled one of your team mates as you climbed from the bath. 'Watch out for the bum-wash,' you heard someone else call as, laughing nervously, you headed at a half-trot, breasts jiggling and seal-wet skin glowing pinkly from the hot water, for the open door.

The first surprise was to find yourself not in another room but completely out of doors, in a tiny courtyard, no more than eight feet by twelve feet, formed by the juxtaposition of the school's ancient buildings and paved with small square flagstones. Overhead, the sky was a bright blue, the thin wisp of an aeroplane's vapour trail, slowly dispersing, a lazy white slash against the blue. You felt a sudden frisson of excitement that struck, low down between your navel and the junction of your thighs, at the thought of being naked, having to walk, move, run thus naked, out of doors, even in such confined surroundings.

The buildings' walls, on three sides, were several storeys high and, save for two barred windows at second floor level on one side, were blind. To your right, forming the fourth side of the yard, a high brick wall topped by a rounded parapet.

The yard must at some time have been part of the stabling which would have once accompanied such buildings, for the flagged floor, glistening wetly, was laid round a central gridded drain, slightly sunken, so that water quickly drained away.

There was another narrow door, open, in the corner of the yard formed by the building you were just leaving and the high wall, and at this end, near a large brass outside tap, stood a second grey-tracksuited Highpark prefect, the bottoms of her tracksuit trousers tucked into short black rubber boots, of the sort worn by porters at Billingsgate fish market. She held in her hand the brass-fitted end of a bright green garden hose, the other end of which snaked towards the tap on the wall.

34

'Been here before?' she asked brusquely. You shook your head in reply.

'OK. Face the far wall and spread your feet apart. Lean forwards, support yourself by your hands, keep 'em up above your head so I can get into your armpits.'

You obeyed, standing as if for a military search, leaning forward against the wall, your weight on your hands, your breasts hanging slightly because of your forward-leaning stance.

The water from the hose was icy cold, hitting you first between the shoulder blades, spraying across your back and shoulders, causing you to gasp loudly for breath. The solid jet played heavily down your spine, across your buttocks and on down the backs of your thighs. Then as the prefect moved towards you, you felt the hose-jet spray against your rib cage, wash coldly up under your right arm and splash, hard and icily, against the side of your breast.

Swiftly, the prefect moved to wash down your other side as, forcing yourself to hold still, you began to shiver with the coldness of the water, your breath drawn in rapid gasping pants. Your skin tingled, goose-pimpled, and your nipples hardened, hurting, against the chill.

The water stopped.

'Step back three paces.' Again, you obeyed, mechanically, not looking round, standing now with your back still to the prefect, your arms by your sides.

'Bend forward from the waist so your tits hang straight down. Feet apart – wider than that. Further yet. Come on. I want them really far apart. Good. Now, reach back and pull your bum cheeks open.'

The demand stunned you, as much for the coarseness of the language as for the outrage of what you were being told to do. There was nothing like this at your own school. Yet even at your school, as at any other in that system, seventeen-year-olds did not argue with prefects. Numbed, your cheeks burning with humiliation, you did as you were told, bending forwards to present your buttocks, suddenly sensitive of the way in which your breasts did, indeed, hang heavily down, parting your feet wide, pulling apart your cheeks to show, not only the crinkled ring of your anus but, beneath and pushed into prominence by your stance, the plump split fig of your brown-haired sex.

The jet from the hose, still icy cold, was even harder this time, more concentrated, and thumped into your buttocks before hammering into the widely opened groove of your behind, hitting with accuracy the pink and puckered entrance. You tensed in automatic response, tightening your sphincter muscles against the pummelling intrusion, the force of the water jet almost causing you to lose your balance.

'Relax. Let it get up inside or it's a full enema,' called the prefect. Horror-struck, you obeyed as best you could, relaxing your clenched cheeks, relaxing your sphincter to allow the soft entrance to open, feeling the water drill against the inner membranes of your bottom-hole. Your stomach churned, full of butterflies, and you found yourself, mind reeling, not merely steeling yourself but revelling in this wanton display of obedience. Suddenly, you felt you wanted to allow this anonymous, bossy girl complete freedom of access not just to your body but your will. Your clutching fingers gripped your bottom cheeks more tightly, pulling harder to keep them apart.

The hose jet moved downwards, drilling onto the lips of your sex, the force of the water parting the outer lips to hammer its way inside. The sensation was exquisite, hanging mystically between pleasure and pain.

The water stopped again.

'Turn round, face me.'

You obeyed, still panting under the shock of the cold water and faced the prefect. Unbidden you placed your feet wide apart again.

'Cup your tits.'

You misunderstood the instruction, cupping your hands over your breasts, the palms protectively covering the rigid nipples.

'No. Not like that. Squeeze them from underneath, lift 'em high and push them together. Point the nipples at me,'

36

the prefect called. You obeyed, blushing hotly once more, your senses swimming.

You saw that the brass fitting on the end of the hose was some sort of control nozzle, capable both of turning the hose on and off and of regulating the flow of water, from fine hard jet to a wider but softer spray. She turned the hose on again, spraying the front of your body, starting you shivering again, before twisting the nozzle to bring back the hard, punishing jet.

The jet hit your breasts, accurately pummelling the nipples which, tightening even harder, passed quickly through hurt to numbness.

'Hydrotherapy,' called the girl, a hint of sarcasm tinging her humour. 'Movie stars pay a fortune for this. Does the tits and nipples a power of good. And it's all free as part of the Highpark service.'

The jet swung away from your breasts, which none the less you still clutched, raised high and pushed together, the frozen nipples pointed forwards like some odd weapon, and splayed across your torso and then belly, just below the navel.

'Firms up the tummy muscles, keeps you trim,' continued the now running commentary, 'and can give the thrill of a lifetime . . .'

The jet swung lower, splashing against your pubic mound, plastering the hair flat against your lower belly. It shifted down another inch, hitting squarely against the top of your sex slit, landing hard and accurately on your clitoris. You jerked your hips back, both in surprise and in order to escape the sensation.

'Come on, push it out, not back. Give me ten.'

Reluctantly, you shifted your hips forward once more as you watched the hand twist the hose nozzle again, narrowing the jet further, into a single silvered line. It splayed hard against the ground by your feet, drumming wetly on the flagstones.

'Right out, so's I can do your twat properly. Bend your knees a bit. And more – the twat lips need to be open for maximum effect. You're still closed like a Scots nun's purse,' said the prefect, matter-of-factly. 'You still a virgin?'

You nodded, hot-faced.

'Well don't worry – this won't break anything. Do a full squat to open it up, then come up halfway, but don't straighten fully.'

You obeyed, holding yourself bent-kneed and with your thighs wide parted, your hands still ludicrously cupping your breasts.

'That's much better,' said the prefect. 'Quite a little clit we've got there. Can even see your inside lips now. They're still closed. Your maidenhead's safe with me. You'll enjoy this. Now count to ten.'

And so you stood, shivering and gasping, feet wide apart, your hips and pubis thrust brazenly forward, hands holding your breasts in an ever tightening grip as, panting for breath, your voice sounding to you barely more than a squeak, your eyes closed, the hard, solid jet from the hose pounding against the core of your being, pummelling, hurting and not hurting, you began to count aloud:

'One, two, three . . .'

By the time you reached ten, you were groaning loudly, your hips jerking as the drumming water pummelled against your rigid clitoris, tears shining in your eyes. Yet when the water stopped, you stayed in your wide-thighed, bent-legged stance, fixing her with your challenging gaze.

'Want to go on? I'm not supposed to give you more than ten seconds – but you want it, don't you honey? You are a game stag, and no mistake. If you were a Highparker I'd take you all the way – the water jet is Highpark's way for a girl to lose her cherry, but you probably have your own rules about that.

'So I'll just keep on going. You step back when you've had enough. But bend a bit more first; open it right up: let's see what you're really made of. That's right – really wide. Your clit's up like a poker, you know – sticking right out. And your inner petals have started to open. I told you you'd enjoy this.' And you lowered yourself further, rendering yourself more exposed, while the hard, stinging

38

spray of ice-cold water again slapped direct onto and around the swollen stalk of your clit, moving occasionally to pummel the soft lips and even the tender flesh of your inner membranes. You swayed, your entire consciousness centred in the core of your being, your belly taut, your inner muscles quivering. And in that moment, you felt a total surrendering to what was being demanded of you, a bond of almost mystic intimacy between you and the girl with the hose. You shuddered in a deep climax, oblivious to the girl with the hose, oblivious to your surroundings.

The wave of emotion swept over you, past you. Suddenly you were acutely aware again of where you were, what you were doing, of the picture you must present. You took a step backwards, away from the drilling water jet. The water stopped abruptly. And with it, the bond was broken. You felt suddenly foolish, exposed both literally and metaphorically, standing dripping wet and shivering with your feet wide apart, totally naked in some strange school's backyard, your sex pushed forward like a fishmarket strumpet in a Hogarth painting, half frozen, holding your breasts as if your life depended on it.

You felt yourself blushing hotly, despite the cold. If the prefect sensed anything, sensed the sudden foolishness you felt, she did not show it.

'Right – through that door, twice around the quad and in for tea. Next . . .'

Blushing to the roots of your hair, you headed for the door, hearing the next name being called from inside the bath-house, hearing the accompanying cheer as the next naked girl came out to be hosed down. As you passed the prefect with the hose, she glanced swiftly at you, and you sensed the bond again, briefly.

'You're quite a girl, Chloe. Pity you're not staying. You could go far here.'

Through the door was a second, larger courtyard, half the size of a tennis court, with a grassed lawn and a paved pathway around the perimeter. There were windows at ground floor level in all the buildings, some with doors, brass-furnished, evidently offices or private rooms, leading

39

off the perimeter pathway. All the windows had net curtains, you noticed, but behind one a figure, surveying the quadrangle, watching. The Victorian games-mistress, you later discovered. In the quad, yet another prefect was waiting for you.

'Twice around, full speed – then into the changing room. Warms you up and dries you off.'

And, naked, ignoring yet acutely aware of the eyes following your every movement, you sprinted off, running fast around the paved walkway, bare feet slapping wetly on the paving stones, bare breasts bounding wildly. Had you been told to run thus not round a private courtyard but down the High Street, you would have done so.

The memory stirred you and, under your prompting, your lover led you naked but for your knee-length, tan boots into the open stable yard, the air cool on your sweat-damp skin despite the warm summer sun. Although you were sure no one was around, it felt daring to be thus nude and out of doors. Your heartbeat quickened and those tiny jitters that hover in the triangle between your navel and your pelvis jumped and fluttered. You laughed, and your knees trembled, as you walked. You almost fell. Yet your nipples stiffened, and you felt the cool breeze waft across your belly and ruffle the soft curls on your pubis, caressing between your naked thighs. You felt yourself full, silkily lubricious once again.

You had stood, arms held high, feet apart, gasping while he had roughly, crudely, washed you down with a coarse horse sponge and cold water from a bucket, as if you were a horse which had rolled in a muddy field. As the water splashed on to your chest, trickled down your belly, your nipples hardened even more, aching dully, while the usually full, soft pink cushion of their wide haloes tightened and puckered, shrinking visibly, darkening. The nipples themselves hardened and lengthened until they stood out from the ends of your white breasts as large, as long, as purple as loganberries.

You wanted to be treated . . . how? Harshly is too strong

a word – the wrong connotation. Brusquely, perhaps? You wanted no tenderness, wanted instead a callous indifference to what might be finer feelings, to submit yourself – albeit in only a lover's game – to something that would tax your tolerance. It was, of course, only a game. You had slid your feet wider apart, stretched your arms higher, thrust your breasts more brazenly in invitation to your lover's rough ministrations, giving yourself over to his impersonal handling, your heart thumping.

The water had splashed into your armpits, trickled down your flanks. Your lover stepped behind you. You had felt the heavy cold wetness of the sponge slosh between your shoulders, over your back, cooling you quickly. You had felt it run down over your buttocks, and trickle in between. Your lover stepped in front of you again, and the water had splashed again over your raised breasts, tightening again the puckering of your areolas, emphasising the frozen hardness of your stalk-like nipples. It had run down your belly and through the matted, sweat-darkened hair of your bush. You had bent your knees, opening yourself further as the sponge, heavy with water the coldness of which made you gasp again, was sloshed up into your opened sex, the coarseness of the sponge rough against the sensitive softness of your parted sex lips, and the water had trickled down the insides of your thighs, leaving dark stains on the soft, light leather of your boots.

When your sousing was complete, you had straightened your legs but otherwise remained thus, naked in the open air of the warm, sunny stable-yard, arms high and legs parted, your skin cooling quickly, goose-bumps puckering on your flesh, beginning to shiver. Your lover left you briefly, and it was understood without a word from either that you were required, he required you – you required yourself – to stand thus, to be tested by the cold water and the now cold-feeling air, until he returned.

You were shivering when you heard a tread approaching from round the corner of the stable block, someone coming into the yard. A moment's panic – and you had made an instant decision. You had sucked in your belly, kept your arms high and your feet wide planted, your breasts and pubis displayed, had gazed fixedly ahead, posed thus for whomever it might be. It was your lover returning with a coarse towel, found hanging behind the door of one of the loose-boxes, and he had rubbed your skin until it glowed. Were you disappointed that it had not been someone else?

Then you had been led, skin tingling again, breasts quivering as you walked (and you walked intentionally with a firm heel action that made them jiggle the more, for you knew your lover liked that, and was watching you as he led you by one out-stretched arm), back into the barn, to dress and emerge as if nothing had happened. But within you, a fire still raged and your pulse ran quick.

Later, that evening after supper when the men were elsewhere engaged in conversation and post-prandial whisky, your hostess revealed that she had seen you and your lover go into the barn, witnessed the bizarre, impromptu ritual which had followed in the stable-yard – and to your relief had given no indication that she might have found your whim shocking. On the contrary she told you of some of her own 'games', and asked a question.

'Have you been kissed with leather yet?' your smiling hostess asked. 'Sorry?' was your puzzled, slightly embarrassed reply – embarrassed because you sensed that not understanding the question might somehow make you seem less, less . . . less what? you wondered, simultaneously, unsure of your ground, sensing yourself not merely at a disadvantage, but displaying a revealing naivety.

'Kissed by leather,' she repeated, adding swiftly, 'been cropped; you know, a riding crop, across the backside? Obviously not, I see – but don't be shocked: it's not nearly so dreadful as it sounds. You should try it, Chloe. In the right circumstances, half a dozen on the bare with a nice whippy little leather switch can really get you going. If one is already fairly steamed up, as it were, one can take them surprisingly hard.

'On the bare seat is the usual place – or elsewhere, if you're game: on the back – bare, of course – if you're feel-

42

ing traditional, or if your man's being a bit magisterial. Six across the shoulders can make you feel you're back with Judge Jeffries if it's for punishment, but it can wipe clean the most overburdened credit card. And make you feel like a raunchy Tudor wench if it's done more lightly, just for fun.

'Getting it on the insides of the thighs can really make you snort, too. I've even taken it full on the plum. A sixer there is hard to hold still for, I grant you, and rather makes the eyes water, but afterwards . . .'

To your surprise, her startling suggestion did not fill you with horror, but rather with more of those wild flutterings in your lower belly.

Next day you rode high on the downs with your lover, your thighs and sex bare on a velvet saddle beneath a heavy, split skirt, both loaned to you, with a knowing smile, by your complicit hostess. And as you cantered, your parting skirt flew high around your waist, to leave your belly, your bush and your opened thighs revealed, if only for your lover's eyes.

You called at a pub for lunch. As you were leaving, a local lad held the head of your horse as you mounted and as you swung into the saddle you made sure that your skirt parted discreetly, revealing to him that you wore nothing beneath. Mounted and apparently with your attention taken by something else, so that you looked only ahead, for a long moment you stood high in your stirrups, knowing that from his viewpoint your skirt would be pulled open by your straddling thighs, knowing he had only to look up at you to have an unrestricted view up between your legs, then slowly you lowered yourself onto the velvet seat. From your saddle you looked down. He was still standing, open-mouthed, staring at the place his vision had so briefly appeared. He looked into your face, his own still frozen. You smiled and turned your horse away.

On the way home, you stopped and dismounted again, tethering your horses, and there on the high open downs you took your lover to you, and left him drained.

Beginnings 2 – Uncle Cedric

'Uncle Cedric,' you breathed, 'it's lovely.'

'Well, Chloe,' said the elegant, silver-haired man you addressed, 'we've been such special friends for so long, I knew you wouldn't think it improper to get such a birthday present. I had Mrs Maple get it for me for you – I don't get out now so much, and anyway, I think retired admirals buying ladies' underwear rather too likely to end up in the Sunday papers for it to be an activity in which I should indulge personally. But I'm glad you like it.'

'Uncle Cedric' as you call him had been your favourite uncle for as long as you can remember, although you knew he was not a real uncle at all: a long-time friend of your late father who, since your childhood, had been a highly indulgent semi-official 'godfather'. In deference to the age between you, and to his special status in your affections, you had called him 'Uncle' since you learned to talk. To change now would have seemed very odd. As a small girl, you had loved to play in his beautiful house with its well-polished furniture, its oil paintings of old ships, its twinkling brass and its delicious smell of cigars and, you eventually recognised, brandy.

As a bigger girl, in summer holidays, the garden with its trees and semi-wild apple orchard was often your haunt, despite the fact that Uncle Cedric was often away more than he was home, still a serving naval officer. But his housekeeper, Mrs Maple, always made you as welcome as did he.

After he had accepted a land-based posting, you had come to see him often, enthralled by his tales of ships, and the sea, and faraway places. As you had grown older, some of his tales became even more exciting when, obliquely at first, then more directly, he had told of balls, and parties and – intriguingly – of their occasional amorous consequences, until, eventually, once your sixteenth birthday had passed, he had told you openly of his lovers and their adventures together. In return, you told him openly of your own girlish amorous adventures, starting with crushes on school mistresses, your first boyfriends and finally, in your first year at university, blushing but puzzled, your first lover. It was not, you had confided, quite the magical experience his affairs had seemed to be.

'It will come,' he had said, 'if only slowly. Your mistake, my dear Chloe, is to take a lover your own age. What can he know, or have learned? He thinks only of himself, little if anything of your pleasure.'

'Ah, if I were just twenty years younger – indeed, fifteen would do it. Thirty-five is a fine age for a young woman's first lover. At nineteen, you do not need another nineteen-year-old.' And he had laughed.

'Now, I'm afraid my dear, I don't think my gout would stand the strain, even if my constitution would.'

So instead, Uncle Cedric had bought you your first 'French lingerie', as he had called it.

'I've decided,' he had said to you, presenting you with the large, gift-wrapped box complete with enormous pink, bow-tied ribbon, 'it's time you had your first big-girl's teddy – and who better to give it to you than your favourite uncle?'

You held the lace-trimmed silk in front of you, smoothing it incongruously over your shirt and jeans. 'I think it's gorgeous – I shall wear it next week, on your birthday, when I come to see you. I'm going to a very smart supper party next week, and I've bought a very smart "little black number" already, to wear to it. It's close fitting, especially at the top – quite low cut too. It shows off quite a lot.' You blushed a little, gave a tiny, half-embarrassed giggle. 'Especially as I don't wear a bra with it. I wasn't going to tell you about it – just turn up in it when I come to see you

45

next week, as a birthday surprise for you, to let you see how grown up I've become.

'I wasn't going to wear anything under the dress – well, not on top. Now I shall wear my teddy under it, for the supper party, and when I come to you next week.'

Your uncle had smiled conspiratorially. 'I shall look forward to it, my dear.'

Standing before his armchair, you turned to face him. Your hand moved behind you, to grasp the zip of your dress which, keeping your eyes on your uncle's face, you pulled downwards, your other hand easing the thin straps over your shoulders. For a moment you held the dress still before you, then let it fall in a pool at your feet.

Bending at the knees, pressed demurely together, keeping your upper torso vertical, you sank down to pick up the dress. With one arm, outstretched, you dropped it on a chair, aware of the way the movement jiggled your breasts, naked beneath the lace-trimmed black silk. You could feel your nipples hardening, knew their outline showed through the thin material, pointedly obvious. The thought merely hardened them into further prominence.

'Well Uncle – what do you think of teddy?' you asked with a smile.

In the black one-piece chemise, black stockings and black high heels, you made a stunning picture. Although in theory the chemise covered your torso, the soft suppleness of its material moulded over your breasts, revealing their shape and youthful firmness. Your erect nipples were outlined clearly, pushing boldly against the black silk. Through the lace cups which barely half covered the swell of your breasts their pale pinkness was tantalisingly revealed.

At the top of your thighs, just above the gusset of the chemise, the garment was made with an inverted chevron of lace which matched the lace covering your bosom and the trim around the loose-fitting high-cut leg holes. The top of the triangle of your pubic hair showed as a dark shadow through the black lace.

The stretched black straps of the suspender belt which was all you wore beneath the chemise, emerged from the lace which trimmed the leg openings and contrasted starkly with the white skin of your thighs, the taut stockings emphasising the length of your legs, the high heels of the shoes, your feet placed demurely together, making the muscles of your calves and thighs tense.

'Ah my dear, if only I were indeed thirty years younger,' your uncle replied, smiling. 'Regrettably, I am not, but what a picture you make, if only in still life.'

'Perhaps I should model it for you properly?' you prompted, on cue. 'Then I shall be more than merely "still life".' Without waiting for his reply, you turned and walked to the far end of the room, aware of the sway of your hips and the tensing of your buttocks beneath the silk. Your uncle watched, enthralled. You did indeed make a picture, as he described it. Beneath the silk, your buttocks rolled voluptuously, you walked as a ballet dancer walks, toes pointed, one foot placed directly in front of the other.

You turned, pirouetting on tiptoe, and posed, again one foot before the other, emphasising the length of your legs. As you walked back down the room, your breasts, the nipples still hard as flint, two pencil stubs pushing against the black silk, quivered with each step, confirming their nakedness beneath your chemise.

You stopped again before your uncle. Quite deliberately (for you had practised this before the mirror, assuring yourself of the visual effect), you bent forwards, facing him, placing your hands on your thighs, sliding them to hold your knees as you hunched your shoulders, deliberately causing the low bodice to fall open so that your breasts and their pale pink nipples were fully on view within the black silk top. Deliberately holding the pose, you pursed your lips, and planted an affectionate kiss on your uncle's head.

Tearing his gaze away from the close-up view of the bare bosom with which you present him, he looked up into your eyes, returning your kiss with one of his own – a chaste, avuncular kiss, albeit, but appreciative none the less.

'You make an old man very happy, my dear,' he said. 'A cliché I know, but apposite for all that. Come. Sit beside me,' and he patted the plump cushions of the settee.

You perched on the end of the settee, your back against the arm rest, half-turned to face him. Provocatively, quite intentionally, you kept one foot on the floor but, kicking off your shoe, pulled your other up, half under you, so that your bent knee rested against the seat-back of the settee, your open thigh toward your uncle. You tucked the foot you had raised under your other knee, so that your legs were parted provocatively. Your uncle's hand stretched unselfconsciously to rest briefly on your knee before stroking up the inside of your opened thigh, lightly caressing the bare flesh above the stocking top.

You had played games like this before with your uncle, perching near him wearing provocatively short skirts, cuddling up to him in just shorts and a T-shirt, even once (with a mendacious naivety, affecting innocent impetuosity while knowing exactly what you were doing), pulling the T-shirt over your head to demonstrate the results of topless sunbathing in the secret privacy of his orchard, your firm young breasts, bouncing as you pulled the T-shirt free, glowing as pink as the rest of your torso. None, however, had been so daring, so blatant as this. Your pulse was running quickly. Your uncle's conspiratorial smile, and the direction of his gaze, confirmed what you suspected and indeed intended: that within the loose, lace-trimmed leg opening of the chemise there peeped, just visible, the wispy brown curls of your pubic fleece.

'You have grown to be quite the young lady, now,' he said, 'and still growing, I see.'

You laughed, an easy laugh with this dear man of whom you were so fond. 'I hardly think that sitting like this, even with my favourite uncle, can be called ladylike,' you said, 'but I also hardly care. If I make you happy with how I look, I am pleased.'

Your uncle's fingers travelled higher, stroking the soft, tickly skin at the inner junction of your thigh and lower abdomen. As you talked to him, telling him of your party later this week, of your latest boyfriend, his fingers lightly combed the curls at the edge of your mound. You talked to your uncle, as you have always been able to do, with complete freedom. This new boyfriend was only your second lover, if such a word can truthfully be used of a young man whose idea of lovemaking was to put you on your back, thrust into you until you were just becoming aroused, and then pull free so that his spurting fluid jetted hotly across your belly. As he listened, sympathising, your uncle's fingers moved more and more freely, running through the curls of your fleece, stroking across the curve of your lower belly until – and you shifted your position slightly, tilting your pelvis more toward him to facilitate the caress you hoped was coming – his finger trailed at last full across the junction of your lips, touching the hard nub of your stiff clitoris. You gasped, smiling, closed your eyes and unequivocally pushed your hips up further. You parted your thighs wider, so that he might have complete access between. You moaned with pleasure . . .

'Aha, my dear – I trust at the least that this Terry has discovered this for you.'

'Terry wouldn't know what to do with it even if he knew what it was, Uncle. I know it's naughty, but you do it so nicely – please don't stop.'

'So. You still have to do it for yourself do you?' he asked as his questing finger stroked lightly back and forth across the hard nub.

You managed little more than a moan in response. 'I'd rather have you do it, Uncle.'

'I must say, it's a long time since I've had the opportunity to help a young lady in this way.'

Swiftly, the finger slid down the length of your slit, parting the plump lips, meeting no resistance, sliding swiftly inside you, helped by the liberal secretions caused by your own tingling excitement. You felt yourself close to orgasm.

Your voice was faltering seriously now, breathless, despite the game you had been playing, trying to keep your conversation normal, so that no one listening, but not watching (you know there is no one else in the house, of course) would guess what was really happening.

'I do believe, dear Uncle,' you were saying, 'that if this goes on much longer, you are going to have to buy me another set of undies: these will never recover. We'd better stop. You'll make me ... you know,' (and, though you blushed to use the term, you decided none the less to say it) '. . . Uncle, you're going to make me come!' And reluctantly you pulled away.

You stood again before your uncle, your cheeks flushed, your bosom rising and falling with your heightened breathing, and laughed. A nervous laugh, for you were nervous. Your games with your 'Uncle' had never gone this far before.

'Perhaps if you took it off altogether, there would be less danger to it,' your uncle suggested, his eyes twinkling.

You laughed again, moving your head from side to side in mocking admonition.

'You really are a wily old bird, Uncle. Perhaps that's why they made you an Admiral!' But already your arms had crossed over your bosom, not protectively but rather to brush the slim straps off your shoulders. Dropping your arms to your sides, you tugged the chemise downwards at each hip. It slid from your breasts, the lace trimmed top catching momentarily on the pegs of your still stiffened nipples, bending each downward before pulling free, causing your nipples to flick upwards and your breasts to quiver as the material pulled away. It landed in a pool at your feet.

For a moment, you stood thus, the chemise at your feet, facing your uncle, boldly, brazen, your hands at your sides.

'So there you are, Uncle Cedric. Another nude for your collection. How do I compare with all those lovers you used to have?'

His admiring gaze travelled the length of your bared body, taking in the bob of your auburn hair, your breasts, the firm stomach and the horizontal band of the suspender belt which, with the straps for your stockings, framed the auburn bush of your pubic hair. You had not yet learned to trim your pubic fleece, and it grew in a profuse reddish-brown mat across the swell of your mound, completely filling the padded triangle at the apex of your thighs, its upper edge a flat horizontal bar, like the top of the letter T, across your lower belly. Although your hair was long, untidy even, it did not grow so thickly that it concealed the fold of your labia and the tight slot between, disappearing back beneath your body, between your thighs.

'I suppose I should pick these up, and put them out of harm's way, shouldn't I?' You stepped out of the garment crumpled at your feet, then very deliberately turned so that you stood with your back to the seated man. Keeping your feet together, your legs straight, you bent forwards from the hips, your upper body hinging downwards as you reached down to pick up the chemise. Staying fully bent you knew, again from your earlier session before the mirror, exactly the picture you now presented, your stance emphasising the length of your legs, the full swell of your buttocks, and the womanly thrust of the lightly-haired fig of your sex pushing back between your close-held thighs, the dew of your arousal glistening visibly.

'Uncle Cedric?' you asked, still bent double.

'Yes, my dear Chloe,' replied the admiral, his voice considerably more husky, considerably less gruff, than usual.

'Are you sure there is nothing special you would like for your birthday?' You remained bent, touching your toes, with your back to your uncle. You heard the sound of movement on the settee behind you.

'Stand up, my dear.'

You obeyed.

'Now, just step backwards a pace or two,' said your uncle. Again, you obeyed, feeling the backs of your knees touch his, still seated. You were trembling, tremendously excited by what you were doing, by the game you were playing. You felt wanton, sophisticated, daring – and at the same time vulnerable, as if about to lose your virginity all over again. Indeed, you reflected later, this – not the fumbled minutes at that sixth-form party – was the true moment of your sexual initiation, the true loss of girlish naivety, the first beginnings of self-discovery.

Firm hands clasped your hips, guiding, leading. You

shuffled your feet apart, moved back further, then allowed the pressure of the hands on your hips to cause you to lower, slowly, your knees bending. You felt one hand move from your hips, stroke gently between your parted thighs, a finger slid full along the slippery length of the slot of your sex, other fingers spread your lower lips. The warm hard-soft flesh – the skin itself as soft as silk, the flesh itself as hard as iron – nudged against your lips. Slowly, you sank yourself down, felt the rod begin to fill you and you shuddered at the sensation. You pushed yourself downwards until the rod was wholly within you.

A kiss was planted, lightly, between your shoulder blades, hands came round your front to cup each breast, squeezing gently, tugging lightly at your nipples. He may have been fifty-five years old, you reflected, but your uncle had lost none of his touch. Rhythmically, he continued to caress your breasts, squeezing one in each hand, his fingers moving from the base to the tip of each firm cone, tugging at each itching nipple at the end of each caress, before sweeping his fingertips featherlight in swirling patterns on your skin to begin again.

'Ah, Chloe,' he said, 'you are a naughty girl.'

'Yes, Uncle Cedric.'

'And you know that naughtiness always brings retribution?'

'Yes, Uncle Cedric.'

'Remember the teachings of our brother Calvin, Chloe: there can be no joy without sorrow, no pleasures unpaid for.'

'No, Uncle Cedric.'

'The curious difference,' mused your uncle, still kneading your tingling bosom, 'between the Calvinist and the Anglican approach is that to the Calvinist, penance is the payment for pleasure; to the Anglican and the Catholic the exculpation of sin. Are you ready to pay for your pleasure, Chloe?'

'Yes, Uncle Cedric.'

Your uncle ceased his caresses, taking instead each nipple between finger and thumb, rolling each back and forth. Lightly at first, then more firmly, he pinched the already stiffened pegs of your nipples, increasing the pressure whilst at the same time drawing them forwards from your body. The effect was to pull your breasts outwards and upwards, stretching them while squeezing ever harder on your nipples. You began to gasp aloud, panting audibly.

'I shall exact the payment, Chloe,' he whispered, his voice hoarsely quiet, compelling, in your left ear, 'but you yourself will set the price. I shall keep squeezing, harder and harder, until you tell me to stop. When you think you can bear your nipples to be squeezed no harder, just say "stop". Do you understand?'

'Yes, Uncle Cedric,' you panted.

'I shan't stop of course. But I shall not squeeze any harder. You must then start to count aloud. When you get to ten I shall release you, and you will have paid your fine. Understand?'

'Yes, Uncle Cedric,' and you closed your eyes, leaning your head against his own neck and shoulders. The grip on your crushed nipples became harder, the pull on your stretched breasts firmer. Drawing your breath in through bared teeth, you absorbed the pleasure-hurt until eventually you had to say, in a half-cry;

'Stop!'

'Now,' your uncle reminded you, 'you count to ten.'

Grimacing and smiling at the same time, panting between each word, you began to count aloud. You did so very slowly.

At ten – you dwelt a long while after nine, uttering the word in a laughing, triumphant groan – your uncle released your burning nipples, cupping them instead in the palms of his hands, holding your breasts gently, protectively, his lips planting butterfly kisses on your neck, your shoulders, between your shoulder blades. The thought flitted swiftly through your brain of the hurried, conventional screwing you had known so far. This was altogether more interesting. Your nipples burned and tingled. You gripped tightly with your inner muscles.

'Happy birthday, Uncle Cedric.'

Beginnings 3 – Swimming Lessons

In your first large company there was a sports club, which you joined. One activity was swimming, which you enjoyed, so you joined the swimming section. The company sports club rented the local municipal swimming pool for private sessions, of which there were several – and there was one, in particular, you regularly attended, on an evening once a month when the department you were in – you were merely a junior executive, then – habitually worked late. After work, about 9 pm, you went in a group, in a company coach, to swim. In summer, when you joined, the group was quite large – ten to fifteen quite often. By November, numbers had dwindled so that on some evenings there were only half a dozen, sometimes even fewer.

Company rules required that the swimming be supervised by a qualified instructor: there were several, but for these late-evening sessions the regular was a middle-aged woman who during the day supervised the typing pool of junior office girls and trainee secretaries. Typically, it was rumoured she was lesbian, and took occasionally a more than professional interest in, particularly, her prettier charges, a rumour to which you gave full credence after not merely one but several incidents in the swimming baths.

Curiously, you found a certain *frisson* from these incidents: not an attraction to your own sex, per se, rather the *frisson* of sexual arousal from the submission of yourself to the will of another in some mildly bizarre requirement (inevitably in these incidents, but not necessarily so in all). It was the early stirrings of that need which thrills you still, and which has brought you thus far and will take you yet further along this particular path to self-knowledge, self-fulfilment.

The first occurred one typical November evening, foggy, with the pavements damp underfoot and the early chill of night turning to that damp cold which reaches through to the bone even though the temperature stays above freezing.

On such a night, the thought of going swimming deterred all but the most stalwart, and there were but four of you, including the supervisor. Yet in the swimming bath itself, where your footsteps, your voices and the splashing of your swimming echoed emptily in the high-roofed baths, the echo amplified by the water and the tiled walls, the atmosphere was warm, steamy – almost drowsy. You were already swimming when the supervisor – who occasionally, as on this evening, did not swim but remained fully clothed – called to you and asked you to climb out of the pool. You did so, and went to her: she motioned you to a small office, the floor without carpet and bare of furniture, wherein you were both hidden from the view of the other two girls who, perhaps guessing what was happening – perhaps they too had been so summoned – remained in the pool, apparently preoccupied.

The supervisor spoke to you, trying to sound official, although later you would confess yourself not fooled by her quasi-authority.

'Ah, Chloe, my dear. Thank you for coming in. Ahm . . .' she was clearly nervous, on edge, unsure of her ground '. . . Ahm, this is a little delicate . . .' a short, nervous laugh, '. . . or perhaps indelicate would be better. I do apologise for having to raise it with you, but my supervisory duties, you understand . . .'

You were truly perplexed, and frowned, feeling suddenly nervous, frightened even, that you had done something wrong, broken some company rule. You racked your brain to think what it might be.

'I'm sorry, Miss Jackson – have I done something wrong?' The woman inclined her head, spread her hands, bringing them together, prayer-like, before her. She drew herself upright – but avoided the directness of eye contact. Her voice, even so, assumed a detached tone, as if she were delivering a prepared speech, carefully thought out, even rehearsed.

'You may be unaware, but the municipal authority does not encourage ladies to swim in the pool during their "certain time" of the month. I can't help noticing your costume seems very, well – very full, em, ah – well, underneath. You are not, by any chance, wearing a monthly towel?'

The impertinence of the question for an instant outraged you. You knew full well there could be no such ridiculous regulation. So why was she raising the subject? Instantly, for reasons you only later began to wonder about, your outrage turned to curiosity. You decided to see where this was leading, what purpose she really had in mind.

'No Miss Jackson – I'm afraid it's all me.'

There was a tiny bead of perspiration in the centre of the dimple just above her upper lip. You could barely keep from smiling and giving the game away as she said: 'I think I ought to check, if you wouldn't mind: I do have responsibilities to see that the rules are obeyed. Perhaps a manual check – or you may care to just move the gusset of your costume aside, so that I may check visually. If you don't mind, of course.'

You did not want her touching you – but the thought of having to bare yourself in front of her you found instantly and, at this stage of your development, surprisingly, arousing. You realised that your nipples were hardening, beneath your swimsuit – and you saw Miss Jackson's eyes fix upon them doing so, which merely made them harden all the more until they pushed against the fabric of your costume like small stubs. You were suddenly aware of the way in which your breasts swelled into the vee of the suit's rather low-cut neckline.

'I'd rather you took my word for it,' you replied, game-playing rather than serious.

Emboldened, Miss Jackson decided to stake all: 'On this occasion I shall not ask you to remove your costume completely, which of course the regulations entitle me to do. But if you would just be so good as to slip the top off your shoulders and lower it, say, to mid-thigh, so that I may check the inside of the gusset, please my dear, no more need be said.'

'Very well,' you replied, feigning reluctance. Crossing your arms before you, you brushed the shoulder straps down so that, as you pulled your elbows free, the top of the costume pulled downwards across your nipples, the hard edge tugging at their increasing erectness, before folding beneath your breasts, baring them.

You pushed the costume over your hips, down to your legs where it gathered, inside out, in a band across the top of your thighs. You stood thus, feet together, arms militarily straight by your sides, holding the swimsuit, and stared her straight in the eyes – save that her eyes were too busy sweeping the length of your nakedness before fastening on your mound and the bush of your pubic hair, both of course revealed by the partial removal of your costume.

And you wondered at the feelings of acute sexual arousal which caused your nerves to jangle, almost to the point of orgasm, which your situation, your game of mixed exhibition and submission sparked within your taut, trembling body.

There was a long silence – then 'thank you, Chloe.' Miss Jackson's voice was strangely taut, husky and authoritative at the same time. There was, too, still a note of hesitancy, as if she were still nervous of you, unsure. She knew that you knew she was greatly exceeding her authority in demanding that you undress before her. You knew, and she knew, that were you to report her to real authority, her position would be acutely embarrassing, at the very least. The question was, did she know that you knew? The game intrigued and excited you: here was this woman, apparently having such authority over you that she could command you to strip yourself naked before her. Yet in reality it was you who then had complete power over her. Were you to complain about her, either to the pool authorities or to, say, the personnel officer of your firm, the resulting embarrassment to her might even have cost her her job. The power, in fact, was yours – not hers.

Yet the feelings which were aroused in you by being thus

commanded to display yourself, and in such incongruous surroundings and circumstances, excited you, compelled you forward. You were blushing hotly, butterflies fluttering in your lower belly. You wanted this woman to make you do something – something outrageous, something you wanted to do yourself, but must have the excuse of being told to do by another. Without conscious decision, yet knowing you did not have to, you heard yourself saying, in a voice barely above a whisper:

'Will that be all, Ma'am?'

You remained utterly motionless, staring straight ahead, your arms still by your sides, your naked torso, your breasts, your taut nipples, your pubic fleece, displayed.

You did not know what you wanted to happen next, what Miss Jackson would do – but you knew, you hoped, that she would not simply bring the moment to an end. You wanted to be told to do something else.

Miss Jackson paused, assessing you. Your question, the tone of your voice not merely gratified her – it was more than she dared hope for. Could you be for real?

'Eh – thank you Chloe,' she said and made a decision to try one more risk.

'I see I was mistaken – you must forgive me. But you are rather well developed, if I may say so, "down there" for a . . . well, for an unmarried lady. I take it you are not wearing, um, internal protection? That, of course, would also be an infraction of the pool rules – although of course not quite as serious.' She paused again, wondering, and decided to push her luck just one notch further.

'Perhaps if you could just part your legs a little, so that I can ascertain there is nothing, as it were, hidden . . . then I would have discharged my duty completely.'

You shuffled your thighs apart as far as the stretched fabric of your bunched swimsuit would permit – and an imp, a demon, put an idea into your mind.

'I'm afraid I can't Miss Jackson – the swimsuit . . .' Then, suddenly, impetuously, saying the words even as you – before you – fully considered the consequences, you heard yourself saying.

'I'm afraid if you need to inspect me there fully and thoroughly I shall have to take it off completely. I hope it won't be necessary – but I don't want to be in trouble, Miss Jackson. If I have to show you everything . . . if you say you need to see . . . I shall submit to whatever is required.'

The woman could barely believe her luck. And perhaps it was just as well, for who knows, had she pushed you too far at that first encounter what different consequences there might have been rather than what then emerged, and what latent seeds within your still maturing psyche, only now being brought fully to flower, might have been trampled underfoot by too hasty and bungled an attempt at cultivation, to remain buried and unenjoyed forever. And so, to return to our reminiscence – what happened next?

Miss Jackson decided to try one step further. Forcing herself to move slowly, lest she should find that she had misread the signals she hoped you were sending, whether knowingly or not, she approached you.

'If you wouldn't mind, Chloe – it would be only for the briefest moment. And of course, entirely confidential.'

She wanted to make sure of you, wanted whatever happened next to be your move, not hers.

For your part, you were trembling with a mixture of excitement, nervousness, and a sudden, overwhelming urge of exhibitionism that compelled you to be as utterly outrageous as you could. There was, in the tiny, tiled office, only a single wooden table, a hard-seated, square-legged chair with curved, slatted back.

Unspeaking, avoiding her eye, you stooped to push the swimsuit fully down your legs, stepped out and, knees demurely together, stooped to pick it up. Half turning, you placed it on the table and, completing the turn, pulled the chair forward, turning it so that it faced the woman who stood motionless, watching you.

You sat on the chair, shuffled yourself forward so that your buttocks overhung the edge – then leant back, grasping the back of the chair where the outer edges of the slats joined the hard seat. Your firm breasts, the nipples still enormously erect, sagged slightly to either side of your torso.

Keeping your feet together, you rolled them outwards, so that they rested on the edges of your little toes, your heels raised, and swung your knees fully apart, revealing the full-haired intimacy of your sex, displaying yourself blatantly. Blushing, you closed your eyes, turning your head demurely to one side.

'Will you have to inspect me physically, as well?' Your voice was almost a moan. You were at once embarrassed and daring, apparently submissive but in reality assertive: yet within, you did not really know whether or not you wanted her to touch you, or what your reaction would be if she did. Seized by a sudden, lustful urge to exhibit yourself – to shame yourself, even – you tensed your buttocks and, pushing down on your hands, you actually lifted your hips upwards, almost off the chair, pushing your opened thighs and opened sex upwards. Your knees rolled further apart, opening you even more. Your thighs were shaking, visibly – but you held your self-imposed position of display rigidly, despite its awkward strain.

Miss Jackson did not move, but put her own head a little on one side. She too, although you could not see it, was flushed in the face. She looked directly, desirously, at your displayed and opened sex, noted the trembling of your parted thighs. She took in the heavy folds of your sex-lips, fringed as they were with the curls of your auburn hair. And she noted the single, heavy droplet of crystal dew which had gathered at the lower junction of those lips, visible now at the closed petals of the bright pink slash which was incongruously revealed within the thicket of your heavy thatch. It told her all she needed to know.

You held your blatant pose for a full minute. It seemed an age. Finally, you turned to look directly at her – but still kept your hips uptilted, thighs apart, your sex still opened towards her.

'Do I have permission to close my legs now, Miss Jackson – I'm afraid holding myself like this is rather tiring.'

'Yes indeed. Thank you, Chloe. I do apologise if I have caused you any embarrassment – but the regulations, you know – I do have to check. You young ladies nowadays –

so well-developed and womanly already. You may put your suit on again, now, and join the others. There is no need to mention this to them – it's perhaps better if you don't . . .'

The Interview

It was one of those archetypal London clubs, set behind a heavy oak door in an elegant Queen Anne façade, one of a dozen such doors and façades in a quiet street within an easy walk of Piccadilly. In the days when gentlemen in town had little to do but move between their club, Piccadilly, Shepherd's Market and St James, it had been a gentlemen's club. Now, although ladies were admitted both as guests and as members, the change appeared to have had little impact beyond that of rendering more varied the list of members' names.

Indeed, with some of the lady members it was almost a case of 'how can one tell their sex?' as you had mischievously remarked to yourself as you walked through the entrance hall, with its glass-fronted porter's kiosk and its polished brass, towards the heavy double doors of the downstairs bar.

Your lover was waiting for you, as arranged. He rose from a deep, well-worn and comfortable armchair to move across the dark, burgundy carpet towards you. What other colour could such a carpet in such a place be? You wondered if the place had been re-decorated since the old king – the old queen, even – had died. (The answer, as a close look at the fabric of the room and its furniture swiftly revealed, was 'yes' and 'no': 'no', the decor had not been significantly altered in close on a century, but 'yes', the fixtures, carpets, furniture and furnishings had been renewed as often as was necessary to prevent age becoming decay.)

It was, you decided, the sort of place you rather liked, in which you would feel instantly at home as, so obviously, did your lover, but one where at least some of the inhabitants would irritate you.

You did not have long to wait to meet one of the latter.

You and your lover had just seated yourselves, cosily (such a place, you thought, invited such a word, not normally part of your everyday vocabulary), in a pair of deep armchairs, a low table between them and drinks, ice tinkling in cut crystal and brought to you by a silent-footed, blue-jacketed waiter who had clearly spent a lifetime being the very soul of discretion, when you were peremptorily joined by George.

George was clearly a buffoon of the first order. He talked loudly, and inappropriately, about your presence and of the fact that you were in your lover's company (though, more correctly, your lover was in *your* company) in such a place. His lips, he announced grandly, were sealed. He called his wife 'the old trout', and immediately regaled you and your lover with tales, barely believable, of his own indiscretions which were obviously frequent and – not the least reason being his obvious willingness to talk about them loudly within his own club – indiscreet to a remarkable degree. He was a man, you decided, who clearly felt that everyone was entitled to his opinion: so long as those opinions agreed with those of George himself.

At last he left, and you and your lover could speak alone. The soul of discretion bought another drink (George, at least, had not been miserly in his hospitality). The low-level, brass-bound lamp with its green shade cast a warm glow across the table, across your lover, elegant in his City clothes, and across yourself, no less elegant.

You had dressed, at least from the suggestion of outward appearances, as for a high-level job interview, in a tailored suit, with a high-necked, close-buttoned blouse with long sleeves beneath the open jacket. You and your lover had discussed what you should wear for this occasion – but you had swiftly cut the conversation short, not permitting him to go into detail. You had your own ideas, knew perfectly well what would be expected, and what would be appropriate. Beneath the blouse and skirt, you

63

wore no underwear, save a matching half-slip, your stockings and the lace-trimmed suspender belt which supported them. Beneath your blouse your breasts, without a brassiere, quivered with your breathing.

A certain tension, an apprehension, grew within you, despite the warming drinks, as you watched the face of the tall, eighteenth-century Dutch clock in the far corner of the room, the heavy tick of its slow-swinging pendulum faintly and intermittently audible in the quiet conversation (quiet, now that George had left), in the room.

At seven-thirty precisely, you and your lover rose, went back into the high-ceilinged hallway with its polished tiled floor and its scattering of Indian rugs (one, you noticed, complete with tiger's head), and turned off the hall and into a narrow corridor, where the walls were lined with framed prints of water-coloured yachts of a bygone era, and gentlemen with stern looks and impressive whiskers.

The single door was halfway along, on the right. Your lover opened it for you, and ushered you inside, following and immediately closing the door behind him.

The room was smaller and warmer than that in which you had just been sitting, and it seemed even more emphatically from another era. It was a library or reading room of some sort, its walls lined with glass-fronted bookshelves, its carpet, curtains and furnishings were a heavy green where the other had been red.

Two men and a woman were sitting behind a long, leather-covered table situated against one wall, facing into the room. An open fire in a fine tiled Victorian fireplace glowed rather than blazed within a chimney set in the corner diagonally opposite the door. The mantelshelf was broad, surmounted by a large, framed mirror with bevelled glass. Before the fire, stretching from one side of the chimney to the other, was an ornate, leather-topped fender – almost a bench – complete with heavy brass fire dogs, long brass tongs and all the rest of the paraphernalia of a Victorian room.

In the same corner of the room, set parallel to the angled chimney breast, was a low coffee table, long, with the stout, curving legs of early Victorian furniture. The top of the table, you noticed, was mirrored, an incongruous touch, out of keeping with the period of the rest of the room.

Large, leather-covered settees, the arms and backs curved as broad and wide as the back of a horse, were arranged along the wall opposite the leather-covered desk.

In the middle of the room, facing the desk, was a straight, high-backed chair, its seat also leather-covered to match the deep green of the rest of the furniture. It stood, alone.

Your lover spoke. 'Gentlemen, Madam, allow me to present to you – Chloe.'

The men were of indeterminate age, somewhere around fifty, the woman likewise. The men were dressed as you might expect the admissions committee of an exclusive gentlemen's club to be dressed, in dark suits and sombre ties. The woman too wore a dark jacket, with a collar and tie, her short-cropped, jet-black hair slicked to the sides of her head, her face lightly touched with make-up. She wore a monocle ('My God,' you said to yourself, 'a monocle – I don't believe this!'), in her left eye, a device which gave that eyebrow a slightly arching effect.

'Welcome, Chloe,' said he who was apparently the senior member, the chairman as it were, of the group, 'please be seated.' He gestured, unnecessarily since you have been fully briefed by your lover on what you must do, how you will be expected to disport yourself, to the single chair in the middle of the room.

With a glance at your lover, you shrugged your jacket from your shoulders, allowing your lover to take it as it slipped from your arms. He placed the jacket on the arm of a settee. You moved toward the chair, turned to face your examiners, and prepared to sit. To an onlooker, one unprepared for what was to follow, or one watching from the front, as were the three whom you faced although they, unlike our fictitious onlooker, knew precisely what they expected to see, it appeared you were merely hitching the hem of your skirt slightly, to facilitate your sitting.

But your fingers, dropping lightly to the sides of your

thighs, did more than merely hitch. Deftly they gathered the material at the sides and rear of the skirt, as far as the hem, discreetly raising it up the back of your thighs to reveal (but only from the side, where your lover stood, watching also), the tops of your stockings and, sliding further, higher, that which was above the tops of your stockings.

In one movement you sat, just as your fingers completed the raising of your skirt, so that it was the bare flesh of your buttocks which touched the cool leather of the seat, the material of your skirt tucked discreetly away. He who was, presumably, the chairman of the three facing you, your examination board, as you have already mentally dubbed them, gave an all but imperceptible nod of his head, the ghost of a smile, in approval of your action. Clearly you have been well schooled.

Still your fingers remained by your thighs, a hand at each side, gathering now the rest of the material of your skirt which thus slid, obediently, up the face of your stockinged thighs, to rest completely in your lap, your stocking tops and the fronts of your pressed together, bare thighs now also visible to the onlookers opposite.

You raised the skirt further, bunching the material tightly at your waist, the creamy whiteness of your hips and even your belly now revealed.

Your hands left your skirt, to separate and rise, clasping together again behind your neck. At the same time your thighs opened, widely, to display the softly-haired flesh within, the lips parting with the stretch of your limbs as the muscles at the tops of your inner thighs tautened with your movement.

You sat bolt upright, boldly displayed, your innermost secrets presented for inspection. Your eyes prepared to lock into the eyes of those seated before you, knowing that the strength of the eye-contact would prompt them to wonder just who was testing who – but the gaze of all three was directed elsewhere.

Your lover had moved behind you. Swiftly his hands came round beneath your own uplifted arms, to undo the buttons of your blouse. The eyes before you followed his movements.

The front of the blouse parted. You felt your lover's strong hands (their touch invariably making your flesh tingle with anticipation), pass across your midriff, pulling the silk of your blouse to either side, exposing your breasts, the nipples large and relaxed. The blouse was pulled free of the waistband of your skirt, pulled back on your shoulders as far as your raised arms would permit, swept free of the front of your body. There was a perceptible intake of breath from those at the table in front of you.

No one spoke. Your lover displayed your breasts, sweeping his hands up your rib cage to cup and lift them before letting them swing free. He brushed the flats of his hands downwards, from your throat across your nipples towards your lap, flattening your breasts roughly against your chest before releasing them again to demonstrate their resilience, their firmness. The roughness of the action began to stiffen your nipples.

At a word from the woman, she of the slick-cropped hair and monocle (where, you wondered mischievously, was her gold-and-ebony cigarette holder?), he grasped each of your swiftly stiffening nipples between finger and thumb, pulling them outwards from your body, stretching your breasts into elongated cones, then lifted each high, stretching them until your in-drawn breath warned him that you wished to be stretched no further.

With a final, cruel tug that burned your nipples, his fingers squeezed and slid off the hardened, sensitive ends, releasing your breasts to fall again and quiver softly, the nipples reddened and now prominent.

The Monocle was the first to move the interview on from the mere display of your charms, and of your willingness to comply.

At her behest you rose and, your blouse still agape and your skirt still bunched high on your hips, you approached the three seated at the table. Of course, you made no attempt to cover either your breasts, which swayed provocatively as you walked, nor the bush of your pubic fleece, plainly on show.

You stretched across the table as directed, your hips pressing into its rounded edge, your breasts flattening against the cool leather top. Upon the Monocle's instruction, you extended your legs stiff and straight behind you, angling downwards so that only your toes touched the carpet. On the Monocle's instruction, you moved your feet apart.

The Monocle rose, and moved around the table until she was standing by your left side. The other two rose also, and moved to your right side. Craning your neck backwards, somewhat uncomfortably, you obeyed the Monocle's command to raise your head and gaze straight ahead, at the wall before you. Following instructions, you did not allow your chin to rest on the table top, but instead, again upon instruction from the Monocle, you spread your arms wide to grasp the edges of the table. The action forced your shoulders down on to the table, so that the weight of your upper body now pressed heavily on to the desk top, flattening your breasts further.

As a final touch, the Monocle folded back the sides of your blouse, gathering the material to rest high between your shoulder blades, leaving your back bare so that the swell of the sides of your breasts, the skin tautened and shining by the way your breasts were crushed by your own weight against the desk top, could be plainly seen. The wide parting of your legs emphasised the creamy swell of your buttocks, revealing the dark valley between.

The crop was light and whippy, its bite sharp but unbruising. To the obvious satisfaction of your examiners you evinced no surprise at its appearance, nor made any protest at the obviously intended next step. You wondered, apprehensively, whether it would be applied to your buttocks (your original assumption – the traditional target), or your back, now bared above the bunched material of your skirt around your waist by the Monocle's actions in gathering the material of your blouse.

Later, to your lover, you would confess your relief that it was not the taut skin of your bared back which had felt the leather's wicked kiss.

It was the Monocle herself who commented, approvingly, when you made no 'silly fuss' as the crop was plied across your offered buttocks. Instead, the sharp intake of your breath, the way your eyes shut tight, then opened again, was exactly the response your examiners wished to see.

So too was the way in which your buttocks clenched, hard, immediately following the stroke, the way you held them clenched for the few moments it took to absorb the sharp, stinging hurt – and the way in which you allowed them to relax again, giving the deliberate, incontrovertible signal that you were ready to accept the next.

After the fourth stroke (at each, the clenching of your buttocks was more pronounced, held longer), you again relaxed, in all other respects holding your position, spread-eagled, your neck arched back, your gaze set at the blankness of the wall. Four clearly defined red marks crossed the bright whiteness of your buttocks. Your mind concentrated on containing the flaming heat spreading through your bottom, while more directly your brain willed the incipient tremble of your parted thighs to be still. You waited thus for a fifth, a sixth – relying implicitly upon your lover to intercede on your behalf, to judge the degree of your discomfort, should you wish to take no more. Your own fortitude in these moments and these matters is your special gift to him.

In fact, it was the Monocle who, unbidden, lay aside the crop. 'Excellent,' she said, as if remarking upon the work of some student whom she had been unable to fault, but was none the less reluctant to be seen to praise.

Next you were required to stand, feet apart, on the mirrored top of the low coffee table, your skirt bunched still on your hips, the heat from the fire palpable on the backs of your bare thighs and buttocks, your hands again clasped at the nape of your neck, while each in turn subjected you to an intimate inspection, tugging at your sex lips, stroking between to test the degree of your slipperiness, your arousal, your further willingness to submit. The Monocle parted your lips at their upper juncture to expose the stiff stalk concealed within, stroking, then pulling, then squeezing, which drew from you a sigh, then a gasp, then silence between gritted teeth as the muscles of your parted thighs knotted and bunched in the effort to keep still, not pull away.

You exhaled deeply, loudly, as her punishing fingers released you and she stepped back. Your breathing had quickened, the muscles of the insides of your thighs trembling in tiny spasms of their own. 'Excellent,' she said again. 'Truly excellent.'

You were then made to stand and face the settee which backed against the wall opposite the table over which you were bent for the crop.

'Bend forwards please Chloe, and put your hands on the seat – keep your feet apart and legs straight.'

You did so, your bared breasts hanging free from your still opened blouse, your skirt still rucked over your hips.

'A little too high, I'm afraid,' said a cultured male voice from behind.

A large, soft-topped leather footstool was slid between you and the front of the settee, the hand which pushed it into place rising to caress, gently and reassuringly, a breast so readily proffered by your pose.

'Rest your knees against the stool, and rest your elbows on the settee.' You complied, the flexing of your knees completing the offer your bent posture and parted thighs made so obvious. Unbidden, you gave confirmation of your own complicity by lowering your head and shoulders further, so that your face, turned to one side, rested on your folded arms, the dip of your curved spine tilting your proffered hips perfectly.

You remained motionless as hands parted your buttocks, revealing the crinkled orifice which lies within. A finger – it must belong to another, for the first hands were still pulling your cheeks apart – stroked upwards, from your cleft and through the valley of your parted buttocks and across the wrinkled eye. The finger stroked your sex-slot again, transferring the slipperiness from your sex to the dry eye above, probing your anus, pushing past the

70

tight ring of your sphincter. You tried to relax, but the dis-
taste you instinctively felt at such an intrusion tightened
further the ring of muscle. You clamped your lips against
involuntary protest, and tried to relax again.

'She will need training there,' remarked a disembodied
voice, 'if she is to be of any use in that regard.'

No one replied. Instead, the hands let go of your parted
cheeks, and moved to caress, briefly, the lips of your sex,
rendered prominent by the pushing back of your hips and
already plump and slick with the juice of your arousal.

You sighed as the first – you know not who – entered
you, sliding into you easily and gently, without haste, filling you deeply. He stayed within you for a few moments,
then withdrew, completely, leaving your now fully opened
sex lips gaping, the air of the room unexpectedly chilly on
the glinting, sensitive skin.

The next – you did not need to turn to know it was not
the first, returning – slid into you no less assuredly, pushing
deeply until you felt the prickle of his pubic hair pressed,
mat-like, against the inner sides of your parted thighs, felt
the weight of the heavy sac of his balls against the thrust-
back curve of your pubis and clitoris.

Tensing your inner muscles, you gripped tightly, squeezing hard, and were rewarded by a sound – half chuckle,
half moan – of approval.

He stayed within you, pressed deep and fully home but
otherwise unmoving, for what seemed like several minutes,
although in reality it was less. For both of you, time stood
immobile. Then, his phallus already pulsing, he too withdrew.

As the hard flesh slid from you, you squeezed more
tightly with your inner muscles and were rewarded by feeling the heavy, helmeted knob give one more strong,
involuntary pulse of power. You were rewarded, too, by a
barely stifled groan which, its perpetrator struggling to
maintain his self-control, his apparent authority in the situation, became half a grunt, half a cough. A blustered (in
other circumstances you might describe the sound, the gesture, as pompous), clearing of the throat, as when

71

expressing unspoken acknowledgement, approval, satisfaction.

It was, for the moment, enough. A minor victory. It was satisfactory.

There was a brief murmur of conversation, indistinct, behind you as you remained unmoving, half kneeling on the footstool, your face buried in your arms in the softness of the settee's cushions.

Footsteps sounded, heading toward the door, which you heard being opened.

Instantly you realised that anyone walking past in the corridor outside which you fully knew was used frequently by persons moving around within the building, anyone walking thus at that moment and glancing, as one naturally would, through the open door, would have an unrestricted view of you, bent thus, kneeling thus, your opened blouse flung up across your shoulders, your breasts hanging, conical, plainly in view, your knees spread, your thighs wide apart, your buttocks – the red marks from the crop still clearly visible – raised and bared, your sex gaping, the hairs on the thickly swollen lips glistening, matted, with your own juices. You remained motionless, unmoving.

'I think I can safely say,' you heard the voice of the senior of the three say, to your lover, 'that we find Chloe eminently satisfactory in every respect. Admirable, indeed. We would be delighted to accept her.'

The door closed. Footsteps approached. Your lover's hands took you gently by the shoulders, raising you, turning you towards him. Your own arms responded. As he bent to kiss you, your bare breasts crushed against the buttons of his suit. You ground yourself against their hardness.

'As always Chloe,' said your lover, 'you were magnificent.'

The House

So now you are to return to the House. Your lover has suggested it, and you have agreed. You want to taste the fruits for longer, not for just a brief afternoon or evening interlude that leaves you intrigued and, next day, disturbed and distracted so that you seem vague to clients, even miss appointments, forget important tasks.

So you have asked your lover to arrange a longer visit – a week – and have taken leave from work for that time. After that, we shall see where you go next.

You arrive by train and are met by Hassan, Stephen's valet: tall, black-haired, dark-skinned: a Pathan, from the northern part of India, near Afghanistan. He greets you politely, takes your bag – but otherwise says nothing. He is impassivity itself. You are intrigued, not least – and because of an intensely private sexual fantasy involving yourself, a broken-down car and a group of Asian men – because you find Hassan at once both highly attractive and dangerously menacing.

At the house you are met by Stephen. Your lover arrives later, meanwhile Stephen and you chat in the garden.

When your lover joins you, he explains that during the week, you are – if you agree – to be 'trained' (trained in or for what is never mentioned). The training will involve your being tightly corseted again, and you will be expected to place yourself entirely in the hands of others for their use. You will be attended by Madeleine, a French girl at the House whose precise position never becomes quite clear, save that for your visit she is both at your command and in charge of you. She will attend to all your needs: you must follow all her instructions. Your training will begin tomorrow; for this evening, you enjoy a relaxed supper party with your lover, Stephen and some of Stephen's friends – a charming evening of wit and pleasant conversation with good food and wine, the very normality of which contrasts enticingly with the more bizarre nature of what you have all planned and agreed to.

Next morning at seven, Madeleine knocks and enters the bedroom where you and your lover are still asleep, and invites you to accompany her. You glance in question at your lover, also wakened by Madeleine's knock. He indicates that you must do as Madeleine instructs.

You climb from the bed, where naturally you have been sleeping naked; Madeleine treats your nakedness with no more than a matter-of-fact sweep of her eyes up and down your body. You stand by the bed, arms at your sides, without speaking. She proffers a big, fluffy towelling robe.

You accompany her out on to the patio outside your suite of rooms, and across to the pool. The paving stones are still cold with the chill of night under your feet, the early sun is pale and unwarm, but the birds are already singing and the day promises to be fine. It is a beautiful morning. Madeleine removes your robe and the chill air fans your body, stiffening your nipples and bringing tiny goose-bumps to your flesh. She gestures towards the still, clear water of the swimming pool; you advance, and begin walking down the steps. You try the water with your foot, and immediately withdraw with a tiny gasp. It is cold, not yet warmed by the sun.

Madeleine places a hand on your elbow, without speaking, and draws you forward. Steeling yourself against its coldness, you step again into the water, down the steps until the level is at the top of your thighs, kissing the lips of your sex. With a shiver, you lower yourself completely and push forward.

Naked, you swim in the still-cold water under Madeleine's instruction.

You emerge and she has you stand with your back to the pool, feet wide apart, hands behind your head, while she dries you briskly with a rough towel. The vigour of her drying restores your circulation, makes your skin tingle; the early sun warms you and just as you are beginning to relax Hassan appears, carrying the breakfast tray. You have to remain still and posed thus, facing Hassan, while he prepares the breakfast table. Hassan, unspeaking, can see plainly while Madeleine continues to rub your body with the rough towel and you must stand still, unflinching and clearly displayed.

While Hassan watches, Madeleine uses the excuse of drying your torso to display your breasts, standing behind you and, her cupped hands holding the towel, raising them high and then letting them fall, moving her hands away quickly so that Hassan can see how they quiver firmly. She crushes them together, then again quickly pulls her hands away so that Hassan can see them spring apart, swaying. To demonstrate their firmness, she pushes them downwards, flattening them, so that Hassan can see, as she quickly moves her hands and the towel away, how they spring upwards.

Finally, with each breast in turn, she tugs hard at the nipple, pulling it firmly several times until you gasp, leaving each in turn standing rigid, reddened and burning.

Then Madeleine does the same around your thighs and hips, pulling her towelled hands across and up your mound, stretching the flesh, making sure Hassan sees not merely her rough handling of your mound but that he is even treated to the sight of your sex lips being pulled and opened, revealing your clitoris, which has stiffened rigidly, partly from her manipulation and partly from your own excitement at being thus so deliberately, lewdly even, displayed.

You realise, of course, that the timing of Hassan's appearance is quite deliberate, the pretext of preparing the breakfast things merely that. It is the first of many such small tests: each morning, you will be made to swim, naked, in the cool pool, each day be displayed in this and in other ways to whoever happens to be present.

Later, Madeleine comes to fetch you from the rose garden,

where you have been relaxing with your lover, enjoying the beauty of the house and its grounds. You soon realise that this will be the pattern of the week: a conventional, somewhat old-fashioned, country-house visit, with walks, outings and evening dinner parties, punctuated by unannounced interruptions which signal the commencement of an interlude involving something considerably less conventional.

Madeleine takes you to your room, where you undress, put on your robe and follow her through corridors and down stairs to another part of the house. You enter a large, bare room in the centre of which is a curious chair-like contraption. Beside it is a table.

The chair has arms, and a back-rest, which in the manner of a dentist's chair are clearly adjustable, but instead of a normal seat it has a shaped stool not unlike the hard, narrow saddle of a racing cycle. Madeleine instructs you to sit on the saddle, and you do. It forces your buttocks apart, pushing against your sex lips. A waist-strap secures you to the back rest. Your arms are raised and Madeleine tells you to grasp your neck, behind your head; your wrists are fastened. Your feet are placed in stirrups, more straps are put around your calves and thighs, your legs are raised and moved apart, the chair is tilted back.

The effect, highly contrived, unnecessarily complicated and far from comfortable, is to hold your pubic area open and still and to display and leave vulnerable your breasts, although for what purpose you are still unsure. You realise that your discomfort on the narrow saddle, as well as the way you have been secured, is wholly deliberate, part of yet another minor ordeal to test, not your submissiveness to others, but your willingness to submit yourself to what others can devise. The submission is not passive, but active.

Madeleine pours warm water from a jug on the table into a bowl, and uses this to soap and then shave your armpits. She carefully rinses and dries each before moving on, and your realise that in this instance the raising and displaying of your breasts when your were told to put your arms behind your head was entirely incidental to the main purpose, which was of course simply to render you immobile, place you in the hands of another, even for such a mundane yet intimate personal chore. You smile inwardly at your mistaken assumption. While you fully expect that your breasts and nipples will bear from time to time the brunt of what your lover called your training, this, it appears, is not the moment. Realising that your breasts are not – this time – to be punished, you relax.

Madeleine now uses scissors to cut your pubic hair, trimming carefully across your mound and down the sides of your parted, opened slot so that you are all but shorn. Then more hot water, shaving cream and a razor to depilate your pubic mound and the lips of your sex completely, washing away carefully any remaining vestiges of soap and loose hairs. Your mound and sex lips are left completely bald.

When she has finished, you are removed from the strange stool and told to bend forwards across the table, feet wide apart. You are instructed to reach behind you and hold your buttocks open while Madeleine carefully shaves between them, removing all traces of hair from the dark valley and even around the puckered mouth of your anus which, red-faced, you must keep displayed. She applies a soothing cream, then you rise, turn and lean back against the table while she applies the cream to your mound and sex, her gentle massage starting in you yet again the tremors of arousal.

Finally, you lean back against the hard edge of the table, legs splayed, while Madeleine holds a mirror between your thighs and you see for yourself your completely smooth mound and the pink, puffy lips of your parted sex. As you shift position, raising one leg a little, bending the knee, the movement opens the outer mouth of your sex to reveal the bright, pink petals of your inner labia which normally lie completely hidden within. You are not surprised to see, in the mirror's bright reflection, a fine trail of silver dew hang like a spider's thread across the entrance to your body.

She takes you, still naked but feeling even more so now, back to your room, and selects for you a sleek and flattering one-piece swimsuit, cut very narrow between the legs and high on the thighs, low at the back. Made of sheer, soft material, the suit has neither cups for the bra nor gusset to cover and shield your sex. The cream which Madeleine has used has softened and smoothed your skin; the material of the swimsuit slides silkily against it. Glancing at yourself in the full-length mirror of your bedroom, you realise that a suit cut thus and made of so sheer a material can only be worn over a pubis as smooth and devoid of hair as yours has now been rendered. To have allowed even a small tuft of hair to remain on the mound of your sex would have resulted in its texture showing, mat-like, under the sheer material; instead, the padded hump of your mound swells smoothly, the divide of your sex lips can just be discerned.

It is a hot sunny day, and you join Stephen and your lover on the patio, near the pool for lunch.

As you do so, Stephen gestures towards the pool, saying to your lover that he would like to see you swim.

Unspeaking, without waiting for your lover to reply, you walk toward the pool, step gently down the marbled steps, and glide off into the clear water.

You emerge after a few minutes, climbing from the pool sleek and dripping, droplets of water glinting on your shoulders and torso. Madeleine is waiting with a large fluffy towel, you walk towards her. The water has rendered the sheer material of your swimsuit almost transparent, so that your nipples, hardened by the cool of the water and pushing against the light material, can be seen plainly, the surrounding haloes showing darkly through.

Below, the depression of your navel shows against the taut muscles of your abdomen, and at the junction of your thighs the sheer clinging material reproduces faithfully the smoothly rounded swell of your mound, the unbroken smoothness and the absence of dark shadow showing that you have been shaved; the shape of your sex lips, the length of your slit, can be seen clearly.

Stephen, you notice, watches you carefully as you walk toward Madeleine. She takes you indoors and swiftly peels the wet swimsuit from you before towelling you off. Vigorously, almost roughly, she towels your torso, thighs and legs dry, leaving your skin tingling. In a few moments, Madeleine having produced a dry swimsuit of an exactly matching cut and material, you return to the patio and seat yourself for lunch in the warm sun, a fresh, fluffy towelling robe flung carelessly over your shoulders.

After lunch, you are introduced to the brush. Without apparent instruction from anyone present – clearly, therefore the result of some prearranged programme for you to which Hassan must be a party – Hassan carries onto the patio and places near the end of the table, where it can be seen clearly by Stephen and your lover without them having to move, a device consisting of a long-handled, soft bristled broom, the handle and head of wood, the brush of synthetic fibre. The handle is mounted in such a manner that the brush is held upright and upside down, through a vertical tube supported by a metal tripod the legs of which are on a flat base plate. There is a horizontal, cranked handle where the legs of the tripod meet to grasp the long handle of the inverted brush. The bristles of the brush have been trimmed to form a broad wedge with a horizontal upper ridge, like the roof of a house. Hassan positions the brush so that those seated at the table are looking along the ridge and the V-shaped top of the brush.

Madeleine asks you to rise and come with her. You go over to stand by the brush, your back to the table and to Stephen and your lover. Madeleine stands behind you and removes the robe, then slips her hands under the straps of your swimsuit, easing them off your shoulders, down your arms and past your elbows. Her hands move round to your front, sweeping the garment down over your breasts, which quiver and bounce in reaction, your nipples – which had softened and relaxed over lunch, after your swim in the cool pool – stiffening once again. Without pause she sweeps the swimsuit on downwards over your belly and thighs and obediently, with no word spoken, you step out of it. Now you are naked once more.

Madeleine moves you so that you are standing behind

the brush, facing your lover and Stephen. She draws you forward:

'Please stand over the head of the brush, Mademoiselle,' (Madeleine is unfailingly courteous, deferential even, towards you even though you both know that you have been told always to obey her), 'and place your feet either side.'

You do so. This is the first opportunity for your lover and for Stephen to see you in your depilated state, and your wide-legged stance reveals you totally: the unnatural baldness of your mound and sex lips makes you feel doubly naked.

'Please cross your wrists behind your back,' instructs Madeleine, and you obey. You feel them lightly but firmly wrapped with a soft, heavy cord, secured behind you. Unseen by you, but of course watched by your lover and Stephen, Madeleine drops into a deep curtsey to enable her to reach the handle which she cranks slowly. The brush rises, still unseen by you, between your opened thighs until you feel the first prickle of its bristles at the soft underflesh there.

'Please raise yourself on your toes, Mademoiselle.'

You rise thus, and the broom follows, pricking you lightly. When you are fully stretched, Madeleine reverses the handle, lowering the bristles by half an inch. She rises, walks away, and returns a moment later with an elegant, wide brimmed hat, trimmed with an open-weave black veil. She places the hat on your head, and takes her leave.

Looking steadfastedly ahead, you know you make a devastating picture, as incongruous as it is erotically potent. Poised high on tiptoe, the muscles of your thighs and abdomen are held taut, their tautness rendered even more aesthetic by the absence of your pubic fleece and the thrust of the pad of your pubis. Your breasts, their firm conical shape enhanced and rendered more prominent by the position of your hands behind your back, rise and fall with your breathing. The wide brim and veil of the hat partly obscure your face, hiding what expression there may be, giving – to the onlooker – a highly-charged air of mystery. Who is this beautiful, naked woman: why is she posed so bizarrely?

After a few moments, barely more than two minutes, your arches begin to tire, your calf muscles start to ache. You relax – and instantly jerk back on tiptoe: even the slightest relaxation results in your lowering yourself onto the prickly head of the brush, the ridge of which aligns exactly with the opened inner membranes of your sex and the parted crease of your buttocks. Until that moment you had been unaware of the alterations made by Madeleine to the apparatus over which you had so unquestioningly placed yourself. The full implications of this latest test of will now begin to dawn upon you.

Of course, you cannot strain on tiptoe for long. Perspiration begins to bead between your breasts and shine on the swell of your naked mound; your straining calf muscles cause your legs to tremble violently, almost making you lose your balance as you struggle, arches throbbing, to remain poised and clear of the nagging little bristles. After fewer than five minutes, you have to give your tiring muscles a respite, and gingerly begin to lower yourself.

You quickly find that the action of shaping the bristles into a wedge has sharpened each into a tiny, stiff spike, as sharp, almost, as a needle. Gasping you allow as much of your weight as you feel you can bear to rest for a few seconds on the brush. Your breath comes in short panting gasps and tiny sobs as your weight presses your most tender flesh onto the uncomfortable perch. After mere moments you rise again on tiptoe.

But the respite is shorter this time. Again your aching muscles cry for relief; again you lower yourself. This time you last a little longer on the brush, before lifting yourself clear.

The process repeats itself, your self-imposed ordeals on the ridge of bristles becoming longer, your defiant attempts to remain on tiptoe becoming shorter.

Finally, your trembling calves and straining arches will support you no longer, and reluctantly, slowly you let your entire weight sink onto the bristled cushion. You cannot prevent a soft sound, half sigh, half groan, escape your lips as you settle onto your uncomfortable perch. Even using your straddled legs only for balance, your feet do not rest flat on the floor. The cruel brush, so devilish in its mundane simplicity, bears your whole weight. The spikes of the bristles feel as though they have invaded your every opening, but surprisingly, now that you have allowed it to happen, the discomfort of your perch is not nearly as bad as you had supposed it was destined to be. The initial contact was the worst part.

You are no longer aware of the individual bristles onto which your own weight presses your tenderest, softest flesh, only of the acutely sharpened throbbing, hovering curiously between pleasure and pain, which now possesses the core of your being so that you can think of little else. Your head tilts back, you moan once more and gaze at the sky through your veil, thinking only of the heat between your thighs. In the sunlight, a film of perspiration imparts a silver sheen to your skin. Soon, tiny rivulets of sweat appear, first on your thighs and between your breasts, later in the hollow of your spine, trickling between your buttocks, wide-spread over the invading brush-saddle, even onto your flanks, from beneath your arms.

'Mademoiselle?' It is Madeleine. You do not know how long you have sat – or is it hung – thus, gazing at the sky, concentrating on absorbing the throbbing heat beneath you.

Madeleine is holding a tall mirror before you, its lower edge resting on the table, which allows you to view yourself reflected from shoulders to parted thighs; and you see your bared, spread sex lips, now puffed and spread wider, as they seemingly devour their tormenting perch. You marvel, both at the effect and at yourself. Through misted eyes you look for your lover. He and Stephen have left. You have undergone this ordeal, apparently, for nothing.

Laying aside the mirror, Madeleine moves out of your vision. She begins to unwind the mechanism which raises and lowers the brush, and immediately the pressure on your sex diminishes. You utter a tiny cry as the bristles come away from your soft flesh.

'Pauvre Mademoiselle,' says Madeleine, who until now

has been strictly correct in the way in which she addresses you, offering no remark which might betray her own feelings or even show that she finds, in your relative situations, anything out of the ordinary.

'Pauvre Mademoiselle – it is only a very little sore, *n'est-ce pas*? Monsieur Stephen – last week he keep me one hour upon the brush; and for me, you know, it is worse. I am not allowed to tiptoe, I must stand on a box, one each side, and must even hold open myself wide as I lower onto the brush. Then the boxes – they are taken away. But come, Mademoiselle: now we must put you straight away into a tight corset. It is the tightest you have worn so far – but very beautiful in its effect. There are special guests for dinner ce soir, and you and I will be sharing a secret. Pauvre Mademoiselle – we shall both suffer agonies. See – I am already fastened.'

And with that, as you gaze in fascination, Madeleine unhooks the waist-band of her skirt at the side – you had not particularly noticed until now it was of the wrap-around sort – and holds both sides apart for your inspection.

Beneath and emerging below her blouse, you recognise instantly the lower part of a corset similar to that in which you had been encased on your first visit to the House. Taut suspenders support Madeleine's black stockings and from the shape of the busk of the corset at the front, it is of a design even more severe than that to which you have submitted yourself.

It also has an additional feature, to which your eyes – with your groin still throbbing from your ordeal on the brush – are drawn with horror. Running in a steel-tight band vertically downwards from the busk of the corset, disappearing into the mass of flaming auburn hair which, in contrast to your own shaven mons, crowns Madeleine's pubis, is a wire-thin strip of polished leather.

'Pauvre Mademoiselle,' repeats Madeleine: 'the worst, as your English saying is, is yet to come.' And, with a barely perceptible wince of discomfort, she places her own feet wide apart.

'Observe.'

Dropping onto one knee, your face level with the bush before you, you see how the strap sits deeply between the parted sex lips which, unlike the mons above, have, like your own, been carefully shaved. This and the effect of the strap exaggerates their already puffy fleshiness.

The strap pulls deep into the crease between the lips before disappearing between Madeleine's legs, into the crease between the buttocks where, behind, it has evidently been pulled very tight, presumably to a buckle at the back of the corset. So deeply embedded in her sex is the strap that only the unnaturally deep division at the base of the girl's parted lips gives a hint of its presence: the strap itself is almost invisible.

At the upper juncture of the lips, at the base of the red-haired mound and forcing wide those heavily swollen lips, the strap widens flatly, leaving a parted aperture, an inch-long slit, through which thrusts the clearly inflamed morsel of the French woman's glistening clitoris, almost unnaturally purple in its colouring.

Your fingers trembling slightly, you reach out your hand and brush your fingertips along its swollen length. From above you comes a tiny cry, but whether of pleasure or of something else you cannot tell.

You will, you know with a spasm of excitement, know soon enough yourself.

Preparation

Before dressing you, Madeleine informs you that she has been instructed to shrink your waist even more, a process that causes you no little discomfort as it is accomplished. Grasping the upright pillar of the four-poster bed in which you and your lover sleep, you press yourself against the upright while Madeleine tightens the laces at the small of your back.

Still not entirely satisfied, your maid – for Madeleine, despite the control she exercises over you is still no more than that – binds you firmly to the post, a broad leather strap being passed around both the wood pillar and your hips, the buckle pulled tight across your buttocks and another being passed around your upper torso, just under the arms. Tightened, the straps hold you fast, pressed against the pole.

It is the latter which is initially the least comfortable, pressing your upper body hard against the unyielding pole which in turn presses hard against your rib cage, between your breasts which are thus thrust bizarrely either side of the upright. You grasp the higher part of the post with both hands, above your head, resting your head on one arm.

The binding holds you rigid, immovable and unmoving, and permits Madeleine the necessary purchase to heave, her knee raised and placed unceremoniously in the small of your back, upon the strong tapes which, through hand-sewn brass eyelets ranged in pairs down the back of the heavily boned corset, enable the garment to be pulled even tighter.

85

As the corset is pulled tighter, you find yourself pushing harder against the upright to which you have been bound, the pressure of your body pushing, grinding the plump lips of your sex, held open by the parting of your thighs round the pillar. And with them, pushed hard against the unyielding wood, is your rapidly stiffening clitoris.

There comes a moment when you realise that it is not Madeleine's knee, nor yet the broad leather strap around your hips, pulled tight across your buttocks and buckled fast, which is pressing your mound and vulnerably exposed clitoris against the hard wood. It is your own stance. You are back again to that childish game with the loosened tooth, testing yourself, pressing the tooth with your fingers to make it hurt, to see how much you can bear before you have to stop. Except that this time it is not your tooth you are playing with. You are deliberately rubbing the reddened nub of your clitoris against the pillar, grinding it hard against the wood to make it hurt, seeing how much of that hurt you can inflict upon yourself, how much your second self will accept, before you have to stop. You are, as it were, two people: the abuser and the abused, violator and victim in one.

It has taken you some time to realise that this is the game you enjoy so much. But the realisation is slowly dawning upon you.

Gasping, released from the straps which have bound you to the upright of your canopied bed you share with your lover, you stand naked save for your corset, high-heeled shoes and dark-topped stockings.

Turning you gently, Madeleine admires her handiwork, adjusting the set of your breasts on the half-cups of the garment, once again using your nipples to lift and stretch each breast in turn, but not as brusquely as before. You notice that this corset holds your breasts higher than the previous one did, pushing them upwards and, because of higher sides to the cups, making them more rounded, although still leaving your nipples and their surrounding areolae completely uncovered.

A short, vertical bone between the cups presses between the orbs of your bosom, holding them carefully apart.

Madeleine lightly caresses the tips, the swelling sides and tops, and the thrust-out undersides of your breasts with the palms of her hands. The sensation is not unpleasant. Using a soft-haired brush, which tickles slightly and which to your mild surprise causes your erect nipples to relax, softening, rather than stiffening further as one might expect, Madeleine applies a blush-pink rouge to the tips of your breasts, heightening the natural colour enough to render the change of tone more noticeable, but not so much as to be garish.

You stand with your feet apart, straddle-legged. Madeleine has placed you facing the full-length mirror so that you may observe what is to happen next. The suspender straps of your corset have already been clipped to the tops of your stockings, which now stretch smoothly. The thin leather strap which Madeleine produces, which, ever since you saw the strap that she herself is wearing, you knew would be produced, which you knew that you, too, would be made to wear tonight, is attached to the front of the corset by a tiny D-ring sewn into the flat, board-hard panel which pushes into your belly. It hangs vertically, bisecting the padded hump of your shaven mound to dangle, incongruously ominous, between your parted thighs.

You see that, in addition to the flattened section of the strap which you saw and touched on the version which Madeleine wears and which on your own now serves to obscure your mirror-view of the junction of your sex lips and what lies between, the hard, rounded surface of the strap has for a few inches immediately below been frayed and roughened to give it the bristled appearance of coarse, rough-haired rope. It is, of course, that part of the leather which in a moment Madeleine will pull through and between your parted sex lips.

In the mirror you see Madeleine move to stand close to one side. You look straight ahead, watching in the mirror, as you feel her hand pass downwards over your mound to press the strap to your flesh. Skilfully, she uses her first and second fingers to part your lips, slipping the strap between, as with her other hand she reaches between your thighs from the rear to catch the free end of the strap, pulling it swiftly through and up behind, to lie in the cleft of your buttocks.

You feel the roughened leather prickle against the sensitive flesh of the inside of your opening, still tender from your ordeal on the brush.

There is a moment as she threads the end of the strap into the tiny buckle sewn to the back of the corset. She pulls the strap firmly secure. You wince. You sense there may be yet some way to go before she has completed her manipulations.

Madeleine has in her hand what appear to be a tiny pair of ornamental tongs, their pincer-end fitted with small rubber pads. She kneels before you, again slightly to one side and, tongs in right hand, places the flat of her left palm against the swell of your mound.

'Bend your knees, please, Mademoiselle.'

You obey, semi-squatting lewdly, wide-open, hands on your hips for balance. The pose is unequivocal; Madeleine, kneeling before you, concentrates on what she has to do.

Pressing flat the flesh either side of the broadened part of the strap, thus pressing also on the leather, she opens the narrow split in the strap, through which the nub of your clitoris is immediately exposed. She firmly grips the swelling flesh with the tongs, tugging lightly first to one side, then the other, to worry it through the narrow opening. You moan at the sensation: the padded ends of the tongs allow Madeleine to grip your clitoris firmly without hurting, blunting the sensation which, though blurred, still causes your hips to writhe in response, in spite of your attempts to hold yourself still.

She has pulled most of your now erect clitoris through the narrow slit in the pliant leather. The tongs shift their grip, grasping more securely, and there is more tugging. Your breath comes in hissed, short gasps.

When Madeleine has finished tugging at your sex you see, in the mirror, that more clitoris than you thought you possessed has somehow been exposed, isolated from its immediate surrounding flesh: the hood of soft skin which normally enfolds and protects the delicate stalk has been pulled back, the stalk itself is displayed from its tip to its root, deep within your normally secret flesh. The edges of the slit in the leather, pushing against each other, serve to grip the root of the stalk tightly. The inevitable physiological response is that the tiny blood vessels within the sensitive organ can fill, but not empty: your clitoris becomes enlarged, distended, almost painfully stiff. The skin tautly stretched, it quite literally shines.

Madeleine lightly passes the fingertips of her right hand along your parted sex lips, which already glisten with evidence of your arousal. Pressing more deeply, she ensures the roughened strap has slid neatly between and into the slot your stance creates, ensuring that no fold of sensitive skin has been nipped or trapped beneath the strap. The intention of the 'saddle-strap', as you describe it to yourself (an accurate thought – that is precisely its name), is to concentrate the mind, rather than to hurt or punish. (There are other forms, less benign, should such a punishment ever be ordered for you.)

Your knees still bent, your thighs still parted widely, Madeleine moves behind and (you feel her fingers slide between the strap and the small of your back, at the base of the corset), with a quick tug, tightens the strap two, three, four notches on its buckle. The strap pulls deeply into you. You wince. It is very tight.

You stand, straight again, before the mirror. The sensation the strap causes is of an intense heat deep within your loins, rather than of simply cutting into you. It is uncomfortable, but only as the corset was at first uncomfortable, before you learned to relax into its firm hold.

Even with your thighs together the visual effect of the strap, and its bizarre peculiarity, is evident. The bulge of your divided lips, where they disappear between your pressed-together thighs, is exaggerated, the presence of the strap drawing the eye inexorably to the centre of your lower body. Between the swelling lips, your purple clitoris thrusts brazenly. It actually glistens.

The effect is not entirely illusory: before you closed your

thighs, Madeleine took another of her quiver of soft-haired brushes and liberally coated the exposed morsel with a pungent oil, laced with a small amount of (your horrified senses tell you, recognising the undisguisable smell), horse liniment. On the sensitive flesh the burning sensation is acute. Tiny muscles at the base of your stomach and the tops of your thighs twitch involuntarily. Your buttocks clench, thrusting your mound forward and upward. The singularised clitoris pushes outward, swelling into further prominence.

'Come, Mademoiselle – we shall dress you for dinner.'

Cumberland
HOTEL · HARROW

```
          The Cumberland Hotel
               Harrow
          VAT Reg No. 222 2703 11
          Order Number  1340130
          17/2/99  Mario      20:50
          Table Number 11  Covers 1

    1         3 Course Dinner        13.50
    1         Gordons Gin             1.75
    1         Stella Dry              2.40

Room Number 108                      17.65
    Cadman
TOTAL SALE  1340130                  17.65
V.A.T. @17.50%                        2.63
CHANGE                                0.00
```

_____
Signature

St. Johns Road, Harrow, Middlesex HA1 2EF
Telephone: 0181 863 4111 Facsimile: 0181 861 5668

VAT Registration Number: 222 2703 11 Registered Number: 570690 England

Amanda

The gown in which Madeleine dresses you for dinner leaves
your shoulders and throat bare, cut low at both back and
front so that its upper line matches closely that of the tight
corset which rigidly controls your figure. To the onlooker,
it merely defies both gravity and nature. The skirt is full,
but with the waistline lowered so that the slimness of your
own waist, enhanced by the reduction imposed by the iron
will of your corset, is emphasised. The material is rich, its
black colour setting off the whiteness of your skin to perfection. A black velvet choker set with a single pearl within
a circlet of small diamonds is your only jewellery.

Full length black lace gloves which reach to above your
elbows, their length matching exactly the level of the top
of your gown, emphasise the bareness of your upper torso.
To describe the effect – and you – as eye-catching, even
sensational, is to understate the case gravely. The picture
you present to yourself in the mirror, before you descend
to join Stephen's guests, pleases you enormously.

Cleverly concealed hooks attach the upper edge of the
bodice of the gown to the upper edge of the corset, at the
sides, under the arms, while the front of the bodice, in stiff
and patterned lace through which glows the whiteness of
your skin, barely covers your nipples which, rouged by
Madeleine, make intriguing shadows. Only an inhuman
spectator can resist the need to look, and look again, to decide whether or not your nipples can indeed be seen through
the material, not quite on display, yet almost so. The roughness of the stiffened material scratches your nipples, causing
them partly to become erect. The effect is compelling.

Raised and offered up by the shaped platform of the corset, the swelling tops of your breasts, above the lace, are bare, provocative, the separation afforded by the rigid central divider of the corset rendering the cleavage deep, inviting.

There are about a dozen guests for dinner: yourself and your lover, Madeleine, Stephen. There is also a woman whom, with a jolt, you instantly recognise as the Monocle, from your bizarre interview at the Club: she is introduced to you as Lady J. (the monocle is not, this evening, in evidence), and is clearly if not Stephen's companion then at least a friend of close and long acquaintance.

With Lady J. is a young woman of, you guess, about twenty-one years – her ward, Amanda, according to the introduction – and a young man of similar age, Mr Ivan. Lady J.'s godson, he is Amanda's attentive but somewhat awkward, if not to say awed, escort.

There is also a Japanese couple, Mr and Mrs Ishigawa: he is tall and tanned, not at all a stereotype; she is also tall, for a Japanese woman. They are expensively and elegantly dressed in Western fashion, and speak accentless English with complete fluency.

Madeleine has schooled you in the manner in which, introduced to each male guest, you must curtsey low, bending forward a little while using your upper arms to press lightly against the carefully sprung sides of the corset. By this means the corsage of the gown is caused to move discreetly, displaying to anyone glancing downwards the tips of your breasts and the full succulent berries of your pale-rouged semi-erect nipples, answering for each in turn the question posed by the lace. This offering is compulsory; you may not flinch, nor decline. To each of the men in turn you are required to show, discreetly, your breasts.

One, a German by the name of Gudeweir, unabashedly asks you to repeat the movement despite the presence at his side of a lady companion, tall, blonde and exquisitely beautiful. Your quizzical glance towards Madeleine, effecting the introductions, elicits a nod of her head, indicating you must obey and as you do, instictively lingering so that he can examine fully what you discreetly display, he quite openly reaches to brush a fingertip across the tip of your nipple, which instantly hardens further in response.

At each low curtsey, the saddle strap beneath your belly, between your thighs, presses even more deeply into your sex, pulling at the tightly gripped and swollen clitoris, hurting deliciously.

Again, Madeleine has warned that you should evince no sign of discomfort, nor allow the – quite intentional – sweet hurt the strap affords to interfere in any way with the sweep and grace of your movements. Rather, you are expected to exaggerate those movements, to curtsey with that inch or two of extra depth, to stay in position that moment or two longer than absolutely necessary. The requirement is, in short, that you demonstrate to those who know of your predicament that you willingly accept the imposition that has been placed upon you.

With this instruction you comply, the butterflies low in your belly fluttering with each self-immolatory sweep, the wide material of your dress gathering, pool-like, around you on the floor.

The dinner itself, with its attendant sparkle of good conversation, is enjoyable but otherwise unremarkable until, sometime after the main course and the cheese (Stephen orders his table in the French manner), and thus during the dessert, Lady J. is talking animatedly with Ishigawa, the Japanese seated on her right, on the subjects of discipline and self-control. She raises her head slightly to include her ward, Amanda, seated on the far side of Ishigawa, in the conversation.

'Amanda my dear,' remarks Lady J. with an almost casual insouciance completely at odds with the burden of her words, 'perhaps you would be kind enough to help me demonstrate what I mean.' Amanda, with a gracious dip of her head, smiles at Lady J. in complicit acknowledgement.

'Madeleine,' continues Lady J., 'be so good as to help Amanda dispose, for the moment, of the upper part of her gown. I require her partly bared for this small demonstration. I am sure no one will object.'

To a murmur of interest from the other guests (Ivan, you notice, who is seated beside Amanda, clearly can barely believe his ears), Madeleine rises, elegant and swan-like (you admire her grace, sharing as you do the mutual secret of the cruel disciplines you each are bearing), from her place beside Stephen at the far end of the oval table, and moves behind the younger girl. Amanda has rich, ash blonde hair, blue eyes and the face of a pretty cherub. Madeleine unhooks the top of her gown at the back, and Amanda eases it off her shoulders and down her arms, to sit naked to the waist, the material of the gown gathered in her lap, framing her bared torso.

Her breasts are spectacular, larger and firmer than your own, and rounded where your own, more mature, are more conical in shape. Your own breasts already possess a natural heaviness which gives them a rich fullness, much admired by your lover, while the youthful firmness of Amanda's breasts causes them to sit high upon her torso, without even that natural crease of flesh beneath. Her skin is pale, almost translucent, and as notable as the snow-white globes of the breasts themselves are Amanda's nipples, or more particularly the areolae surrounding the nipples. The nipples themselves are small, button-like, but the areolae are large – almost three inches in diameter, you judge, seated, as you are, directly opposite – and clearly delineated, their colour a blushing pink.

'Notice Amanda's nipples and their surrounding haloes,' continues Lady J., somewhat unnecessarily, every eye round the table now being already focused thereon. 'Note their distinctive coloration – I hope you find it attractive, as indeed does Amanda. She has been to some trouble to ensure that you should.'

'Indeed?' queries Stephen, as much, you suspect, to keep the conversation flowing, to keep his other guests involved, a part of the extraordinary tableau which has suddenly developed, as out of curiosity on his own part. You also suspect, quite rightly, that Stephen is already as familiar with Amanda and her person as he has recently become with your own. You have realised, already, that it is no co-

94

incidence that tonight you should be meeting Lady J. again, realising too that she and Stephen probably, as the vernacular expression has it, 'go back a long way'. Lady J. interrupts your train of thought.

'Left simply to their natural colouring, the haloes of Amanda's breasts would be almost invisible, so pale did they remain as she began to mature. Yet their unusually large size makes them a most uncommon but attractive feature of her bosom. But a feature is attractive only if it can be seen, and be admired, and if nature has provided us with a feature which might be admired, but which might with advantage be enhanced, albeit it with the aid of a measure of artifice – should we not then be prepared to take that artifice and bend both it and ourselves to our will – our desire, if you prefer – to be seen and admired to best advantage?

'I certainly think so and Amanda, having spent much of her formative years with me, shares my view. Amanda has lived with me since she was ten, and at the age of sixteen agreed to enter a regime of strict discipline and training in return for such advantages and opportunities as my experience of life could offer her. As a result she has, despite the deceptiveness of her very feminine appearance, an iron will, especially where she herself is concerned. She has, in short, been brought up with discipline: both mine and, more importantly, her own.

'And so, to return to the matter of Amanda's admirable breasts: both she and I, as her breasts developed, agreed that admirable as they were, their appearance would be enhanced if only her nipples and, in particular, the quite remarkable size of their surrounds were a little more immediately obvious.' Lady J. pauses to take a small sip of wine, while the company utters not a word, but waits. The effect of the pause lends a dramatic effect to her tale, entirely intentionally. Clearly, there is about to be made a revelation which Lady J. fully intends will shock her listeners – or at least compel their attention irredeemably.

'Once she became of an appropriate age,' continues Lady J. after her little moment of theatre, 'Amanda therefore voluntarily submitted herself to the not inconsiderable discomfort of having the haloes of her breasts, including the nipples, mechanically tattooed, to leave them permanently, though only by a shade or two, darker than the colouring nature had provided.

'That is the sort of self-discipline of which I speak.' Lady J. turns to Amanda with a smile, genuine in its warmth. 'Thank you, darling.' Amanda, however, makes no move to replace her gown, continuing to sit bare-breasted.

'In Japan,' interposes Ishigawa with an inclination of the head, 'tattooing is much more highly regarded than here in the West, where it appears to be seen simply as a lower-class phenomenon. In my country to submit to the tattoo – without, of course, the benefit of any form of drug-taking, by way of opiate or, as so often with those who visit tattooists here, by way of alcohol-induced numbness of the mind – is regarded as a worthy demonstration of self-discipline. It is something willingly undergone, for that reason, both by gentlemen and by ladies, often intimately, to enhance the pleasures of the bedroom.' Ishigawa glances again at Amanda's bared breasts.

'Amanda was given an anaesthetic, perhaps, to dull the sensation before being tattooed? The nipples are, quite obviously, an acutely sensitive area.'

'Yes indeed and not at all,' Lady J. swiftly replies, reversing the reference. 'An acutely sensitive area as you suggest, and no, Amanda was not assisted in such a manner in any way. She simply sat, much as you see her sitting now except with her arms over the back of a high-backed, upright chair.'

Amanda's position shifts in mute demonstration; withdrawing her arms completely from the folds of her dress, she places each over the back of her chair, grasping the chair uprights with both hands and pulling her shoulders back, thrusting her breasts into even greater prominence and locking her torso firmly against the chair's rigid back. As she does so, the material of the dress falls lower, revealing the top of an obviously tightly-laced waist corset, its upper edge reaching to the lower part of Amanda's rib cage. Having her breasts tattooed is, it appears, not the only discipline to which Amanda willingly submits.

Lady J. is still speaking. 'It was, as you say Ishigawa-san, simply an exercise in self-discipline.'

Lady J. continues, permitting herself a wry smile. 'Though I must admit to being a little hard on the dear girl, for which she has since generously forgiven me. It was Amanda herself who volunteered the suggestion, while discussing her appearance, that actually having her nipples and their surrounding aureolae tattooed would be the best and most permanent method of improving upon their too-pale colouring. I was of course impressed that she would think of, let alone seriously consider, such a solution, and pointed out the possibility that undergoing such a procedure might be rather uncomfortable. She assured me she had already considered this, and remained undaunted.

'It was clear, however, that Amanda was thinking in terms of having the operation done in a private clinic, expecting naturally to be either locally or even generally anaesthetised. I, however, saw in the suggestion a most delightful and unusual opportunity to assess the effectiveness of my training regime by putting her through a small ordeal, a rite of passage as it were; to gauge the measure of her self-control, to try the strength of her will.

'Amanda, when I put to her what I had in mind, quailed somewhat at first – but it was a measure of how far she had already been trained that she accepted, albeit with some foreboding, my suggestion, and asked me to make the necessary arrangements for her. I did not, therefore, engage the services of a cosmetic surgeon, nor even a normal beauty salon. Rather I sought out an old-fashioned but very discreet tattooist, arranged a private session, took her to the appointment myself and of course remained with her throughout.

'I also suggested to Amanda herself that, as part of her training, she endure what was to be done without taking or using anything to deaden the sensation. I am pleased to say that, having committed herself to submitting to her "trial-by-ordeal" she instantly accepted this further little challenge. However, without, I confess, telling her, I decided for my own purposes to make things a little more –

shall we say – *demanding* for her than they need be, to see how she would react.

'I therefore obliged the tattooist to follow the old, traditional method, using a single mechanical needle rather than the electronic multi-heads that are currently in vogue, requiring therefore a much greater measure of fortitude on the part of the subject, especially when being used on – as you have said – so sensitive an area.' Lady J. pauses to sip her wine. There is complete silence around the table, the entire company now intent upon the story of Amanda and her tattoos. After a brief pause, Lady J. continues.

'It is one thing to be the passive subject, however acquiescent, in such a situation; it is quite another to be the active architect of one's own immolation. Despite my presence as chaperone, as it were, I quite intentionally made it a requirement that it should be Amanda herself who should take command of proceedings. She discussed with the tattooist precisely the area she wished to have coloured and the precise coloration to be achieved, bared her breasts at the appropriate time herself (rather than being disrobed by another), and offered them for the tattooist's inspection and opinion, then, seating herself so as to present each in turn for the procedure to be carried out, she invited the tattooist to begin or, indeed, to desist, if she should have had enough.

'In fact it took about half an hour to colour each of Amanda's breasts in turn, beginning – for no particular reason – with the left. Over an hour, all told, allowing for a brief respite between. It turned out indeed to be just the ordeal I had intended. While her self-possession to begin with was only to be expected, it required commendable and impressive effort of will on her part – she was but eighteen years old at the time – to hold herself steady while being worked on for such a long time and endure what was obviously an increasingly acute discomfort without movement or complaint. And especially I think, to resume her seat and offer her right breast for the same treatment, once she had rested after the left was finished, knowing then as she did what it was going to entail and how long it would take.

98

'I could, of course, have taken over, instructing both Amanda and the tattooist – but that would have defeated at least part of the object of the exercise. I therefore preferred to remain aloof, allowing Amanda to dictate the pace. I am pleased to say she passed her little test with flying colours: there were some small tears by the end, of course – it was obviously quite uncomfortable to endure – and a certain amount of gasping and head-tossing as the tattooing itself became more difficult to bear unaided – but not a squeak, and not once did she really flinch, or pull away. Rather, she held herself still and almost quiet for the entire duration: I was extremely satisfied with the display.'

Ishigawa, clearly anxious to hear every detail of Amanda's ordeal, interrupts: 'She did not have to be held at all?'

'Not by way of restraint,' confirms Lady J. 'other than for the operator himself to grip her breast firmly as he worked. And when tattooing the nipples themselves, it was necessary for me to assist, but only by holding the breast itself steady, and to tauten the skin, to prevent the nipple moving around too much under the needle. Like this.'

Lady J. rises swiftly, to step behind Amanda who is still sitting in the pose she adopted as Lady J.'s description of her ordeal at the tattooist's hands began. Lady J. reaches down across Amanda's left shoulder to take hold of a white breast with both hands, gripping tightly with her fingers either side of the rounded globe, squeezing hard so that the halo itself becomes an even tighter rounded ball, her thumbs horizontal and touching tip to tip, her fingers pressed flat and downwards. Her hands, surprisingly strong, form a solid circle around the halo. Holding the breast firmly, she uses her thumbs and forefingers to stretch the skin of the halo tight so that it gleams tautly in the soft lighting of the room, the small nipple standing solid and hard. Amanda leans her head back and to one side, against her guardian's arm, and closes her eyes. No one speaks.

Lady J. releases her hold and returns to her seat. The imprint of her grip is pink on the white skin.

'Amanda herself did the rest,' she resumes speaking as she sits, the sudden tension in the room caused by her dramatic demonstration quickly subsiding. 'Highpark certainly taught her a thing or two.'

'Highpark?' you repeat incredulously. You turn to Amanda. 'You were at Highpark?'

Amanda nods. 'Not you too, Chloe?'

'Yes – well, only for a brief visit. But I got the cold shower treatment and all that. 'Tell me,' you continue recklessly, emboldened to ask both by the company you have been keeping and by the turn of events at table, 'I heard something about the place, after I left: they called it "Tits and Twats"' (Ivan, seated next to Amanda, gulps.) 'or "Prefects' Choice", or something like that: the prefects are allowed to administer corporal punishment, but they use a wet towel, flicked, you know what I mean? And on the breasts or, well, right up between the legs? Is that true?'

'Oh yes,' concurs Amanda, ruefully, 'it's true all right. And anything else you ever heard about Highpark – including the speciality canings.' Amanda glances at her guardian, as if for permission to continue. Lady J. nods.

'I did an exchange term there once, and got to know their system rather well. I was eighteen – it was my last term at public school, before I went to finishing school.'

'You mean you were caned?' remarks Ivan, unable to contain himself any longer. Lady J. has brought along her godson, you are already beginning to surmise, purely so that he may be plunged into something beyond his comprehension. Another of her 'little tests'.

Amanda turns toward him, her air of quiet dignity entirely uncompromised by the present deshabille of her dress. 'Mr Ivan, is that not a rather indelicate question to ask a young lady at dinner? Even one sitting beside you with her breasts on display for you and all else present to see and, if Lady J. later gives you permission, which I rather suspect she will, to handle and perhaps even cane for yourself?'

Amanda smiles, thoroughly in control of her remarkable situation. The young man Ivan blushes, stammering lamely, finding the prospect of being allowed to handle or – as, Amanda herself had hinted, almost promised – to strike with a cane that astonishing bosom almost too much to contemplate.

'Oh, I say, I mean – do you think, I may?'

You intercede. 'I believe. Mr Ivan, that it is a fairly safe assumption that anyone who has been to an English public school, particularly one such as Highpark, has been caned, be they male or female.'

'Quite so,' adjures Amanda, warmly grateful for your support. A bond of fellow feeling is developing rapidly between this cool young lady with the spectacular bosom and yourself. You sense you are not merely birds of a feather but probably birds presently – even if of their own volition – very much in similarly gilded cages.

'As you rightly suggest, Chloe,' continues Amanda, as if discussing the weather, 'I did indeed make the acquaintance of a Highpark cane, but only once with any severity. Of course, I took occasional minor canings from the mistresses. Nothing special – and naturally I was a regular target for the phenomenon you have already described, the Prefects' Choice. These' – she cups her breasts lightly – 'were, as you can imagine, very popular, being already somewhat well-formed, but I wasn't neglected lower down. They really do mean Tits and Twat, and divide their attentions equally. It is always delivered to the bare flesh, you know, and they are quite merciless, even when applying the wet towel between the legs, which one is required to open completely wide while standing otherwise still, and holding position with no complaint. They are also uncannily accurate. The outer lips of my sex – plump enough, if I may say so myself, when I started – were quite markedly thickened and toughened up by the end of the term, as well as being left somewhat darker in colour.'

Mr Ivan almost chokes on his meringue.

'And your breasts?' you ask, as much for the benefit of your own curiosity as for that of the company. 'They received the Highpark treatment as well?'

'Only once,' replies your companion, 'and I can tell you,

101

to be caned on the naked bosom is not at all like being caned on the bottom.'

Lady J. intercedes, encouraging her ward and, you rather suspect, seizing the opportunity to regain control of both ward and situation, a control which has, in truth, been somewhat slipping from her. She had not, perhaps, expected to find you and Amanda so at one; had clearly intended to shock, if only mildly, and for the sake of some light diversion, the company with her command over her charge's demeanour and behaviour, the unquestioning obedience she can clearly command.

'Amanda, my dear, you have clearly struck a chord of response. Perhaps you had better give us chapter and verse.' She turns to the rest of you, embracing in her remark Stephen, yourself, Ivan and the others. 'While of course Amanda was subject to some measure of normal discipline at home, it was when she was at Highpark, really, that we both learned that she had a facility, an aptitude if you like, for discipline and self-control of a more developed kind.

'Continue, my dear.' She smiles at the still awe-struck Ivan. 'In gory detail if you please.'

Chapter and Verse

Seated between the young man Ivan on her left and the elegant Oriental, Ishigawa, Amanda seems content enough to oblige both her guardian, and the rest of the by now fascinated table. Bare-breasted, smiling and seemingly quite unconcerned at her unorthodox deshabille, she continues her tale.

'About two weeks before I was due to leave Highpark, I got a note to go see the head,' she begins. 'I thought I was for it – and I was, but not in the way I'd imagined.

'She told me I'd been a model pupil, but she felt that to gain the full benefit of being at Highpark I should experience the full extent of the Highpark curriculum, as she put it. There was no reason, she emphasised – I had done nothing wrong – but was I game to see if I could take all that Highpark had to offer not merely in the classroom and on the playing field, but in the more privately tutored matter of personal discipline and self-control?

'Well, you know how girls at school feel about letting the side down. She didn't say so in so many words, but she obviously wanted me to agree to take a full caning, Highpark-style. I, however, while knowing only that the head sometimes caned senior girls on the breasts, as well as on the buttocks, had no idea what it all might entail.

'So I said yes, as long as it didn't go on my record that it had been necessary for me to be punished, I would submit myself to whatever she regarded as an appropriately demanding test – although being eighteen, what I actually said was that I'd "take the works".' There is laughter, and Amanda smiles, clearly enjoying being allowed to hold centre stage for so long in what is – the young man Ivan excepted – company rather senior to herself.

'She said that was fine: "Glad to see you're a gal of spirit, Mandy; you probably won't enjoy it at the time, but it'll be good for you, and you'll be glad you did it when it's over. Every senior Highparker gets it once – sort of graduation ceremony, if you know what I mean. Sets a gal up for life, know you belong to a special club" – and much in that vein.'

You smile at how easily the now elegant and soft-voiced Amanda can recall with such accurate mimicry that mode of speech peculiar to a certain type of English girls' school.

'She told me I was to go to see the games mistress, and tell her I would be reporting back to the study that evening, at punishment roster, for a Highpark "top set". She would tell me what to do.

'It wasn't until I got to the games mistress I discovered what I had let myself in for – a full half-dozen, bare, on the boobs, followed by "six for Highpark". When I said did that mean six on the behind as well, she just said: "wait and see".

'It was quite an experience. By the time I got there I was, quite frankly, scared as hell. I'd been fully briefed what to do by the games mistress, who always attends to see fair play, and it was quite a little ritual, and indeed still is. I know a girl who left Highpark just two years ago – I met her at a party at Aunt J.'s – and we compared notes. She told me that nothing has changed. It's still the same headmistress, and still the same routine.

'One queues outside the study, waits one's turn to be called in. A girl for "topping", as they call it, always goes in last of that day's punishment group, however many there are. One may thus have to stand in line for twenty or thirty minutes while one's mind, despite one's best efforts to get it to think of something else, insists on producing the wildest possible imaginings of what one is about to receive. A mistress supervises the line, so of course no talking is permitted, and that merely serves to make matters worse.

One is in an absolute flutter of anticipation by the time one's name is called. One goes in, curtsies and says, "Top set, Ma'am, if you please". Then it's stand at attention until one is told to strip and present.

' "Strip" comes first. That means going over to a table in the corner, facing the wall: you remove tie, blouse and bra – all to be carefully folded, and put on the table – so that one is stripped bare to the waist, then you turn, face the headmistress, walk three paces forward, stand to attention.

'One may have to stay thus, breasts displayed but standing quite motionless, for several minutes, while she deals with notes and files on her desk, lying across the front of which are two canes. They are very traditional: light bamboo, very thin, shaped at one end with a curved handle, like a walking stick. As I say, there are two: a thicker one, used for the more conventional, ahm, procedures – on the bum, as it were; and a much lighter, thinner one which, since one has now been fully primed and warned about it, one knows is known simply as "the upper sixth" and is the one one is going to get across one's bosom in just a few more minutes . . . It's very unnerving.

'Eventually she looks up, gets up from the desk and comes across. I'm sure it's all part of the ritual, designed to test one's nerve and all that, but anyway, she always "checks" the target area manually, if you know what I mean. She cups and lifts each breast in turn, gives a squeeze or two – "to test the resilience", she calls it – pulls and pushes them back and forth for a bit, tweaks the nipples to make them erect. All that sort of thing.

'When she stands back and says "Present", it's put arms behind the back, palms of hands flat on the buttocks to make one's breasts protrude as fully as possible; head up, lean forwards just enough to make them hang slightly, but not enough so that one's head and shoulders get in the way, pull shoulders back so one's tits stick out as much as possible: then say "Ready Ma'am" – and hold still for the duration or come back tomorrow and try again. You have to be able to take the whole lot in one go, or you haven't passed. That's the test.

105

'The headmistress has some clothes pegs ready. Before using these, however, and to make one's nipples fully prominent, she simply takes hold of them again between her fingers, squeezes really tightly and pulls hard while one counts out loud to ten, in Latin.' (Unbidden, a lightening thought flits through your mind, causing a faint smile to flicker across your face. 'I think I preferred Uncle Cedric's arithmetic lessons' you say to yourself.) Amanda continues.

'When one reaches "Dix", she lets go and one has to say – and word perfect, mind – "Thank you, Ma'am. May I respectfully suggest pegging, please". Then she puts the clothes pegs on one's nipples and one has to count out loud again, this time to twenty, in Greek. The slower one does it, the more kudos one gets – but it doesn't let you off any of the strokes.

'The first two flick the clothes pegs off, which is murder. What's worse is they don't count towards the dozen.'

Ivan, you notice, has twice had to shift in his seat, his right arm betraying some subtle movement of his right hand – easing, you know, his inevitable erection into a more comfortable position; he listens awe-struck, his mouth slightly open, his eyes never leaving Amanda's exposed bosom.

'Then she starts in earnest,' continues Amanda. 'It's not too bad on the top, but underneath, when she does the uppercut as she calls it, it really rather smarts. One's boob bounces quite alarmingly – and the cane on one's nipples is absolute purgatory. She does one side at a time, pretty hard, from the side – three strokes, alternating down and up, then moves round to the other side. One mustn't move while she shifts position, just keep pushing them out for more, and needless to say no yelling or blubbing. I can tell anyone who has never experienced it that after the first couple one thinks one's bosom is going to explode. And she always leaves the nipples to the last. And at the end one has to stand there until she says, "Stand down".

'One stands upright, then, arms by the sides, at attention – no rubbing allowed – and then, as if one might by now not have had quite enough, one is expected to say "Thank you, ma'am. May I take six for Highpark, please?".'

'The specials the games mistress wouldn't tell you about?' you ask, horror-struck yet ghoulishly eager for every detail.

'Indeed. There is a piano in the study, and the head-mistress takes the music stool and moves it into the centre of the room. One is led over to it, told to kneel on the seat and take hold of the handles at the sides. Then one is directed to kneel up with back straight, head turned to the right, arms stiff at the sides and hands holding tight to the handles of the music stool. The games mistress goes and stands behind and reaches round one's front, grips one's nipples – which are so sore by this time one almost faints at the touch – and pulls each tit outwards, away from the chest and then hauls them up as high as they will go. She holds them taut like that, stretched fully upwards. It is acutely uncomfortable.

'Six for Highpark is three backhanders to each, fast and hard on the underside, taken in complete silence. If there were no tears in one's eyes already, there are by the time that's over: it's probably the hardest part to take, but one knows by then that one is almost through – and to give up at that stage would be to fail the test completely. If that happens, you either try again each week until you get through it in one go – or be forever known as a "gal" who couldn't hack it. It's a tough place.'

You listen, fascinated and, strangely, curiously excited by such a tale. You find yourself wondering if you could take such a strict regime, uncomplaining, and your stomach churns at the thought of giving it a try, just to prove yourself. Prove yourself to whom? You are, even now, beginning to ponder the answer to that question.

'Isn't it dangerous?' you ask Amanda. 'I mean – doesn't such harsh treatment cause damage? Breasts are so delicate, there must be a risk of permanent harm?'

'Not really,' replies Amanda. 'It's a very light cane, which stings more than anything else. Afterwards, one goes back to the table and puts on one's blouse – in itself something of an ordeal, as you can imagine, given the state of one's bosom by now – and one's tie. The head keeps the bra, and gives it back next day, in assembly, as a sort of certificate of graduation, so everyone knows that one has been given a topping, and passed, and then one goes to the matron.

'She checks for bruising, and has bowls filled with iced water. One sits – feeling extremely foolish, I might add – at a table with one's boobs dipped in a pair of those for about twenty minutes, to prevent any bruising and make the swelling start to go down. Or one can use ice packs.

'Next day, one's boobies are fairly colourful: mine were bright red. But it only hurts for about a day, and the marks all fade in less than a week. By the time I went home at the end of term, you would never have known. Certainly Aunt J. didn't notice anything – except that she remarked, when I turned out for my morning exercises next day, that they seemed even bigger and firmer.'

'Exercises?' you query, enthralled and fascinated by the story of Highpark's extraordinary regime, and now intrigued by this latest revelation.

Fresh Air Is Good for You

Your question, hanging briefly on the air, causes the well-nigh breathless flow of Amanda's enthusiastic reminiscences to falter. Blushing pinkly, she glances nervously towards her guardian. It is clear that, despite the fact she is over twenty-one, the young woman holds herself in thrall to her guardian. She spoke freely enough about her Highpark experience – but only once Lady J. had, very pointedly, given her permission. Now again Amanda falls silent, face turned to her guardian, waiting to see if she may tell more – or perhaps indeed watching to see if she may have suddenly said too much. There is a *frisson* of tension in the air. It is not, you note, fear of that embarrassment which is sometimes felt by others in a company when one – or more usually two – fall foul of each other's rules, and what should be private rebuke becomes public reprimand. More, it is a *frisson* of being permitted to share something essentially private, out of the ordinary – and expectancy at what may come next.

You find yourself wondering what consequences might befall Amanda later in the privacy of her home with her guardian, should intimacies be revealed which should not be. Such thoughts stir you, and intriguingly you find you have instinctively tightened the cheeks of your buttocks, so that the hard strap you wear, almost forgotten during Amanda's tale, suddenly pulls hard and between the lips of your sex. You gasp suddenly, privately; you glance around, but no one has noticed.

'I should explain,' says Lady J. picking up the thread of Amanda's tale, 'that once Amanda's sixteenth birthday had passed and she was with me during the vacations, she was exercised for half an hour each morning in the stable yard. I place great emphasis, Chloe, on physical fitness – especially for a girl or young lady in training, and Amanda was by this time undergoing the strict training regime which she herself had chosen.

'I keep a small and very discreet staff, all of whom have been with me since Amanda became my ward at the age of ten: they know her as one of their own family. Once she was in training, it was natural that occasionally I would hand her over to one of them to be dealt with; that was in itself an integral part of the training. She could hardly be described as "trained" if she was prepared to do only what I told her.'

Lady J. turns slightly, embracing the remainder of the company in her explanation, and continues. 'So unless we happened to have house guests whom I did not wish to take into my confidence or close friendship, Amanda exercised each morning in the Greek manner – that is to say, quite naked.'

'Really?' It is the turn now of Mr Ishigawa to re-enter this extraordinary conversation, interposing for the first time for several minutes. 'You say the Greek manner – classical Greece, I take it you refer to – but it is something of the Japanese manner too. I too, and my wife and daughters – separately, of course – provided the proper proprieties can be observed, are in such a habit still.'

'Fresh air, Ishigawa-san, has, since antiquity, been regarded as beneficial to all the body,' replies Lady J. 'Amanda, as a girl, was quite used to such exercises each morning with, as you say, the proper proprieties being observed: one is not running a peep show. None the less – and I do not know how you view family servants in Japan – within our own, small household, there were two of my own close staff to whom the more intimate aspects of Amanda's training could safely be entrusted: my secretary – an unmarried lady of mature years who has been with me for a long time – and my head groom, a married man with two daughters of his own, each a little older than Amanda.

110

The fact that some of those aspects required Amanda to be without some or all of her clothes was quite incidental.

'In any case, it is good for a young woman to have to display herself naked on occasion, provided it is in properly controlled and in disciplined circumstances. That too is part of her training. She thereby learns pride in herself, along with discipline.

'If I could not put Amanda through her exercise routine myself – I usually did so, of course – I would leave the matter to my head groom. He has been with me now for more than twenty years. He trains all my horses. I knew a seventeen-year-old girl would be no problem to him. And, as I say, I felt it was good for Amanda to have to show herself and to exercise nude under orders.'

'So. Amanda,' asked Mr Ishigawa, 'you raised no objection?'

'Well, no,' replied Amanda. 'I mean, I didn't really think much about it. One simply did as Aunt J. bid. I thought myself lucky – and still do, by the way – to have such a mentor. I had – still have — my own flat, above one of the stable blocks, overlooking the yard. I came down each morning, six-thirty in summer, seventy-thirty in winter, and did half an hour of exercises. A bit like circuit training, really.

'I'd get up, shuck off my pyjamas, go to the loo, brush my teeth and hair then put on a pair of knee-length white socks and lightweight training shoes and run down the stairs. Absolutely starkers apart from shoes and socks was the rule.'

'So you were kept naked at all times? You did not wear a robe, for example, when going to and from your place of exercise?' asks Ishigawa, warming to this tale. 'But there were others who might have seen you thus, no?'

'As I said,' repeats Amanda, 'I was absolutely starkers, apart from shoes and white knee-length socks from the moment I left my bedroom until I got back: that was the rule. The stable yard was closed off, the gates kept shut overnight, and Aunt J. kept only a small staff. So apart from Aunt J. or Pelham waiting to put me through it, there

111

would be no one else about at that time. Miss Markham, Aunt's secretary, never actually took me for exercises.'

'You exercised out of doors? In all weathers?' continues Ishigawa, adding solicitously, 'Your English climate can be so unkind.'

'If it wasn't actually raining, I'd be exercised in the yard – and sometimes even if it was raining. If the weather was too bad, it would be in the tack room of the stable block. It could be a bit brisk during the winter, although one soon warmed up. And anyway for much of the winter we would move into the tack room for most of the session, especially when there was a frost on the ground – certainly until I was properly warmed-up. Exercising in very cold air can actually cause both muscle and lung damage – and I have to say that both Aunt and Pelham knew what they were doing. All that working with horses, I suppose.

'Although I also have to say that Pelham, especially, always seemed to take a particular delight in finding some pretext – usually press-ups or a sprint – for taking me out of doors for at least part of the session when it was really frosty, either back into the yard or occasionally through a side door from the tack room onto some rough pasture at the back of the stable block. As a concession to the cold, I would be allowed to wear gloves in addition to my shoes and socks, but otherwise, I still had to be completely nàked.

'He once had me run the whole length of the drive – almost a quarter-mile – and back on a very frosty morning: but looking back I suspect he knew there were neither house-guests nor other staff on the estate that morning, so it was highly unlikely anyone would be around to see me. Although he was very tough on me, he was also very protective.' Amanda pauses, momentarily reflective, then continues. 'I must admit that running completely naked through a pure white world, my breath hanging in little silver clouds in the totally still air, all the tree branches glittering crystal and every long blade of grass frozen white and stiff was actually rather beautiful. It was barely light, the ground still very misty. Warmed up, one didn't really feel the cold despite being bare: it nipped and stung a bit, and made one's nipples ache most awfully, but otherwise it just left one's skin tingling and prickling – and I remember especially enjoying this tremendous feeling of total freedom.

'Even so, I was also as nervous as anything in case I would be seen. I mean, running down the drive buck-naked at daybreak would take some explaining. At the same time, I got quite a buzz from being made to do it, and the thought that someone might indeed see me. I think Pelham realised this,' she continues quickly, 'for he soon developed his "Jack Frost Special", as he called it. It meant taking me outside on the frostiest mornings for a run across what we termed the back pasture – starkers, of course, apart from the shoes, socks and gloves – to the far fence then back by what we called the stony path, but stopping along the way for ten or even twenty press-ups. And with Pelham, press-ups really meant press: even with the ground thick with a really heavy frost, like a deep-pile white carpet, I wasn't "down" as far as he was concerned until my chin and elbows were on the floor with my hands clasped behind my neck. The object of that, of course, was quite unashamedly to ensure my boobs were pressed hard and uncomfortably into the ground. He used to pick the really stoniest bits of gravel or roughest bits of pasture to work me on, and of course, I had to pump my bare front down just as if I were on a feather bed.' Amanda laughs again. 'There was no gingerly easing myself down onto the cold, hard ground either – "They're not rare ostrich eggs, Miss Amanda, they won't crack or break," he used to say, "an' a little prickle or two won't do 'em no 'arm. So let's get 'em toughened up. Down you go." So it was *thump*, straight down hard onto whatever was there: stones, rough grass without so much as a second's hesitation or a wince at whatever I might be landing on. And of course, in the frost the ground one was laying oneself upon was damned cold.

'But there was no complaining, otherwise it was double the dose. It was pretty spartan, in that regard. And he'd usually finish a press-up session with what he called a "spread-eagle": arms and legs spread wide out, chin, shoulders, hips and knees – and all bits in between – pressed hard onto the ground for a count of twenty. I'd usually end up with small stones or bits of twig stuck to me all over my front, and might well not be given permission to brush them off until I was dismissed to go back to my room.

'He once even, quite deliberately I know, just to see if I would go through with it, made me do ten press-ups on to what looked like just a tuffet of frozen grass: only thing was, we both knew it wasn't grass. It was a small prickly bush – *juniper horizontalis*, to be precise, a dwarf member of the pine family – which has particularly sharp prickles coated with a natural resin that makes them quite painful to touch. My whole tummy and boobs ended up a mass of spiky little green pine needles, and after my shower my breasts were covered in little red scratches which lasted two or three days.

'But that was the exception, really, rather than the rule. To be honest, in the spring and summer I generally found it rather pleasant to be naked out of doors on a bright, warm morning, once I'd got over the initial embarrassment bit. It wasn't nearly so bad as it sounds.'

For Exercise

During Amanda's dissertation Ivan, you notice, has had increasing difficulty maintaining his equanimity. Once, you felt sure, he was almost ready to explode there and then, and saved himself only by turning away from the nubile young woman on his left, tearing his eyes away from the still stiff-nippled bare bosom at his side, and pouring himself more wine. You were not the only one to notice, and be amused by, his discomfiture. With a wry smile Stephen, catching your eye and seeing your amused glance at Ivan, had motioned to the young man to extend the courtesy to others near him, yourself included. And you realised, as Ivan had with trembling hand refilled the crystal goblet before you, the heavy lip of the decanter ringing briefly, bell-like, against the rim of your fine glass, that, although you had not really noticed until now, Stephen, though apparently as absorbed as everyone else in Amanda's tale, had not actually been watching her at all. He had been watching you, your reaction. Every time you had glanced away from Amanda, it was you upon whom the head of the table's eyes had been resting, not the bare-breasted young blonde. Stephen has, you realise, colouring suddenly, not taken his eyes off you from the moment Madeleine had risen to stand behind Amanda, and had at that young woman's request undone the buttons at the back of the dress and eased it from the creamy shoulders, baring for all the high white globes of the young woman's breasts, with their tiny nipples and their startling, wide, pink haloes.

Even as you begin to ponder what significance, if any, this realisation might have for you (the strap between your thighs, pulled hard between your sex lips, is suddenly uncomfortably noticeable, pulling tight beneath you), Amanda's tale, barely interrupted, continues, though it is actually the Japanese, Ishigawa, who pulls it forward.

'And the exercises themselves, if one may ask, Miss Amanda: they were all rigorous? Like the press-ups on the gravel?'

'Not really,' Amanda answers, shrugging noncommittally so that her firm breasts quiver, moving together on her bare torso, rising so that they almost touch, then parting again, 'but enough to have one glowing, as we English ladies say, at the end of half an hour even in the coldest weather.

'Once into the stable yard, it was warm-up first. Starting with feet together and simple stretches, arm swings, side bends, back bends and toe-touching. Then the same, but feet apart. Then star-jumps: that's when you stand at attention, jump to feet out, arms out, then back, for twenty, quite fast. Really warms one up. It does rather make the boobs leap about a bit, though, which can be a little disconcerting, and actually rather uncomfortable if done for too long. Quite amusing to watch, though, I suppose,' she adds with a cheerful chuckle. 'Then more bending and stretching exercises – a bit more strenuous. Then the usual routine: squat bends, press-ups, running on the spot.'

'And you were not at all embarrassed?' pursues Ishigawa, determined to extract every last iota of information from the matter-of-factly candid Amanda. 'I mean, at having to display yourself naked in this way, before a male – and a servant, at that?'

'One didn't think of Pelham as "a servant", of course. He had been my guardian's groom for as long as I could remember, and indeed for many years before I came to live with her, and he was in complete charge not just of the horses but of all that side of the household, so he was as much a figure of authority as a servant. But yes, I admit, it was a bit embarrassing at first, especially the first time coming downstairs and presenting myself completely starkers to him: you know, breasts and pubes and everything on show. And of course it was acutely so when I started to exercise: boobs bouncing around all over the place, and all that – and everything else displayed any time I had to part my legs or bend over. Still, he had daughters of his own, so I reckoned he wasn't seeing anything he didn't know about.' Amanda laughs, remembering. 'Anyway, he soon ensured I got over any girlish shyness: touching toes with feet spread wide apart and him standing behind me had me blushing the first couple of times I had to do it. But I got used to it.'

'And the exercises,' pursues Ishigawa again, 'after the warm-up and the stretching and so on. What of those?'

'Some hop-ups, on the bench,' replies Amanda. 'Then onto the back, legs cycle, scissors – all that sort of thing – and finish off with a fast sprint three times round the yard and some final stretching to calm down. After a while I didn't think anything of it, really.'

'Scissors?' enquires the relentless Ishigawa, urging Amanda to leave no detail unexplained. 'What is "scissors", please?'

Amanda replies, matter-of-factly: 'You lie on the back, hands out to either side for balance, feet towards the instructor. Then you swing the legs straight up in the air, feet together, toes pointed, and hold. On the command one, move feet to eighteen inches apart and hold; on command two, open full stretch and hold; on command three, bring feet together again. Holding open like that, especially full stretch, which is legs as wide apart as you can get them, can be murder on the backs of the knees and on the muscles on the insides of your thighs, especially if whoever's in charge is feeling a bit sadistic, and takes their time before allowing you to close.

'And of course, one is rather showing off everything one has. That really was a little difficult, the first time I had to do it in front of Pelham – and the old goat made me hold myself fully-open for ages before giving permission to close. And he had me do it half a dozen times. There was nothing about me he didn't know by the time he'd finished. Especially after he had me trim.'

'Trim?' queries Ishigawa, on cue.

'Oh, yes.' Another giggle. 'My pubes – pubic hair, you know. He had me remove it all but completely.' There is no need for Ishigawa, or indeed anyone else, to prompt Amanda further with a question. A raised eyebrow and attentive silence are sufficient to keep the tale flowing.

'Pelham had supervised me a couple of times while Aunt J. was at home, but too busy to take me herself. Then, after the second week of my new regime, Aunt J. had to go away for three days, so I had him for three mornings in a row. She left me a note, saying she was placing me completely in Pelham's charge, that I was not to be surprised if some of his instructions were new or seemed a little unusual and that I was not permitted to query anything he said. I had to do exactly as he directed me until her return – so she obviously knew, and approved of, what was coming.

'At the end of the first morning, just when we were finishing and I was waiting to be dismissed, Pelham told me to place my feet wide apart. Then he took the end of the crop he always carried and flicked it back and forth through my pubes a couple of times, sort of fluffing them up, then quite calmly said he didn't like it, and he wanted it a *lot* shorter.

'I remember it vividly, I can hear his voice now – it was rather scary but exciting at the same time, to be spoken to in such a direct way about one's most intimate person, to be given such explicit and indeed intimate instructions. It made me tingle all over.

'I am blonde, as you see, and was at the time really rather proud of my pubic hair, in a teenage sort of way. In those days I had quite a lot of it. Many blondes have quite thin, wispy pubic bushes, but even at sixteen mine was thick and already very profuse, sort of sandy-gold in colour, a little darker than on my head but not much, but the hair itself was unusually long, very bushy and, well, I rather thought it quite the bees-knees, actually. In fact,' Amanda giggles again, 'having begun to get used to being naked in front of Aunt J. and even Pelham, I had secretly taken to waxing and brushing it before I came down in the morning, to make it as fluffy and bushy as possible. I thought it looked quite good. Pelham didn't share my view.

' "For tomorrow, Miss Amanda if you please," he said, very polite, but very firm. "We should get rid of all of this here old straw. It's thicker than an old doormat, much too long and quite unkempt – all right on a farm-girl, I suppose, but not suitable for a young lady at all." ' Amanda's imitation of Pelham's rustic tones causes laughter, and she continues. ' "Tidy it up, if you'd be so kind: mow it real close across the hump. As for in underneath and along the lips, where it grows much too long, I'll be obliged if you'll trim it away altogether, so's everything can be properly seen. Your female part has developed quite womanly already – indeed if anything I'd say the quim lips themselves is really rather large for a young lady o' your age, and a little too pale, p'rhaps, though that'll change in time I dare say. Still, they're strong looking an' thick, plump as a pheasant, as they say: nice an' meaty and well rolled into the fold. You've got a good long slit too, what should show nice an' high at the front and set tight and close underneath, with the leaves still small and slow to open, like a proper virgin should be", (which I was, of course), "– an' from what can be seen through all this mat when I gets you to open yourself I'll bet you've got a good tough hymen, closely sealed. That'll take a bit o'breaking' in and I dare say your eyes'll water a bit, I wager, when it comes to the time of your deflowerin' – but I've no doubt her Lady-ship'll make suitable arrangements for havin' you seen to in that regard when the time does come. So for now, it may as well all be displayed to best advantage. But with all this here hair it's straggly as a gorse bush in below, it's like looking for a rabbit run in a hedgerow. If it's not all short and neat by tomorrow morn, I'll get Mrs Pelham to come down and shave you bare altogether, quim lips and all, with cold water and an old blade, right here in this very yard. And I don't think you'd like that at all."

'Of course, I wanted to refuse, get quite indignant – "how dare you" sort of thing: and there was absolutely no sensible reason for it, other than to make me, well, even

119

more naked, if you see what I mean. But I guessed he would never had acted and spoken so, well, so intimately, without my guardian's approval, and anyway, there was the note from her telling me to do anything he said without query.

'In a way I found it exciting to be spoken to like that, so directly but in such intimate detail, sort of personal and impersonal at the same time, and to be made to do it, show myself off like that, so specifically I mean, especially imagining what I'd look like when it was finished.

'I mean, it's one thing to know that someone can see everything there is to see "by accident", as it were – you know, as a side product so to speak of one being nude and doing exercises. But actually to be told to remove most of one's pubes – or run the risk of having them forcibly shaved off completely – so that one's quim lips can be studied to see how fat they are, and knowing that having done that one is going to be required each day to hold oneself open practically for inspection, and hear their size, colour and everything else about them discussed in intimate detail – that is rather different.

'And all the time he was describing my "female part", when he was saying about having such long hair round my quim lips, as he called them, and having Mrs Pelham come and shave them, and then went on about how large they were and my long slit and everything – while he was talking about it all he took the crop and slid it in underneath, lengthwise, right along the centre of the fold so it actually slipped in between, and he pressed it there quite hard, then moved it back and forth until I couldn't help but squirm. The horrifying thing was I could feel myself going all, well, you know, squishy, despite myself. He must have realised, for he kept it going, back and forth, back and forth, for a good minute or maybe more. I really was squirming by now and he obviously knew. He slid it out again and it was very obviously darkened, and wet. He didn't say anything: just nodded, and gave a little slap with the leather trainer on the end, full up directly onto my slot, as he pulled it away. It wasn't hard, but it was absolutely square on the lips, and it nearly made my knees go from under me. Instead of getting indignant, as I'd intended, all I could do was say "Yes, Mr Pelham." Even that came out as a sort of croak.' Amanda giggles again, and continues. 'So, after supper that night, I went back to my room early and set to.

'Next morning when I came downstairs I had a crewcut down below which would have looked bare on a Royal Marine. I'd trimmed everything away across my mound and tummy so there wasn't a hair left anywhere more than a quarter-of-an-inch long, and I'd even taken my own little razor – the one I used for under my arms – and actually shaved all along and around the sides of what he'd called my "good long slit" completely, myself. It took absolutely ages, and was surprisingly difficult to do, but eventually I got it so all the hair in underneath, including on the actual lips themselves, was totally gone, just in case he was serious about Mrs Pelham.' Amanda pauses briefly while, quite obviously, young Ivan and indeed one or two others – not all of them men, you notice – gaze at her with expressions that clearly indicate they are allowing their imaginations to picture the scene as the young Amanda courageously shaved off her labial veil for the imperious Pelham.

'Of course, being completely bald like that did indeed make my lips and everything very well, you know – conspicuous. It made me very conscious that I was completely bare and thus on view all the time, even when I was standing up. In fact, when I stood up straight and kept my feet together, the front of my slit could be seen quite plainly.' Amanda giggles again. 'I know, because I checked in a mirror.'

Amanda pauses again, taking a sip of her wine, and the guests remain silent, waiting for her to resume. She laughs and continues: 'And that wasn't all I checked in the mirror. There was one exercise in my warm-up routine, called a trunk bend, where I had to put my feet apart, then bend my upper body right forward and down from the hips until I could rest the palms of my hands flat on the floor while keeping my legs completely straight. It was actually quite difficult: one needs very long hamstrings.

121

'Of course, one way to make it a little easier is to slide one's feet a little further apart: indeed the further apart one can get one's feet, the easier the exercise, so inevitably this is what one does. Equally inevitably, Pelham would arrange things so I always did trunk bends when standing with my back to him. So on that first morning in my bedroom, just before going down to him in the yard, I stood with my back to the mirror, plonked my feet apart, dropped down and put my hands flat on the floor. Then I slid my feet even further apart, until I was comfortable. I looked back at the mirror from between my legs to get an idea of what I would in a few minutes have to show him. Of course, it was a position which I knew already must be rather revealing, but at least with hair on my pussy lips there had been some veil of modesty, as it were. With everything shaved bare completely and my pussy itself totally bald, my lips and the slit between were *very* revealed, as you can imagine – and my feet were not the only things stretched wide apart and open. It was a most unequivocal statement.' Amanda giggles again, unembarrassed – indeed obviously enjoying being the centre of attention still. 'At least he knew I was still a virgin,' she adds, smiling.

'Yet you went ahead without demur?' prompts Ishigawa again.

'To be honest,' replies Amanda 'I found the whole thing rather exciting.' She takes a deep breath, causing her openly displayed bare breasts to rise, swelling as if deliberately emphasising the point: 'I suppose there always has been something of the exhibitionist in my make-up – and certainly Pelham's insistence on my removing my pubic hair, blatantly putting what he called by "female part" so obviously on display not just for the exercises, of course, but for every time I might be required to undress, rather brought it out, if you see what I mean.' She giggled again, 'No pun intended. I definitely decided that since I had to do it, I may as well play it to the hilt.

'All I could think of during that first morning's exercises was what I must look like down there, what he could see when I bent down – and what I would be showing when it came to do my scissors. By the time we got to that stage, I could feel that the tops of my thighs had become so slippery that I knew I must be absolutely dripping – and I knew he would be able to see that, every time I opened up. And of course, that only made it worse. I really stretched myself when opening, I wanted him to see everything.

'That's what I mean when I say he soon knew everything there was to know about me.' She looks around the table smiling, wholly unconcerned about the intimacy of her revelations.

'After that I always kept my pubes trimmed very short when at home and if I knew I was going to exercise in front of Pelham next morning, I'd shave the lips again as well, always being really careful to remove every scrap of hair. Having gone that far, I was rather tempted to see what it would look like completely bald – you know, if I shaved everything off, from everywhere, including my mound. Perhaps foolishly I mentioned it to Pelham, and he was really rather taken aback. "Certainly not" he said " 'twouldn't be lady-like at all, I shouldn't think." And he immediately absolutely forbade it. So of course after that I didn't dare.

'Even so, sometimes, if I felt especially brave, I'd trim my mound extremely close, then shave not just the sides of my slit but up and across the front as well, above the join, then up the sides of my mound and across the top, going as low as I dare, so that all was left was a tiny little wisp of very short hair in the middle of my hump and my slit was completely bald and visible at all times. Of course I would have to let it all start to grow out when it was time to go back to school. It would usually not have grown back completely until halfway through term time, so in the showers and things I had to be a bit careful for the first couple of weeks, in case of awkward questions. But even that just added to the feeling of daring. And as soon as I was home again – out came the scissors and the razor, and off came the golden fleece.

'That was how Aunt J. noticed how thick and prominent my labia had become, thanks to the old prefect's choice, when I got home from the term at Highpark.' Lady J.

smiles in amused recollection, while Amanda continues, now, suddenly, blushing. 'That was a bit undignified – you thought I'd been at it, didn't you, Ma'am?' She turns her remarks back to Ishigawa.

'I don't know if you examine your daughter's maidenhead regularly, Mr Ishigawa, to check it's still there: but from then on until my nineteenth birthday, I had to present myself to my dear Guardian once a week just before bedtime for a "good girl check", as she called it. She'd be in her study. I would go in and curtsy, and she would move to sit on a low settee – a *chaise longue*, we call it. I had to stand with my back to her, take my pyjama jacket off, fold it on a chair in front of me, then the bottoms off and put them on the chair as well. Then bend forward, feet apart, reach back pull my quim lips open and hold absolutely still. Aunt J. would very slowly, very carefully insert a slim glass rod, suitably oiled, to check my maidenhead and ensure I was still what she called "virgin tight".'

Amanda pauses, glances at her guardian, then continues, blushing even more pinkly.

'I had to demonstrate with what dear Aunt called "the maiden's grip". Although the rod itself was quite slim, since of course stretching or actually breaking my maidenhead would rather have defeated the object of the inspection, it was set into quite a heavy handle, made of silver, which stayed outside, if you see what I mean. The rod part was about four inches long, rounded at the end, but only about half an inch in diameter. Once it had been fully inserted, so the handle was just touching my outer lips, I had to stand up straight with my hands on my head, thighs together so I was gripping the rod, then turn to face the front. Ma'am would wait for a moment or two, then simply give a little nod – the signal for me to begin the demonstration: remaining with hands on head, I had to slide my feet wide apart again, while gripping the rod tight to hold it still in place. What an interrogation if it began to slip out!'

Abruptly, you find yourself wondering how Amanda eventually would have lost her virginity, given the closeness of her Guardian's regime. A vision of yourself, well-striped bottom upturned over a whipping horse, and Stephen rampant and ready between your wide-parted thighs, flashes into your mind. Did Amanda, on her nineteenth birthday, find herself thus spread and offered – were these the 'suitable arrangements' to which Pelham had referred? But Amanda is rushing on with her story, not waiting for Ishigawa to gather his thoughts and respond, nor you to indulge your speculation.

'The only exercise I really hated,' she continues, returning incongruously to the subject of her exercises, and chuckling, 'was jumping the block. You know what a mounting block is, Mr Ishigawa? It's a sort of free-standing stone step, about knee-height. You use it to help you get up on a horse: every stable yard has one. Well, jumping the block involves standing by the block, jumping up onto it – you know, one foot, the other foot, up-down, up-down, up-down – on and on. Pretty tiring, especially if you're doing it with a half-hundredweight feed bag held above your head, arms full stretch. Then you had to lift the sack again and hold it high for a count of three while the crop was applied lightly across the shoulder blades – makes one smart a bit – or three times to the tummy if my shoulders or back were already marked from –'

'Amanda, my dear,' interrupts Lady J., the weight of emphasis on the last word of her interruption indicating to Amanda – and to everyone else – that in her guardian's opinion, if none other, the young lady was rushing ahead too enthusiastically now with familial revelations, 'I think Mr Ishigawa has heard enough for the moment – unless you wish to be involved in a further little demonstration of disciplinary control . . .'

Abruptly, Amanda's narrative ends. She smiles at her guardian and you are left wondering whether that smile is not one more of complicity than contrition. Certainly, there is no suggestion in her demeanour or expression that Amanda is in any way cowed by her senior's obvious authority.

Amanda engages the entire table with her smile: 'You

125

must forgive me,' she says, 'I fear I have been somewhat monopolising the conversation. Madeleine – would you mind . . .?'

Swiftly, Stephen's voice takes up the thread of dinner talk so that not a beat is missed, the subject changes, the conversation swiftly moves ahead. None the less you watch as Madeleine steps around behind Amanda once more, and Amanda slips her arms again into the upper part of her dress, covering her bared breasts, holding the dress to herself as Madeleine refastens the hooks at the back.

Later, you learn from Madeleine that young Ivan did indeed have his fantasy realised, and was permitted to cane Amanda – but not on the breasts. Under Lady J.'s direction Amanda and Ivan had, after dinner, withdrawn to a small drawing room. There Amanda had bent over the back of a low armchair, her dress removed and her legs parted widely to reveal plump lips carefully shaved, and presented her creamy buttocks for the young man's first lesson.

Amanda's splendid bosom, Madeleine tells you with some awe, was reserved for Mr Ishigawa, who plied the slim switch a dozen times, six across those high firm breasts – including one each to each tattooed halo – and then six times across the front of the white thighs, beginning at mid-height and ending at the very top of the ivory pillars, the switch striking across the lower part of the neatly trimmed pubic mound, where the join of Amanda's prominent sex lips, carefully depilated to heighten that prominence, was just visible.

Amanda, clad only in a waist-cincher and with her suspenders undone, tucked high and clear and her stockings carefully rolled down to just above her knees, had stood rigidly and unflinchingly, at attention, head up, feet together and arms stiffly held by her sides for the dozen strokes.

Lady J. had, said Madeleine, after sending Ivan away and bidding Amanda rise and don a silken robe, asked Madeleine to fetch Ishigawa and invited him to test for himself the mettle of Amanda's fortitude. With a polite inclination of the head, the tall Japanese had accepted – but it was apparently Amanda herself who had determined the nature of the test, an evidently willing collaborator with her guardian.

It was Amanda – not Lady J. – who, from many in a wide drawer in the handsome, mirrored Edwardian sideboard, had selected and then almost ceremonially proffered to Ishigawa the thin, leather-wrapped switch with which her examination was to be accomplished. She had then, unprompted by either Ishigawa or her guardian, removed the robe and assumed the pose which unambiguously offered that part of her anatomy where she realised her impromptu examiner's interest would lie. It was she too who, again unprompted, had first unclipped the suspenders and rolled down the stockings, baring her thighs in silent, additional, invitation, so cruelly accepted.

Only a slight trembling of her long legs, coupled with a quivering of her firm bosom, had betrayed her emotions before Ishigawa's searching examination began, only a slight glistening in her brimming eyes bore witness to its acerbity when it was finished: that, and the twelve red, horizontal lines which traversed the front of her legs and her upper torso.

Ishigawa-san had confessed himself humbled by the power of Amanda's will.

With These Rings

You have, of course, assumed it will be Madeleine who will pierce you, and affix the rings you are to wear. She has, after all, put you through all that has so far been your lot to endure, however willingly, in the long week which you have spent here in the House.

Your training, as your lover described it to you, is almost over – at least for this week, but already you know, have decided, that your training has really only just begun. It is why you have decided to ask for and to wear the rings. They are the symbol of your wish to go on, to continue along this path you are discovering for yourself, once you leave the House tomorrow.

Thus, it is Madeleine now who prepares you, fetching you after your final, formal dinner from the drawing room and into the privacy of Hassan's butler pantry to remove first the cruel saddle-strap with which your composure, if not your fortitude, has again been tested this final evening. After first removing your gown and accessories she unbuckles, with a gentleness your readily appreciate, the hard leather thong first from the front of your corset, and then the rear.

Unbuckled, the strap hangs from you incongruously, bent double, both ends hanging between your thighs and parted knees, the middle held by nothing more substantial than your own flesh, for the swollen clitoris, enpurpled by the two hours or more it has endured in the grip of the tight, hard-edged split which divides the strap about it, thrusting through, tumescent, now holds the leather still to your body.

128

Madeleine takes the strap lightly between thumb and finger.

'Hold still, Mademoiselle,' she whispers in fond warning, 'a moment's hurt – no more.'

She tugs the strap free with a swift movement and the leather drags roughly over the end of the swollen stem of your trapped clitoris. It stings, sharply, as Madeleine promised it would, but not deeply, not for too long. You clench your teeth, press your lips together and are careful to utter no sound. There is none present save yourself and Madeleine, from whom now you nor your body can have no secrets – yet you are determined to show no reaction.

Your clitoris throbs.

Madeleine next removes your corset, swiftly untying the laces, releasing you from its firm hold, until it too falls away, and you stand naked except for your black high-heeled shoes, your stockings and the black velvet choker about your white throat.

The freezing spray, delivered through a long silver proboscis from the tiny cream coloured can, its label with its scientific compound name clinically objective, feels cold upon your skin. Madeleine sprays, liberally, the nipple and areola of first your left, then your right breast, then kneels on one knee to part, with the fingers of one hand, the thickened lips of your sex – thickened and reddened by the chafing of the roughened portion of the saddle strap from which you have just been released, thickened too by the thought of what lies ahead as much as by the experiences recently undergone.

As Madeleine proceeds, bent upon one knee, to apply the cooling, chilling spray to your swollen clitoris, the thickening morsel stings briefly, as sometimes does the soft skin of your underarm when you apply an astringent deodorant, then it deadens, becomes numb. It is a strange sensation. Suddenly, even as your body begins to tingle with anticipation, goosebumps (though it is not cold), crinkling and tightening your flesh, the fine downy hairs on your arms, your belly, tingling as though suddenly charged with electricity – so even then, at this acute heightening of

129

your awareness of every inch of your bare skin the centre of your sensations, the core of you, disappears. A void. Like a blind spot – what is it the astronomers call them? Black holes. A black hole, at the very juncture of your being, where rightly should be drawn together all your tingling, jangling nerve ends.

And as your central being deadens, so too your mind detaches itself from the immediate prospect that lies before you, and you see yourself from outwith yourself. (It is a curious, Scottish, expression – 'outwith': you had not heard it until your lover used it once, of a Royal Parks policeman who had caught you once, together, as you walked, laughing on a hot summer day, with your breasts bare along a shrub-lined path. 'Indecent exposure' had said your lover 'you may deal with, my friend – but surely beauty's celebration is outwith your terms of censure, if not your jurisdiction?' The policeman had laughed, his eyes, unleering and rather, more, in homage and admiration roaming freely over your pale orbs and air-hardened nipples. 'Just as long as they 'aint loaded, young lady,' he had said, with a smile, adding, 'but I'd put them away before you go much further: my sergeant isn't quite such a connoisseur.')

The thickened lips of your sex thicken – or so it seems – even more as the anaesthetic spray takes effect. As at the dentist, when your cheek and lip seem suddenly fashioned of dull leather, unfeeling, so now you cannot feel the pressure of your thighs closing your sex, or the parting of your thighs allowing that same flesh to swell.

Madeleine still bends, one knee between your two, parted. You glance down, and see her eyes raised towards you, eyebrow raised in question. You realise that she has taken one of your labia and is now pinching it, hard, between finger and thumb. You feel nothing. Unabashed (she has rarely yet handled you quite so intimately, and does so now with a curious dispassion), she takes both your labia, grasping between a finger and thumb of each hand, pulling them out and downwards from your body, stretching them lewdly to check the effect of the spray. You feel the sensation, but nothing more, as at the dentist when one's gum goes numb, before the drilling begins.

At least here, you think to yourself, there has been no injection, as there always is at the dentist. The injection is always the worst part of the visit.

And suddenly you are nervous, wondering if, even with the spray, the piercing of your nipples and your sex is something to which you really do wish to submit. Butterflies flutter in your stomach. Anything you have tried before has been ephemeral, a game. Showing yourself naked, daring yourself to be naked where you might be seen. The cold water, the candle wax – they left no marks: they ended when the game ended. Even your experience thus far under the cane has been but an extension of the game, such marks as there were – and there were marks, true enough – fading quickly. But now you offer yourself for something different. To have your body pierced, and ringed: it is a statement, even a commitment. You realise that now you have a last chance to back away, to decline to take the game further. Now, if you go forward, there can be no going back to before now. Your Rubicon awaits you.

You tremble, and steel yourself. Soon, you will be ringed, and bear your rings with pride. Your rite of passage is at hand.

You are led, naked now, by Madeleine into the dining room. The long table has been cleared of all but four large candlesticks, each with five new candles, tall, white and already lighted, set two to each side. From the legs of the table, thick plaited cords, gold in colour, lead up on to the polished surface and at one end, also slightly to one side, lies, its hinged lid open, the silver box wherein glitter the five gold rings presented to you – and to the other guests, complete with an explanation of their intended purpose – earlier this evening.

Those guests are now gathered around the fireplace at the far end of the room, the fire freshened with new logs that crackle and throw a wavering backlight to augment the candles on the table. The electric lighting in the room

131

has been turned low, so as to create an almost mediaeval atmosphere.

Madeleine leads you towards the group. You wear only the black velvet choker with its single, central, hanging pearl-drop that has become your hallmark. Even your feet are bare.

·There is a tall mirror, a cheval-glass of the sort in most of the bedrooms, before which you had stood to be shown yourself on the first day you were corseted, the mirror standing, slightly angled, next to the group of guests who are idly chatting amongst themselves, as if unconcerned with you or what is about to be done to you.

They fall silent as Madeleine, still leading you with one hand holding yours, the other flat in the hollow of your back, just above the curve of your buttocks, approaches; they turn to look at you, as if seeing you now for the first time. Madeleine leads you to the mirror, bids you stand before it. You stand as she directs, your hands by your sides, your feet together.

It is Stephen who addresses you, not your lover.

'Look at yourself, Chloe, in the mirror, and see yourself truly naked for the very last time. In a moment, you will be pierced and then ringed, at your breasts and at your sex. Thereafter, while you remain with your lover and with us, you will always wear these rings. They will always be with you, be on you – you will never be able to be naked again.

'And even if, at some later stage, you decide to leave us, and have your rings removed, you will none the less always remember yourself, ringed. So look at yourself now, and remember your breasts, and the outlines of your sex, before they are altered irredeemably, forever.'

And you look, thinking to yourself, 'It will be like losing my virginity all over again. No matter how hard I try, I will never be able to get back to this.'

There is silence. You watch your reflection, the perfect globes of your breasts, tipped by the wide pale halo of your nipples, and by the protruberant nipples themselves. Your lover adores your nipples, you know: fusses over them, nibbles at them, pulls them twixt finger and thumb. Even in casual meetings, fully dressed, he will contrive always, and in the first moments of meeting, to pass the palm of his hand across the tip of your breast; and always, your nipple responds with eagerness, hardening instantly. Occasionally, as in a restaurant in the evening, your breasts naked for him under blouse or dress, he will ask you to make them show. You have only – you cannot ever remember refusing, even in the most crowded restaurant – to caress your breast yourself lightly, for a moment, to make the nipples stiffen and show through the material.

Now, those nipples are, as Stephen so graphically phrases it, to be altered irredeemably.

You look too at the reflection of your full, rounded hips, the almost flat plane of your belly – a certain fullness around your navel merely adds to your femininity – and at the mound of your sex, the slit, which normally, veiled by your hair, lies semi-hidden between your thighs, now rendered so visible, so obvious, by the unnatural baldness of your pubic mount, so carefully kept naked since the day of your arrival here.

Denuded of their natural veil, the lips of your sex show thickly, in particular the join of those lips at the apex of your sex, hiding within and beneath them the secret stalk of your clitoris – the core of your desire, as Stephen has called it more than once – a part of you that had never received so much attention until your arrival here, a part of you now that can trigger response more immediate than anything you have ever imagined. Altered irredeemably? Are you not already altered irredeemably?

Stephen turns to your lover. 'May we proceed? You do not wish to reprieve her?'

In answer your lover steps towards you. He takes you in his arms, kisses you as you turn your lips up to meet his. His hand strays to your breast, caresses it, lifts it slightly, squeezing gently in the way you love, the fingers sliding towards the stiffened tip until he holds you by the nipple only. He stretches your breast, pulling upwards and outwards on the nipple, the breast following in an elongating cone until he lets his fingers slip, deliberately, off the very

133

end of your stretched teat, making you gasp, letting your breast spring back to its proper shape, bouncing with heavy firmness.

'Do you wish for a reprieve, Chloe?'

'No,' you say simply. 'I wish to be pierced, and to wear the rings. You have given them to me, and I wish to wear them. You give me the rings: I give you my body, to be marked as you will. If you wish me to wear the rings permanently, I shall do so. If that requires me to be pierced, then I shall be pierced. So please: let it be done, and done now.'

Madeleine leads you, trembling now, for the bravery of your words belies the trepidation you feel as you face the moment, so long imagined, of having your flesh pierced, and the rings fitted to you, by what instrument you still have not seen, have not been told, leads you to the table, helps you sit upon the end and then slide until you are seated almost in the middle. She lays you back so that you are at full stretch, then draws your arms over your head, securing your wrists, drawn wide, with the cords. As she moves to the other end of the table, you instinctively, knowingly, part your ankles, opening your thighs.

Madeleine takes each ankle in turn, stretching your leg sideways until your ankle and foot overhang the edge of the table. She binds the soft, heavy rope over each ankle in turn, so that you are tied, spread-eagled. A cushion is brought – you know not by whom – and eased under your shoulder blades.

You lie, ready and presented, your back arched lightly over the cushion, your breasts thus raised as, flattened by their own weight, they pull to either side of your torso.

You hear the rustle of movement as the guests move from round the fireplace to stand round you at the table, to watch you endure your ordeal. Curiously, you find yourself thinking not of your lover now, but of Stephen, wondering how he will judge your performance, your bearing, during your piercing. But you do not look at those who watch you. You gaze instead simply at the ceiling, waiting for Madeleine to begin.

But it is not Madeleine. There is a heavy tread beside your ear, a face comes into view. It is Hassan who now leans over you, his face impassive.

You feel a moment of panic. Ideally, you would want your lover to pierce you himself. You know that is unlikely – is not, as your lover would say quaintly, in keeping with the mood of the meeting – so you have accepted that once again it will be Madeleine to whom your intimacy, your self, will be surrendered.

Not Hassan again, you think to yourself in sudden despair. Hassan's only contact with you is to shave you afresh each day after your morning swim, still naked, goose-fleshed from the cool water, splayed wide across the table beside the pool for his unremitting razor and impersonal fingers: questing, parting, flattening, drawing aside your most intimate, secret flesh; then turned face down, required to pull apart your cheeks, your most secret place revealed, the valley between your cheeks and the lower join of your sex lips also carefully shaved, dried and powdered with one of those old-fashioned squeeze-bulb powder-puffers of the sort still used in a traditional gentleman's barbershop. It is, as you have thought of it more than once, the ultimate in-dignity, a total denial of your existence as a person, to have to surrender yourself daily and so intimately to your host's manservant. It would not be so bad, you almost feel, if Hassan took you, enjoyed you sexually, at the same time, but the fact is that the passive Pathan face remains unsmil-ingly devoid of all expression save polite concentration throughout the daily, passionless manipulations. Hassan is, at best, your barber, and you realise that having the barber brought in to pierce you is in itself no accident, no coinci-dence, but rather another statement to you on your journey of self-discovery.

So you give yourself over to what is happening, allow-ing, once again, your destiny to be dictated by others.

Hassan leans across you, spreading his hand flat over your left breast, marks with a soft-pointed blue pencil of the sort used by surgeons before they make an incision, two spots directly opposite each other and on the soft flesh of your areola, either side of your nipple and as close to the base as the thickness of the pencil point will permit.

Swiftly, workmanlike, uninterested in your beauty or, apparently, in your sexuality, he repeats the procedure with the pencil on the tip of your right breast.

He disappears from your view for a moment, then returns and, without preamble, grasps the nipple of your left breast, drawing it upward, holding it firmly by the end, gripped between finger and thumb, your breast elongating elastically until it is stretched taut in a tall cone.

He lays the point of the needle lightly against the stretched nipple, close to the base. You feel the tip lightly prick the skin, but feel no other sensation. You did not know what sort of implement would be used to pierce you – you had assumed some sort of needle, but did not know what. This, you now see, is like an oversize hypodermic, without the syringe, but hollow.

You feel and see Hassan push the sharp steel through, feel it pass through your flesh as one feels every movement of the dentist's drill working, but feels no pain.

It is not quite no pain. Effective as the anaesthetic spray is it cannot wholly deaden your flesh, and there is a momentary stab, no more, as the steel passes through your nipple, the point emerging on the opposite side. You are pierced.

The ring can be opened, its ends which normally slot one into the other to close the circle pulled apart. One end is placed carefully into the hollow tube of the hypodermic, which is slowly withdrawn, the ring following through until all that is through you now is the gold ring. Hassan sets the needle aside, somewhere out of your range of vision, and deftly shuts the ends of the tiny gold circle. You are ringed.

'So that's how they do it,' you find yourself thinking with a curious detachment.

The piercing of your right nipple follows. Hassan's grip is hard and unyielding, pulling roughly. It is as if he is being deliberately rough, the callousness of his treatment making to you, and to those watching your piercing, a statement. Here is Chloe. Observe her immolation.

The taut stretching of your breast is of itself something sometimes done by your lover to test you, and Hassan stretches cruelly, until your breath begins to shorten.

The metal pushes through, you feel and do not feel its passage through your flesh. You close your eyes, laying your head back on the table, absorbing the sensation as Hassan releases his rough grip, allowing your stretched breast to relax and then pulls the needle back, the ring following through. The second gold ring crowns your second breast.

The throbbing of your breast, the feeling – despite the anaesthetic – of bursting fullness in your stiff and thickened nipples absorbs you as the lips – the thick outer lips, not the thinner inner labia – of your sex, about one-third the way back from the apex of your slit, are each pierced and ringed, the sensation no more than a tugging and gripping tight of each in turn. Then you feel Hassan's fingers part the flesh of your sex-lips at their apex, exposing the pinker flesh within, grasping tightly the stalk of your clitoris, drawing it forwards, pulling it outwards from your body.

The clitoral ring, much smaller in diameter than those through your sex lips and nipples, is to be put through close to the end, close to where Hassan's fingers grip and pull, holding you fast. Your lover had suggested to you that you might wish this fifth and final ring to be placed through the less sensitive fold of skin just above, or just below, the stalk itself: you had declined, telling him that it was through the stalk itself you wished to have the ring placed. You wished there to be no shirking the full ordeal on your part: now its final act is at hand.

The piercing is made through your erect and stretched clitoris. Unbidden, your hips buck at the acute sensation – it is not painful, but even with the anaesthetic spray, it causes you to wriggle slightly, twisting away as when the dentist touches a deadened but not dead nerve end. Madeleine's hands, from the side of the table opposite that from which Hassan works upon your opened sex, press your hips into the table top, to hold you still. You moan, quietly, as the ring is passed through. Had you not been anaesthetised there, you are sure, you would probably faint.

When it is over, Madeleine helps you from the table. Brandy scorches your throat, burns your inner belly and the throbbing in your breast becomes dulled. Through misted eyes you see your lover, see Stephen – the deep brown eyes locked upon you – see Lady J.; see all of them smile at you, nodding their heads in approval. A hand, you know not whose hand, reaches and touches a ring in your nipple. Madeleine leads you to the mirror again, but though you look at yourself you know, correctly, that you will later remember nothing of what you see or feel.

Given another brandy, you are turned to face the guests, your arms raised to clasp your hands behind your neck, lifting your breasts and their ringed nipples, your feet parted to display the rings through your sex, the two larger, the one smaller, at the very centre of your being.

The familiar pose. You close your eyes. It is done.

Next morning, as the guests take their leave and as your lover waits for you in the garden, pacing slowly, as if in some uncertain frame of mind, you stand naked in the tall hallway by the open door, where you are plainly on view to anyone inside the house, or passing through the hallway, but where the sight of you from outside, where wait chauffeurs and taxi drivers, is masked by the heavy door itself.

You stand in your classic pose, your ringed nipples and sex displayed, and from each ring, even from that smaller ring through your still swollen and protruding clitoris which now, the anaesthetic having worn off, throbs dully, the ache increased by the weight upon it, there hangs, as might a frozen droplet, a glinting pendant of semi-precious stone.

You look neither right nor left, but straight ahead, unblinking, as the guests take their leave of Stephen, who occasionally caresses your opened sex, and who gave you the pendants to add to your perfection.

You are the ultimate odalisque.

Arrangements

You will be moving from your present flat to an apartment which I shall provide, and arrange. Madeleine will move in with you, to act as your maid and companion. Leave of absence has been arranged for you from your employers, and arrangements made to secure your financial future in some comfort.

Each morning, you will visit the basement gymnasium of the apartment block, where Nancy, your physical training instructor, will arrange and monitor a programme of work-outs to enhance your looks and fitness.

Each afternoon, you will be taken, usually by Lady J.'s car and after lunch with Lady J., to M. Alcard's, where the more specialised aspects of your training will be catered for. There will be two, complementary, aspects to this part of your training: figure control, and self-control.

The former will require you to be dressed in ever-more demanding garments, designed to control, enhance and frequently reveal your figure in a variety of ways; not all of these garments will be comfortable to wear. It will be a substantial part of your training (and a substantial element of your attraction, when trained), that you be able to contain this discomfort without visible sign of its existence. The latter will involve various tests and minor ordeals, demonstrating and fortifying your own self-control. Some of these will be easily borne, some will be more demanding. Always, you will have the right to bring any test or trial to an immediate end, without penalty or further discussion.

In the evenings, you will be entertained on a social round which, it is hoped, you will find both pleasant and fulfilling. Occasionally you will be asked to demonstrate your progress; on some occasions you will, quite simply, be put on display. In this latter case, your anonymity will be carefully preserved: the full nature of your life now will be known only to myself and those, such as Lady J., who will be directly concerned with your progress.

Occasionally, you will be loaned, perhaps for an hour, perhaps an entire evening, but certainly no longer. You will be required, of course, to comply with whatever may be asked of you by whoever it is to whom you have been given.

A regime of modest punishments and rewards will be introduced to give point to your training and to mark its success. You must expect to be caned occasionally, but you may rest assured that you will never be harmed, nor permanently marked or scarred in any way. If you are to be punished, the nature and extent of the punishment will be explained to you beforehand, and your permission sought to proceed. You will always have the right either to appeal, or to decline. An appeal may result in your punishment being reduced, confirmed, or, if deemed initially insufficient, increased. A non-acceptance of an offer of punishment will result in your position being reconsidered and, if appropriate, your training brought to an end.

Once you have given your permission, any punishment ordered will be completed in its entirety.

Always, you are free to leave at any time. Nothing will be done to or with you without your consent, continuously inferred from your very presence, continually re-ascertained by explicit request.

The Fitting

You are collected by Lady J.'s car and taken to an old-fashioned outfitters in London, where you are attended by a discreet but demanding corsetier, Monsieur Gerard Alcard. You are to be intimately measured for corsetry of a more advanced, not to say rigorous, design.

But first, you are sent into a room to disrobe, and then present yourself for inspection. At Lady J.'s request, you have worn the corset you were given upon leaving the House – a version of those into which you have been laced, but one with modern zips concealed at either side, so that you may dress yourself. You have also, at Lady J.'s request, worn the rings.

Standing once again in what is becoming a familiar pose, feet apart, hands clasped behind your neck, eyes gazing fixedly ahead, you feel rather than see yourself being studied by Lady J. and Monsieur Alcard. The dais on which you are posed puts your hips at their eye level, so that to look at them – which instinctively you know you are not expected to do – you would have to lower your gaze, tilting your head downwards.

Instead, you keep your head tilted slightly backwards, your elbows pulled back in line with your shoulders, your breasts bare above the supporting, shelf-like cups of the corset, the nipples and their full, swollen areolae fully exposed, the gold rings glinting under the arc lights whose warmth you feel on your bare skin. The raising of your arms thus raises and thrusts forward your breasts, the pull of your elbows on your shoulders causing your breasts also to be pulled apart by the stretch of your torso, so that each is thrust not only out and forwards but slightly to the side.

Below the lower edge of the corset your belly is flattened, your hips spread by your wide-thighed stance. Those same parted thighs, combined with the way in which, upon Lady J.'s instruction, you have turned the toes of your black, high-heeled shoes outward, open the lips of your sex slightly, each pierced by its own golden ring. You have not continued with the daily depilation of your pubic mound and sex lips now that you have returned from the House, but instead have allowed your hair there to grow back soft but, you feel sure, not quite so thick. You now keep it close-trimmed, using scissors at least twice a week both across the padded swell of your mound and along the soft lips of your sex, using the rings to stretch each lip in turn as you trim.

Your buttocks, bunched, almost clenched, by your pose, swell creamily beneath the curve of the corset at the back, framed on either side by the stretch of the suspender which supports the taut black stockings. Your final act, before leaving the little cubicle in which you had disrobed, was to turn your back to the full-length mirror which hangs on one wall and, your head twisted back and round over your shoulder, to ensure that the seams of your stockings are militarily straight. In the two weeks since leaving the House and returning home, those same swelling buttocks have not once felt the kiss of the crop, and the full moon of your bottom is unmarked.

Now, once more, you are presenting yourself for the impersonal inspection of a stranger.

'The waist, of course, is too thick,' Monsieur Alcard is saying, his voice soft but impersonal, discussing what he sees as one might discuss a work of minor art or statuary.

'I would say that with training it should be possible to reduce it certainly to less than twenty inches. She is too old now to be brought down to eighteen, I suspect – what a pity I could not have had her from the age of seventeen, as with your ward – but we might get down to nineteen, or just under.

'It depends upon her, how much she is willing to put herself in my hands and to accept my methods.' You hear an unmistakable smile suffuse his voice, although your fixed gaze does not permit you to see the slight inclination of the head which accompanies it, nor Lady J.'s no less knowing smile in response. 'Methods of which you yourself, milady, will be well aware.' He pauses. 'Do you think she . . .?'

'I have no doubt,' interposes Lady J., quickly, adding in a matter-of-fact tone, 'that is why I have brought her to you. Chloe is already quite well trained, and no stranger, from what I have seen and been told about her, to self-control. I have seen her fortitude demonstrated amply – although of course she has yet to submit herself to what you and I would regard as anything truly difficult. Real training, as it were.'

You notice, already, how Lady J. is swift always to refer to you by name, the corsetier never. Already this tall, formal stranger, at once distant yet intimate, is assuming in your own mind the role of an impersonal, even anonymous, task-master. The thought of having such a task-master, of being placed thus in his charge, being required to perform, to pose, to submit to his will, causes familiar butterflies to flutter, itchily, deep in your lower belly. You sense yourself moistening.

'The breasts,' you hear the cultured voice continue, 'I have to say, are indeed rather fine, well-formed and firm, considering especially that she is no longer a teenager.' At Monsieur Alcard's request, you unclasp your hands from behind your neck, lowering your arms and crossing your wrists instead behind your back, just where the constriction of your waist swells outwards to your hips and buttocks. The effect is to lower to a more natural position your previously raised and tautened breasts. Monsieur Alcard reaches to the narrow semi-circular crescents which take the place of half-cups at the bodice of your tightly-laced corset, and deftly turns them downward, away from your breasts, so that your breasts themselves sit in their natural position, wholly without support. He continues his objective appraisal of your body.

'Yes indeed, her breasts are indeed an exquisite shape, rather unusual and quite beautiful.' He raises a hand, to

143

stroke with featherlight fingertips along the skin of your bosom, then presses lightly against the side of your right breast, which gives a little under the pressure of his touch. 'They are quite succulently feminine – the skin so soft to the touch, the breast itself soft despite its apparent, indeed obvious, firmness. They are youthfully firm but still give the impression of mature fullness. Observe how,' he continues, smiling, clearly appreciative of your physical appearance, 'although their upper slope, the way they sit upon her torso, is that of full maturity, the underside of each is quite horizontal, giving them in profile an almost exaggerated conical shape.' He draws a hand lightly outwards along your breast, curving his fingers over and around first the top, then the sides, then along the underside of your breast once more. Dispassionately, objectively, he raises a hand and casually slaps your breast, quite hard – not hard enough to hurt, but hard enough to sting. He and Lady J. watch your bosom quiver: you shut your eyes briefly but do not otherwise move. 'Unusually firm and resilient. They appear almost to have been made for the crop. She has already been treated thus, I take it? Certainly they should stand well under punishment,' and he repeats his ominous question: '– she has been whipped?'

'On the breasts,' replies Lady J., 'no. They have yet to be baptised.

'It is most important they are not damaged permanently. You well know my views on risks to the breasts, and of the care that must be taken. Still, you are quite right. She should experience the crop there at least once during her training, so that she comes to know the taste fully. It would be a most rigorous test for her.'

You listen, trembling slightly, increasingly fearful yet aroused as Lady J. continues with this objective disposition of your fate. The thought of being whipped across the breasts – you think instantly of Lady J.'s ward, Amanda, and her story – causes you not to run, nor to think of abandoning that course upon which you have just embarked, but rather causes you to pull your shoulders back more, thrusting your breasts even more. 'If Amanda can manage it . . .' you think to yourself.

'The light crop would be best, or the whalebone,' Lady J. is saying, 'to leave them thoroughly marked but to ensure no risk of permanent damage. Remove the nipple rings first, of course.'

'Ah yes, the nipples,' continues Monsieur Alcard. 'They are quite beautiful; exceptionally well developed. You were quite right to have them ringed of course. The training possibilities are (if you will pardon the little joke), greatly extended.'

Lady J. interjects.

'Ah, but my dear Gerard – it was not I who had Chloe's rings inserted. It was she herself. I was there, I am happy to say. It was a most memorable occasion. It was not Chloe who performed the operation, you understand. But she was ringed at her own request.

'And observe,' continues Lady J. You hear the step taken toward you, feel a gloved hand upon your opened inner thigh, the fingers sliding upwards toward your sex, the pressure of a thumb against your flesh easing one heavy lip aside, revealing what lies between, beneath and within the fold of the join of your sex lips. 'You have noticed already, of course, the rings here, through the sex lips: but look closely at the smaller clitoral ring.

'Observe that, unusually, it is actually through the clitoris, there is no faking. It has not been put through the loose skin above or even below, as is so often the case.'

Your lower belly begins to tremble visibly, your breathing to quicken, as you feel a fingertip touch against the sensitive tip of the now stiffening organ. 'See – it is through the stalk itself, quite close to the tip. She insisted upon this herself. A local anaesthetic was used but even so – quite a trial, don't you think, especially during the healing period, when the anaesthetic would have worn off?'

Lady J. pauses, her gloved fingertip stroking your swiftly hardening bud, forcing you to fight hard for the control necessary to hold yourself absolutely still.

'Chloe is indeed rather special,' she says, simply.

'Has she been exercised with weights yet?' the corsetier asks. 'To lengthen either the labia or the clitoris?'

'No, not yet. And I think,' continues Lady J., 'not for the labia, at all. She is particularly neat here, as you see – the inner lips are very dainty, and completely invisible when she is not aroused. She is like a closed purse. It is quite unusual, and really rather pretty. In her case I do not want either set of labia stretched. The outer labia should be thickened a little, however. They are just a trifle thin, especially before she becomes aroused. The gloved finger-tips brush the full length of your sex, reaching far into the crease between your buttocks, and instinctively your feet move apart a fraction further as you open yourself to accept the caress. 'I know you will be careful to avoid damage, it would not do to toughen the flesh with too harsh treatment. Regular urtication might be better – I leave it to your judgement, but use the Singapore nettles if you do decide to urticate. Although their sting is more stringent than the common nettle, it is short-lived, while the swelling they induce is, in my experience, cumulatively long lasting, and eventually more or less permanent. But no weights, on either the inner or outer lips.

'She should be depilated however. Denude the outer labia completely. Apart from any other reason hair there will hide the rings: bare labia will show them off so much better, and emphasise both their presence and her predicament. That can be attended to right away, as soon as we are finished here.' Your pulse quickens further as you listen, your belly tightening. 'Colette and Jasmine, that Chinese girl who has started recently, can attend to it. Have them finish her in one session – she may as well get it over with straight away – including in between the buttocks and around the anus. They will need to spread her well. Also the area around the clitoral junction will need attention.

'Her Mount of Venus should be left covered: however, it is too retroussé to look well completely depilated (I have seen her thus), so have them simply depilate her to the bikini line, and keep the remainder trimmed short, as it is now. And from now on, keep her sex and outer labia plucked regularly, at least once a week I should think. That in itself may serve to thicken them a little. Otherwise, no special treatment for the sex-lips: we shall leave them as they are.'

You listen to all of this with a mixture of fascination and horror, all the while gazing fixedly ahead, if trembling rather more than at first. The effect is lost on neither Lady J. nor Monsieur Alcard, both of whom find your demeanour entirely enchanting. 'She is quite captivating, totally suitable,' Monsieur Alcard murmurs at one point, almost aside, even as Lady J. carries on with her prognosis of your present condition and her prescription for your future. Yet even before you have time fully to contemplate the mechanics of what Lady J. has just prescribed, how the removal of your labial hair is actually to be achieved (and you have no intention of turning now from whatever plough it is to which you have so blindly set your hand), that part of your lower belly which is connected so directly to your sexual responses takes another lurch as you listen to Lady J. move swiftly on.

'The clitoris is quite another matter,' continues Lady J., her tone changing, hardening. 'It is already quite prominent, and she responds instantly to its manipulation – see, it is already stiff, just by listening to us, and by being touched once or twice. You may have a completely free hand with the clitoris. The fact she is already ringed will help you – with weights it should be possible to lengthen her considerably, I should think, without even bothering with other methods. But you need not restrict yourself. Use whatever methods you feel appropriate. Already, when she is aroused, the tip of her clitoris protrudes from the crease at the top of the lips. See, it is already beginning to do so now. One can almost see it growing erect as we speak: she is already quite swollen. Look – it has pushed out between the outer lips already. There is no reason why it cannot be trained to sit so all the time. That would look good, I think.

'Yes, let us do that. Her clitoris is to be lengthened so that at all times it pushes out from between the junction of her outer lips. You must make it quite obvious, as prominent as possible. You may be quite experimental on her here,' repeats Lady J. dispassionately. 'Use whatever gives the best results, as well as the weights. She will be able to take it – she has considerable fortitude, indeed she seems to relish her clitoris being enlarged. The more one does to it, the more erect and prominent it becomes. So. Give the clitoris a hard time. She is up to it. And see –' there is light laughter in Lady J.'s voice now '– she is also most responsive – look.'

You do not need the feel of Lady J.'s gloved fingertip sliding further across the taut skin of your opened thigh, moving in beneath the undercurve of your belly to pull apart your sex lips below the close-cropped fringe of pale hair, to know that this disembodied conversation has begun to arouse you, to cause the silvery evidence of that arousal to bead, like dew, upon your inner flesh and upon the folded lips without. You can feel without touching or being touched that your lips have swollen, that your juices are beginning to flow.

You would not be surprised to hear the voices remark that you are already dripping onto the carpet between your straddled feet.

If It Itches . . .

After the first week of your training, Monsieur Alcard introduces a new and, as he calls it, 'trifling' variation. Curiously, while it may have seemed trifling to him and indeed, compared with some of the other rigours to which you are now increasingly subjecting yourself, or allowing yourself to be subjected to, this is hardly extreme; curiously though this 'trifling' little trial tests your will-power to the very core.

Perhaps it is, as with the ritual with the clothes pegs with which you and your lover had begun this journey, the very mundanity of it all which you find so trying. As Alcard explains what he requires you to do, you blush deeply and, throughout the daily sessions to come in which you must submit yourself to this particular little trial of will, the petty humiliation involved will invariably bring colour to your cheeks.

Perhaps that is why you enjoy it.

You stand as you did for your initial inspection, Monsieur Alcard appraising the afternoon's presentation of your charms. On this day, Madeleine has prepared you with a simple waist-cinching corset which leaves your entire upper torso bare and which extends only to the upper curve of your hips. It does not carry with it any means of attaching your stockings which are thus today of the self-supporting kind, the garters of which, you know, your corsetier faintly disapproves. For this impropriety you expect at least a rebuke, if not some more tangible punishment.

In recompense, the corset itself is exquisitely tight: Monsieur

Alcard's ever-present tape measure pronounces your waist measurement to be a most satisfactory twenty inches.

'A reduction of four inches already, Chloe,' he murmurs, not without approval. 'Excellent.' You recall the efforts of yourself and Madeleine to get you into the corset, and lace it to its necessary level of severity.

Monsieur Alcard continues. 'We have a new, very trifling little discipline for you today Chloe, before we begin. It is not very much at all. However, it will help you learn self-control. Please be so kind . . .'

The elegant hand waves towards a chest of drawers standing against one wall. It has not been present on any of your earlier visits to this room, so has obviously been brought in for this new trial, whatever it is to be.

The chest is in a faintly Chinese style, black-lacquered and with a top which extends beyond the sides and which, at either side, curves upwards. A low footstool has been placed in front and by this Monsieur Alcard helps you to step up, turn and sit upon the incongruous throne.

You see immediately that the flared ends of the top form rudimentary handles, by means of which you can steady yourself.

'Slide forward as far as you can without falling off, Chloe,' your mentor instructs. 'And put your hands to either side. Take hold of the ends of the table-top. Excellent.'

You feel the cool of the lacquered top under your naked thighs and buttocks as you sit, torso erect. Despite the fact that your corset today offers no support, you cannot avoid a twinge of narcissistic pleasure at the way in which your bare breasts thrust forwards, secure in their own heavy firmness.

You sit thus, breasts bare, knees together, feet tucked back against the front of your impromptu perch.

'Open your knees, Chloe, and part your thighs wide.' You obey. .

'Oh, much wider than that, please.' There is a hint of mock laughter in his voice. 'Try to touch the backs of your knees against the front of the ottoman.'

The instruction is, of course, impossible to comply with to the last detail, but the effort leaves your inner thighs stretched and – the object of the exercise – your ringed sex brazenly opened.

Monsieur Alcard has a small round box in his left hand, a fine sable-haired brush in his right. The box contains what appears to be finely-chopped coarse brown hair, tiny shards of which catch the light and wink, iridescent.

The brush, dipped into the mixture in the box, is applied liberally to the outer lips of your sex, first one, then the other, for their full length, but avoiding going inside to the deeper pink of your inner lips, and avoiding too your part-ly revealed clitoris which, despite its exclusion from treatment, is noticed by Monsieur Alcard (not without ap-proval – the heightening of your sexuality is, as you must by now have realised, a major goal in your training), im-mediately to begin to thicken in response to the attentions to your sex. The brush returns to collect more of the tiny hairs, returns to your exposed sex to brush them onto your flesh more fully, spreading across the soft skin at the very tops of your opened inner thighs.

The process is repeated for each of your nipples, the hairs of the brush stirring the gold rings, and for the pale pink halo which surrounds them. Glancing down, you see the tiny brown hairs clinging to your skin: some appear to have stuck lightly into your flesh, standing up like tiny pins. Apart from the not unpleasant sensations caused by the long, soft and gentle hairs of the brush, you feel no-thing untoward. Finally, the swelling fullness of each breast from its tip to half way back to your torso is lib-erally painted with the dry brush and its almost invisible coating of silvery brown hairs.

'Schoolboys' itching powder,' remarks Monsieur Alcard lightly. 'There will be no particular sensation for a few mo-ments, then perhaps you may notice something. I want you to stay in that position, without moving, quite simply for as long as you can manage. You may move your head, and toss that lovely hair of yours around, if you like, but other-wise absolutely still, please. For as long as you can.'

He pauses. This does not sound too onerous a requirement – and that in itself is ominous.

'When you have had enough, you may ask to be relieved. I suggest cold water, from the bidet and wash basin in the washroom on the next floor. You may wear your robe, if you feel you have time to collect it.' He places over a chair back the pale silken robe you removed as you presented yourself for his inspection.

It is fiendish in its simplicity. Yet again it is you, yourself, who is to be the architect of your own trial, the sole arbiter of your own fortitude. The first small itch begins along one lip of your openly displayed sex, the sudden tickling nip taking you wholly by surprise so that it is only with great effort you stop your thigh jerking in response. It is quickly followed by similar small itches along the other lip. Soon the entire outer entrance to your opened sex is itching maddeningly.

Steeling yourself, you feel the sensations increase. The growing itch (the substance was appositely named, indeed), spreads to the sensitive skin in the private hollows at the very top of your opened inner thighs, which it now requires real willpower not to close. At the same time, your breasts begin to itch, beginning with the pale pink areolae surrounding your nipples, spreading quickly to the entire surface of the skin of that part of each breast which Monsieur Alcard has visited with his brush. Finally, your ringed nipples, too, begin to itch.

Within moments, it feels as though your sex lips have grown to incredible thickness, as though you have swollen to three, four times your normal size. Glancing down, you are surprised to see that your nipples are not, as you had felt they must be, stiffened to the size of acorns: in fact, their appearance has altered little, save that their surrounding areolae are suffused with a somewhat deeper blush than normal.

Yet with every passing moment, the urge to close and rub together your thighs, to leave go with your hands of the impromptu grab handles which you now grip with white-knuckled intensity and to clasp your itching breasts, rubbing ferociously at your nipples, grows irresistibly.

Your head tosses, as the wicked Monsieur Alcard predicted it would. You roll your head from side to side, then up and down, then from side to side again – anything, to take your mind off what is happening to your breasts, and to your sex and inner thighs. Your chest heaves with your panting, so that your breasts shake and quiver.

At this point another of the whimsical little cruelties in which Monsieur Alcard specialises is introduced: as you struggle to hold yourself steady, the door to the small room opens and two of Monsieur Alcard's staff appear, carrying between them a tall cheval-glass mirror on a stand. You know, of course, that you must hold your pose of open display despite the entrance to what should be a private place of two outsiders, yet – as always when caught out, as it were, in such a position – you cannot prevent an inward sigh of dismay, an involuntary blush momentarily suffusing your cheeks. Paying you no particular attention, the two women place the glass in front of you, so that you see yourself – the open mouth of your sex, the reddened, quivering breasts – reflected faithfully.

Watching yourself, using the lewd reflection to help you keep control, to prolong your immobility, you tense, gasping for breath, and concentrate on pushing your thighs apart, holding your sex opened. Almost involuntarily, the muscles of your buttocks clench and unclench, as if that might distract your mind from the nibbling at your sex lips and inner thighs. The movement causes your hips to rock back and forth slightly, which in turn induces – again to Monsieur Alcard's interest and even amusement – your sex mouth (for it resembles nothing so much as a mouth), to pant rhythmically, as if gasping for breath. Your clitoris has thickened so that it stands prodigiously erect, the tiny golden ring embedded therein itself apparently erectile as the constriction in the stalk and the spreading of your nether lips cause it to be lifted clear of the surrounding flesh.

Now you are gasping aloud, groaning, moaning – anything to relieve the sensation of enforced inactivity as the itchiness grows to an unbearable level.

Watching, Monsieur Alcard smilingly observes your antics, sees the fine gold rings in the lips of your sex visibly move as your outer flesh spasms rhythmically with your inner movements and the clenching of your buttocks, as you desperately fight for the control to keep still.

You can take no more.

'Please,' you say to Alcard with tears of frustration in your eyes, 'please, enough.'

His response is simply to spread his hands, palm outwards, as he grins in genuine warmth at your contortions. He has told you the rules. You know where – and how – lies relief.

You snap your thighs closed, catapult off your unconventional perch and grab your robe as you head for the door, your cheeks burning with humiliation, your eyes avoiding the reflection of yourself in defeat.

You pray, as you walk with all the composure, all the self-control, at your command towards the washrooms on the floor above, that you will find a bathroom free. These floors contain the fitting rooms associated with the more normal corsetry practice of Maison Alcard, so it is not unduly unusual for ladies to be seen walking so informally attired.

To your relief a room is vacant. Gasping now, able to rub your burning breasts at last, you fling off your robe and squat over the bidet, reaching for the shower nozzle and turning the water to its coldest, most powerful jet in one swift movement, fumbling in your haste. You are still gasping audibly.

The ice cold water pounds against your sex, splashes across your inner thighs. You lift the nozzle and, leaning forward so that your breasts hang in perfect symmetry, you souse the cold water over and round them, unmindful of the fact that you are soaking the front of your corset. Retribution for that, should it be required, can be handled later.

The relief, happily, is no less swift than had been the original irritation, the itching subsiding as quickly as the offending fibres are washed from your skin. Only where you have rubbed at your breasts does any evidence of your brief ordeal remain, where your rubbing has brought a red rash as the hard, sharp but almost microscopic fibres have abraded the surface of your white skin. Here, in one or two places, a slight stinging sensation has replaced the itch. You make a note for future reference – for you realise that this bizarre test will now become a regular feature of your daily training sessions – to be even stricter about scratching your itch, even when safely beyond your mentor's quizzical gaze.

Back in your private training room, Monsieur Alcard glances at a stopwatch which, presumably, he had set at the outset of the test, to monitor your powers of self-restraint.

'Ignoring your somewhat unseemly squirming, Chloe,' he remarks flatly, 'you managed sixty-three seconds before abandoning your test. By the end of the week, I trust we shall see, shall we say, five minutes? And real immobility. Five minutes under the itching test, without moving a muscle. Now – to work.'

He steps to the wall, and tugs the bell pull. Colette, the female assistant corsetierre who is responsible each day for lacing you ever tighter and who earlier was one of the two women who brought in the mirror, comes quickly through the door. She is carrying, suspended from a hanger, what looks to be a one-piece sleeveless leotard, except that this appears to be made of shining black plastic, heavily boned.

The leotard has a high, stiff collar of the same shining black material, which at the front has a tiny shelf: for your chin, you correctly assume. You also assume, again correctly, that once the collar, which you can see is lined with a soft, velvet material, brilliantly scarlet, has been closed at the back of your neck you will be unable to tilt your chin, or your head, forward at all, but must hold your head high, looking only upwards or straight ahead, but never down, at the front of your body.

The waist of the leotard, you can see as it hangs from Colette's fingers, is impossibly small: it will reduce you as no corset yet has done, when fully laced. Its lacing, you correctly guess, will take no little effort on the part of Colette and require no little forbearance on your own part.

You can also see that above the waist, where the bra cups would normally be, there are just two circular holes, ringed by what look like fine steel hoops. The hoops, you observe, are not quite complete. On the outer side of each are two small plates, joined by a threaded rod, with a small butterfly screw at the top, so that the hoops can be tightened, making the breast holes smaller.

That, you correctly assume, will not be done until you are wearing the suit. And to wear the suit, your breasts will first have to be drawn through the steel-rimmed holes.

It is going to be an interesting day.

156

Keep Fit

The schedule of your life has taken on an even tenor, its seclusion and security comforting, its routines established, fixed, yet sufficiently varied for you never to resent their rigidity. You welcome also the flexible phases in your daily life – one evening a visit to a theatre, another a supper party with Lady J. – but always you are accompanied, your life ordered, either by your lover or, more usually, by Lady J. Stephen, you note, you have barely seen since your new regime began, and then only in the most fastidiously normal of circumstances: a supper party here, a drinks party there. Never in any moment where the special nature of your life and being – which you know of course to be known to him, most probably in every detail – is brought into evidence.

There are, too, the fixed rituals in your life, whose inflexibility you welcome just as much as the flexibility of your evenings. Your afternoon visits to Monsieur Alcard, of course, are at the centre of these rituals. Their content varies daily, yet their timetable is rigidly fixed, their logic immutable. Once, through no fault of your own, you feel, you are late. Though you are blameless, you none the less earn and suffer your first punishment. It is your first true punishment – you have accepted, continue to accept, many discomforts, even occasional humiliations – but the concept of real punishment is a new experience. The difference between a punishment and an exercise, you discover, is that even though an exercise may be more demanding than a punishment it can always be stopped by you. You have only to say your 'safe' word, as Monsieur Alcard calls it, and whatever you are being asked to undergo is modified, or brought to an immediate end. A punishment, once you have accepted it (you are never told what it is to be, merely that it is to be), is immutable; once begun, it goes on until it is finished.

It is not a severe punishment, this first. Three strokes of the crop, applied moderately hard, across your bared buttocks – you have voluntarily (but then even your punishments are voluntary), accepted much worse, and will doubtless do so again. It is the fact of it being a punishment which marks it apart from all else.

Your day begins in leisurely fashion. Madeleine brings your breakfast – too light, almost, to be called a breakfast: orange juice and a lightweight ryebread biscuit, but the fact of it being brought to you by another is of itself sufficient significance for your daily status to be reinforced.

It took a few days for you to grow accustomed to not being permitted to bathe yourself, but to submit to being bathed by another – Madeleine, of course – but that too has become a ritual, a central thread in the fabric of your daily life. And now that you are used to the idea, you enjoy the gentle caress with which Madeleine each morning washes you, gently soaping your breast, having you kneel, childlike, to soap your belly and between your thighs, relaxing and relaxed into a cocoon of secure affection.

You enjoy, too, your subsequent daily massage, Madeleine's strong hands and firm fingers kneading your shoulder blades, tensions flowing from you until you float, dreamlike, half-waking half asleep. And turning onto your back, from lying face down: the unspoken but understood signal, when you do it, which is not everyday, that you wish the nominally therapeutic massage to change in its nature. Occasionally, you permit Madeleine to bring you to orgasm, her knowing fingers skilled almost as your own in finding where, how fast, how hard to caress, then knead, then stroke, then press . . .

Your morning fitness sessions with Nancy, your demanding tutor, are another ritual. Nancy is American,

Californian, to be precise, and so physically fit herself as to be almost terrifying. Sleek, with a short-cropped, though stylishly shaped bob of honey-blonde hair, she has the body of a lithely muscled athlete. There is not, you reflect although not especially enviously, an ounce of fat (she refers to it as cellulite – her talk is peppered with the jargon of the gymnasium and the professional physical fitness instructor), on her body – or at least that of her body which you have seen, for there is no sexuality in your relationship with Nancy, as there is now with Madeleine.

Or rather, almost no sexuality. For one day Nancy introduces a curious exercise routine to your regime.

'OK Chloe,' she says, when you have been there about a week, 'we're going to add something a little special to your daily work-outs here. I think you'll enjoy it, certainly you'll find it different, I think. Come with me please. We need a little privacy for this one.' And she leads you to a curtained cubicle in one corner of the airy purpose-equipped gymnasium, beside the partitioned, half-height glass-walled area she uses as her office.

Inside, the curtains are pulled again to form a small room with a tall, roll-fronted cabinet and therapist's massage table. There are some steel-framed stools, a trolley of the sort one sees in a doctor's consulting room, and a small desk, where a consultant might take notes. In the centre of the curtained room, under a cover so that only its splayed steel legs are visible, is what appears to be a low vaulting horse.

'Right,' she instructs, her manner as brisk, as crisp, as all-American as ever – including that curious American phenomenon of spurious politeness whereby a not-to-be declined instruction is invariably phrased as an apparently optional invitation. 'For this series of exercises I wonder would you care just to slip out of everything below the waist: not just the tights, but including whatever you've got on underneath.' She smiles: 'We need you bare-assed, as they say in Texas.'

The instruction, though unexpected, does not unduly dismay you. You have grown used to not being mistress of your own body. You are wearing, as usual, an exercise leotard over tights, with a chaste, athletic bra (your gym sessions are one of the few occasions when you wear any bra, chaste or otherwise), high waisted pants beneath, with knitted leg warmer socks over training shoes. Her request is not therefore entirely easy to grant.

'You might care to modify your outfit in future, Chloe – we're going to be doing this every day from now on,' Nancy advises as you begin to undress, pulling off the leg warmers, then pulling the straps of your leotard to hang around your waist as you sit to untie the laces of your shoes. 'From now on this will be a regular exercise in your routine. We're going to be working on some inner muscles of which you've probably never heard.'

You look baffled. 'In short, Chloe,' explains Nancy, laughingly dropping for once the glib jargon of her profession, 'we're going to be working on the pussy grip – those are all the muscles you use when you clamp down on the man of your dreams – and I'm gonna give you a snatch that you can use to crush cider apples, should you have a mind.'

By this time, you have bared your lower body completely and stand naked below the navel, even your feet are bare. You wait quietly for Nancy's next move, your feet together, thighs closed, your hands by your sides. Nancy, who has been standing with her back to you throughout her talk, as you disrobe, working at some apparatus in the roll-front cabinet which she has opened, turns toward you, her eyes dropping to the neatly trimmed patch of short fair hair which adorns the pad of your mount of Venus, but leaves bare the lips of your sex and the junction of those lips, above your clitoris.

'Love the way you keep your hair – don't mind me asking, you know us Californians, straight to the point – but how come? You shave yourself there?'

You decide to elaborate only a little, you are unsure how much Nancy knows of the rest of the regimen of your life, so you add, simply; 'I have my labia and pubis plucked, and trimmed twice a week.'

160

'Yeah?' responds Nancy, her eyebrows puckering. 'Sounds, well – weird, you know. Can I look?'

Fully aware of the consequences of allowing Nancy to inspect any more closely what yet remains hidden between your close-pressed thighs, you make an instant decision, or, more correctly, a non-decision. You decide simply to let events take their course and your nerves begin to jingle in anticipation of where the course might lead you. It is, to you, the essence of the game: the playing with the fire of the unknown. You sit on a steel-framed, leather-topped stool, your hands clamping the seat edge behind you, and with deliberation you part your thighs, exposing not only your ringed labia but the smaller ring of your clitoris.

'Jeez,' exclaims Nancy, 'rings! Fantastic. May I?'

'Be my guest,' you reply, leaning back, allowing your knees to open further, to facilitate the inspection.

Nancy drops to one knee, her hand reaching to touch, her fingertips as light as gossamer, your shorn lips and the rings held captive in your flesh. Gently, she uses a thumb to part the upper junction of your lips, the index finger of her other hand lifting your clitoral ring in more than merely professional interest.

'This is something else,' she says in genuine admiration. 'I've seen pussy rings before, of course, but never one through the clit itself. Jeez – your eyes must have watered when you had that done. You do it for a man? Wow. You must love him – yeah?'

You contemplate telling Nancy that, no, you did not 'do it for a man', but rather for yourself, but instead you sit silent, unmoving, as Nancy gazes in wonder at what she sees.

'It's beautiful, really beautiful. You must tell me about it sometime, it's something I . . .' and she looks at you for a moment, her eyes full of meaning.

Before you can answer (you wonder how to frame your answer, for Nancy's invitation is unequivocal in its implication – Nancy, you suddenly know incontrovertibly, is a lesbian), Nancy herself breaks the eye contact.

'Still,' she rises briskly, as if afraid of the developing

intimacy, afraid of the jeopardy in which any further approach – at least for the moment – might place her and she swiftly resumes her professional tone and with it her authority. 'They won't get in our way at all. And we have a job to do. Look.'

And with that she pulls off the cover over the low vaulting horse. Its intent, if not its rationale, is immediately apparent. Sturdily set on four stout legs, the horse has a low, rounded top in which is set, precisely in the middle of the seat, its domed head and thick shaft unequivocal in its maleness, a not particularly lifelike but none the less unmistakable metal phallus.

'Meet Ernest. He's fully wired for sound,' says Nancy, uncharacteristically flippant, 'and even centrally heated.' And then, reverting again to her brisk professional manner:

'The probe is electronically pressure-sensitive, and can be monitored remotely, here, on this console.' She gestures with her hand to a small computer screen in the roll-front cabinet.

'It is also spring-loaded in its mounting, and can be lifted – watch.' She grips the probe, as she calls it, firmly with one hand, unconcernedly coiling her fingers round its phallic shaft, and draws it upwards from the base of the saddle. It rises about two inches.

'The resistance on the spring can be varied. Measured in pounds, it too can be monitored on the screen.'

Briskly, Nancy snaps onto her hands a pair of clear, disposable surgical gloves before removing from the cabinet a box of individually sealed antiseptic cleaning wipes. She peels open one of the small packets, and carefully sterilises the probe before coating it lightly with clear jelly from a plain tube. It glistens in the fluorescent lighting of the small, clinic-like room, the message unmistakable.

'OK, Chloe – would you care to get acquainted with Ernest, and we'll see what that pretty jewel box you have there can do?'

All this you have watched, listened too, while a curious phenomenon occurs inside your head. One part of your mind is whirling, feverish, at the incongruity of the situation in which you find yourself; the other is strangely still, empty almost, absorbing and accepting all that is passing before you as you accept all that happens in Monsieur Alcard's private rooms. And it is this latter part of your brain which now guides you forward, has you straddle the horse and its unequivocal 'probe', has you shuffle forward until you feel the tip of the probe – it is pleasantly warm, Nancy's apparent flippancy about central heating was evidently not a joke – against the lips of your sex.

Carefully, your hands on your straddling thighs for balance, you adjust your position over the end of the probe, permitting the end, slippery with the clear jelly Nancy so carefully applied, to slip between your sex lips, nudging the entrance to your inner self. Slowly you flex your knees, sinking yourself gently onto the artificial manhood, feeling it fill you, until it is nested within you and you are fully seated astride this stool.

'OK Chloe, that was good,' says Nancy. 'Now, I want you to squeeze as hard as you can.' You comply.

'Good,' encourages your trainer, her eyes on the computer screen. 'Now give me ten, one after the other and each as tight as you can, on my count. One . . .'

As Nancy slowly counts to ten, pausing briefly between each count, your inner muscles grip the phallus as hard as you can, then relax, repeating the grip to the rhythm of Nancy's count. By the time she has reached ten, your lower belly is glistening with the effort, your jaw set firm and your features tight with concentration. You are also beginning to feel distinctly aroused, not so much at the erotic stimulation of the inert probe, more at – once again – the bizarre incongruity of your situation. Here you are, naked below the waist, revealed in the most intimate manner to another woman who is requiring you to peform physical exercises of which, only a few moments ago, you could not have dreamed.

'Now grip the probe as tightly as you can, then straighten your legs – try to lift it off the seat.'

Again, you comply, squeezing your inner muscles together

in what you hope is a vice-like grip and begin to rise. You feel the probe rising with you, then begin to slip. You grip harder, the probe holds fast for a moment, then again begins its inexorable slide. As you straighten your thighs, the probe withdraws completely. The sense of loss you feel is palpable, tangible, and you laugh nervously, dissipating the inner tension – mental as well as physical – and look towards Nancy, blushing in half-embarrassment. You are not sure why you are embarrassed. Is it because of the ambiguity of your situation, the exercise you have just performed; or is it because you wonder if, somehow, you should have been able to lift the probe further before the resistance drew it from you?

You cannot help asking.

'Well. How did I do?'

'Not bad,' replies your trainer. 'Your straight grip is okay, about four psi – that's pounds per square inch – which is better than average for untrained muscles. But you flag fairly soon. On the pulse test you drop off after four, and you were down to less than half grip by ten. I know it doesn't feel like that – you think you're gripping just as hard – but the computer doesn't lie. And in the lift, Ernest started slipping away from you at only a two pound pull. We can do a lot better than that. In ten days I'll have you pulling ten pounds. OK. Let's get to it. Put yourself back on to Ernest and we'll get to work.'

And so from then on, each day, when your normal work-out is finished, you move into Nancy's inner sanctum, remove your leotard (after the first day you cease wearing tights, so that you present yourself to Nancy – and Ernest, you humorously reflect – in training shoes, leg warmers and bra, your lower torso bare, your neatly trimmed pubic triangle unconcernedly on display, the rings in your labia and clitoris provocatively visible each time you swing your leg over the bench, opening your sex), and, straddling the apparatus, lower yourself onto the shining metal prong.

During the second week of this regime, Nancy introduces a refinement. Requiring you to remain still on the probe, warning you not to rise, but to hold yourself steady through what is to follow, she flicks a switch on the control panel in the roll-front cabinet, and rotates a control. At first you wonder what is to happen, what she is doing; a moment later and the probe within you tingles momentarily. The tingles, pulsing rhythmically, increase in intensity until your muscles begin involuntarily to spasm as the small electric impulses – for that you swiftly realise is what they are – pass up the probe. The sensation is not unpleasant.

'We can use this simply as a muscle toner,' explains Nancy and then, smiling, 'or as a reward.' She turns the control, and the intensity of the pulses increases, definitely erotic now, the probe quivering slightly as well as pulsing. The modest electric pulses are turning you on.

'If you squeeze really hard, you can stop the twitching – try it,' continues Nancy. You concentrate on gripping as hard as you can with your inner muscles, your eyes closed in concentration. Sure enough, the sensations cease. You relax again, and immediately feel the pulses in the probe recommence. The sensation sets you tingling.

'We can also,' says Nancy with a knowing smile toward you, 'make use of this particular facility to provide an incentive to do better next time. On full volume, Ernest is quite a little tickler . . .' and she turns the round knob – it is indeed just like the volume control on a hi-fi amp – fully clockwise.

'Yeoow!' you yell in surprise, your legs jerking straight, pulling you swiftly up off the probe. Standing astride the horse, the probe still pointed at the centre of your body you glare at Nancy. Like a tickle that touches a raw nerve, the pleasant sensations of the pulsing probe had developed a sudden edge, dancing on the very edge of pleasure. The sensation generated deep within you has left your muscles and nerves jangling, your knees palpably trembling. 'I'm not at all sure that's nice,' you complain.

'At that strength,' says Nancy 'it's not really supposed to be. However, it is not dangerous. The voltage is kept low, even when the current is increased, so there is no danger of damage, temporary or permanent. They're just

165

pretty hard to contain without jumping off, or giving the game away. Don't worry, I've worked out on Ernest myself, at full volume. He can work wonders.

'Like I say, we can use the mild discomfort of Ernest at full power as an incentive to do better. There are two ways. You can agree beforehand to take a certain number like that if you fail to meet a test target. Or we can turn the volume up during the exercises themselves, allowing you to hold the full-power pulses at bay with your own muscle grip, as you did just now. Once you relax your grip, you get pulsed like that until the grip tightens enough to turn the power off again. That's the way I work out with this apparatus.

'To start with for you, though, I suggest we use the first method. I'll set you targets each day. You set the number of what we'll call penalty points for missing each target. If you fail to meet the targets, you get nipped the previously agreed number of penalties. Once I'm satisfied your grip is good enough, and you can maintain it long and hard enough, we'll start using the second method as well. Okay?'

You stare hard at Nancy for a moment. This is a new development. Nancy is not Monsieur Alcard, or Colette, or even Madeleine. She has, beyond the role of physical instructor, no authority over you – you have not agreed to submit yourself to her. She is, you are sure, exceeding her brief with these demands.

Nancy, in turn, returns your steady gaze, challenging you to accept. You sense the challenge, and ponder, noting at the same time that the effect of the full-power pulse, mildly uncomfortable as it was at the time, has already faded to a tingling buzz, leaving you with a curious, almost expectant, tingling sensation inside the entrance of your vulva.

'That's not in the deal,' you say, the sensations tickling between your legs notwithstanding. 'This is supposed to just be a keep fit programme. Suppose I say no, I don't fancy that? That I won't do it?'

'That's your prerogative, Chloe. Nobody will force you. But you know what they say: "no pain, no gain". I think

166

you'll do it. I reckon, Chloe,' she says, looking you straight in the eye, her gaze so direct as to be almost impertinent, 'it's a challenge the little devil inside you won't let you turn down.'

You look at her, unmoving, your gaze locked into hers – how does she know about that 'little devil'? – but down below, in the lower regions of your belly, you feel that old familiar churning beginning, joining the itch-like tingling the after-effect of the full-power 'nips', as Nancy calls them, has left just between and within your sex lips.

It is Nancy who is first to break the deadlock. 'We may as well start now, Chloe. You can walk away from this one altogether, or you can accept my terms. You needn't say "yes" and you needn't say "no". If you don't want to do it, just climb off the apparatus.' She pauses. You do not move.

'If you're prepared to accept the new rules – just slide back down on to Ernest. I'll give you a few, now – let's say six, to pick a figure – just to show you what you're letting yourself in for, and to show you that you can take it. And I know you'll take it.' She pauses, waiting for you to move. You do not move. After a moment, Nancy says, very gently, knowing now that you will comply:

'Put yourself back on the hot seat, Chloe. Set yourself over the probe, then bend those knees again and slide fully down. Then hold still. When you're ready, put your hands behind your head. I'll count to five, then switch on the juice.' Her voice hardens with authority. 'The pulses will be five seconds apart, and you must keep still for – what did we say? Six?' And then, more softly again, she said, 'Twenty-five seconds, Chloe – that's all you have to take. Can you do it?'

Without speaking, you once again manoeuvre yourself into position over the probe, feel its warm metal head nudge against your sex lips, hear a tiny click as the metal catches against one of your rings. Deftly, you use the forefinger of each hand to part your lower lips, feeling the rounded head of the probe fit between. Putting your hands back on your thighs, your gaze never leaving Nancy's, you

167

flex your knees and sink back down onto the thick rod, feeling its hardness rise within you, filling you once again.

Nancy watches you, her hand already on the round control knob – the volume control, as she calls it – of the control panel. But it is a different Nancy to the usually cool, detached and clinical professional one. Now her eyes sparkle with unconcealed anticipation, excitement even, her mouth slightly open, the tip of her pink tongue stroking her white teeth. You see that she is breathing rapidly: much more so than your own, calm breathing. The tension in the room is suddenly palpable. It is no longer Nancy in command, but you.

Firmly settled down on the padded bench of the apparatus, the rod fully nested within you, you fix her with your steady gaze, then slowly raise your hands, but not to clasp them behind your head. Instead, you reach behind your back and unclasp your bra, sweeping the straps from your shoulders to let it fall to the floor, baring your breasts. Nancy's gaze flickers from your eyes to your breasts and she sees for the first time that your nipples, like your sex, have also been pierced and ringed. Your nipples are hard, causing the rings to appear more prominent than when the tips of your breasts are soft and relaxed.

Now you raise your arms again, linking your fingers, clasping your hands firmly against the nape of your neck. The movement raises your breasts, stretches your torso, flattening almost to concavity your belly. Your opened thighs splay over the rounded bench, the rigid stalk of your clitoris with its tiny gold ring protrudes visibly, rendered prominent by the way your sex lips part round the base of the silver probe on which you are impaled.

Nancy is breathing now through parted lips. She flicks the switch. A moment, and the first wicked little pulse tingles within you. You force yourself downwards, eyes and face utterly passive, only the fluttering of your sucked-in tummy and a small, involuntarily jerk of your spread thighs evidence of what passes.

When it is finished you lower your arms slowly, use your palms to push downwards on your thighs as you straighten your legs, pulling slowly up off the metal prong which glistens with your secretions as you rise. Stiffly, you swing yourself off the horse, and turn to recover your discarded clothes. Intentionally, you keep your back to your instructer, bending stiff-legged, feet slightly parted, to gather your garments from the floor, affording her a full view of your still opened, ringed sex, the lips thick and slickly shining. Your vulva and your vagina practically buzz, the sensations within tumbling one on top of the other. A few more moments, you know, and the tingling, nipping pulses would actually have brought you to orgasm.

'Same time tomorrow,' you say simply to Nancy as you head for the door, still carrying your clothes.

'Chloe?' calls Nancy after you. You turn. The Californian health goddess is looking at you with what could almost be worship.

'You're really quite something – you know that?'

Groomed

Your afternoons too have taken on a routine.

You arrive, usually from lunch with Lady J., at precisely 2.30 pm. Madeleine will have dressed you – or assisted you to dress, if you prefer – appropriate to the day and to the luncheon venue: Lady J. has a selection of venues round which you, to use her phrase, 'ring the changes', ranging from the club where you first met (the tailored look, is Madeleine's phrase as she ponders what you might wear for such a place), to a summery restaurant overlooking the river. Here you wear what Madeleine calls your ultra-feminine look, wide-brimmed hat, white gloves, full skirted dress, always with seamed stockings and high-heeled, shining shoes.

Always, beneath whichever outfit Madeleine has decided is appropriate, you are tightly corseted, your corseting part of your morning ritual with Madeleine, after your bath and massage. It is Madeleine who decides which corset – your wardrobe, chosen and filled by whom you know not, although you assume it to be Lady J., now boasts a wide variety of such – you will wear. You sometimes wonder if this is indeed Madeleine's choice and decision, or whether she is simply acting on instructions from – again, you assume – Lady J.

Whatever the method, the corset chosen invariably complements – and is varied both in style and indeed degree of severity to suit – the outfit of your day.

Thus, for the tailored look which accompanies lunch at Lady J.'s club, your corset is normally black although on occasions another colour – dark blue, even brown or green

– is chosen for you. It is often of soft patent leather, and of the sort which in particular makes bending or slouching difficult, with stiff back and heavily boned stomach flattener. Occasionally, the corset will cover your breasts, the conical cups emphasising their shape so that beneath the jacket of your suit your bosom is high and pointed.

For your feminine look, your corsets are inevitably satin, in pastel shades chosen to complement the colour of your dress, often matching precisely (the knowledge always amuses you as you sense appreciative glances when you arrive), the accessories you wear with whichever outfit has been chosen for you. Although of a softer appearance than the hard-sided corsets of the tailored look, your feminine-look corsets are laced none the less breathlessly tight, in particular to narrow and constrain your waist, while emphasising the swell of your hips.

Your satin corsets rarely cover your nipples, so that beneath your dress you are normally bare-breasted, your bosom supported by the corset's half-cups (sometimes little more than a shelf beneath the curve of each breast, sometimes a full, lace-trimmed half-cup over which your nipples show like rising suns), or by their own natural firmness alone. Should your dress have a low neckline, your corset will be correspondingly high at the sides, pushing your breasts together in a deep décolletage. A favourite of Madeleine, and of yourself, is a high-sided corset in cream satin, without cups but with a central vertical divider which extends midway between your breasts, separating them. Pushed inwards by the corset sides, yet held apart by the vertical stay, your breasts are thus thrust forward, jutting horizontally, squeezed slightly which in itself lends a measure of support yet none the less permits them to move freely, naturally, beneath your blouse or dress.

Occasionally, the corset – with either the feminine look or the tailored, or the combinations between – is little more than a waist-cinch, a *guepière*, leaving your entire upper torso bare. Under a summery dress, you will normally leave your breasts unsupported, their movement as you walk merely emphasises your womanliness. Or perhaps

171

you will wear a light, lace brassiere through which the rouge applied on such an occasion to your nipples and the haloes of the tips of your breasts shows darkly, emphasising the gold of your rings. Sometimes, over such an ensemble, you wear a translucent blouse so that the dark haloes and their gilded ornaments can be dimly, tantalisingly discerned, hinted at but rarely confirmed.

On other occasions, under suit or jacket, Madeleine, with an air not far removed from mischief, will require you to wear some exotic creation, again usually of the sort which supports your bust, sometimes in exaggerated manner, making your breasts jut astonishingly beneath the shirt or blouse, but which leaves the ends of your breasts exposed.

Tugging the nipples erect, she will then coat each peg of flesh with a clear fluid which quickly hardens, keeping your nipples erect. Under your jacket, the silk blouse which inevitably accompanies such an ensemble does nothing to disguise either the thrust of your nipples or the outline of the rings which transfix them. Seated in a cocktail bar, your jacket hung nonchalantly on the back of your chair, you are conscious of the repeated glances which such an intriguing outline draws, as if those who glance are reluctant to allow themselves to believe what their eyes appear to be telling them.

Between the feminine and the tailored is what Madeleine describes as the bizarre, used occasionally to take you to some dimly-lit, *outré estaminet* where strange men and women float like exotic birds of paradise, sipping drinks of curious hue from strangely shaped glasses, nibbling on snacks which claim, at least, their origins in exotic Caribbean and Oriental parts of the world. The outfits you wear on such occasions are normally no less bizarre than those of your unknown luncheon or evening companions: tight-fitting plastic or leather dresses and jackets, a studded, shining black PVC catsuit – even, on occasions, a high, metal studded collar.

Beneath, your corset of the day will be no less *outré*. There is one, an especial favourite, which Madeleine herself favours for such outings, a gossamer light, entirely see-through creation which, unusually, has full cups at the brassiere through which show your ringed nipples and, lower, the indentation of your navel. Only four lightweight, pliable black stays – two running vertically down the front of the garment, towards the side, commencing under the semi-circular hoops of the same material which undercup your breasts, two running down the sides at the back – appear to give the garment any rigidity, but the effect is illusory.

The lightweight, see-through material is in fact a mixture of nylon, from which so many such basques are made, and Kevlar, that flexible but unyielding material from which are manufactured such diverse objects as the casing of motor car tyres and the linings of bullet-proof vests.

In your case the Kevlar lends a rigidity to the gossamer undergarment wholly out of keeping with its appearance, and it holds you in a vice of unbending severity. To don it, you stand naked and outstretched, arms above your head, while Madeleine first fits the corset round your waist, using a zip fastener set in the elasticated spinal panel – the only pliable panel in the garment – to effect the initial enclosure. Moving to your front, she has you lower your arms to your sides while she adjusts the cups, which hinge incongruously from the front of the basque, over your breasts, fastening each at the side to hold your bosom securely.

Next she moves again behind you to pull tight the waist laces which criss-cross the back, lacing them to tiny hooks set on the rear stiffening rods, the elasticated panel adjusting itself to the new shape so as to leave no spare material.

By the time she has laced you tight, reducing your waist sometimes to an hour-glass eighteen inches, you are left breathless with the constriction.

But the discomfort of being thus tightly corseted quickly passes, unless, as is occasionally the case, an intentional discomfort – a tiny flesh clamp here, a carefully positioned stud, to press into the navel or between buttocks, there – has been added.

After lunch, you take a taxi to Monsieur Alcard's premises

in Mayfair, entering through a side-door and making your way to the second floor suite which comprises the rooms in which your 'training' and, you know, the training of others, perhaps contemporaneous with your own, perhaps earlier, takes place.

Colette is there to greet you. In the small changing room, you disrobe, keeping on only your shoes, stockings and whichever corset Madeleine has decreed you should wear for that day.

A twice weekly ritual ensures the perpetuation of that state of appearance decreed for you by Lady J., when first you stood for your inspection by her and the then unfamiliar Monsieur Alcard. First, you lean backwards against the padded leather trestle over which so much of what you are put through each day is accomplished. Supporting yourself with your arms, your feet placed slightly apart, your stance presents the hump of your pubis and the upper junction of your sex lips neatly for the ministrations of Colette and the tiny-limbed Chinese girl, her shining black hair as sleek as a raven's wing, who invariably assists her on these occasions.

That first day, the depilation of your labia and mound prescribed by Lady J. had been accomplished using strips of warmed and pliant wax laid onto, then pressed against, your skin. When the wax had cooled and become less pliant it could be stripped off with one swift movement, taking with it the hair over which it had been laid. It had been a drastic remedy that had left the soft flesh of your sex lips bee-stung and swollen, a stinging that also affected the tender skin at the tops of your thighs and of your lower belly where the sides of your mons had also been treated.

Once completed, however, the waxing has not again been necessary. Instead, twice a week, the two handmaidens use tweezers to pluck and tidy those areas of your sex which Lady J. has decreed shall be kept depilated. Your mound itself is trimmed with scissors, keeping the hair short, though not exaggeratedly so. The sides of your mound and the upper junction of your sex lips can be attended to as you stand thus presenting yourself. When that

174

is finished you are required to turn and bend over the padded trestle, grasping the familiar handrail on its further side, placing your feet, as so often required for so many purposes, against the inner edge of the two front legs of the apparatus.

Thus displayed, revealed and opened, the entire length of each plump sex lip is carefully examined and treated, errant hairs swiftly plucked away by the questing tweezers before your buttocks are unceremoniously opened to reveal fully the crinkled centre of the shaded valley between. Again, the nipping tweezers invariably find fresh harvest.

Finally, as you remain in position over the trestle, that treatment which Lady J. advised and by which the outer labia of your sex are to be rendered fuller and more plump than their natural contour already bestows is carried out. The stinging nettles decreed for you by Lady J. are drawn lightly but repeatedly up and over each now smooth and bare lip again and again until, reddened and swollen, they pass from flame to heat to numbness.

It takes you almost three weeks to develop the self-control required to hold yourself completely still and compliant for this irritating rite, and a further week until – a mirror held before you to assist you to monitor your own progress – before you can endure the entire ordeal with that calm and serene facial expression which gives little clue to what is happening behind you which is so sought after by your tutors.

Particularly trying is the devilishly contrived climax when Colette with both hands uses your rings to ease open the stung and thickly swollen outer lips, pulling them first outwards then fully apart so that the pink flesh within, including the soft petals of your minor labia, is revealed in all its vulnerable succulence. Invariably, the inner membranes glisten with the dew of your arousal; occasionally, the parting flesh takes with it a thin string of your silver oil, so copious is the flow of your secretions.

Colette's admonitory 'and now hold absolutely still, please, Mademoiselle' warns you that it is time. The nerves of your lower belly churn, firing your emotions further into that state of anticipation laced with fear which is the key to so much of your sexuality. Setting your jaw in determination you push your feet outwards, hard against the legs of the trestle, tensing the muscles of your legs and thighs to try to prevent movement. You lift your heels slightly, tilting your hips upwards even more, to show your willing readiness for what you know Colette and her companion plan to do, and hold your breath in anticipation.

Very slowly Jasmine (for that is the Chinese girl's name) gently draws one stiff nettle stem, stripped of its leaves but not of the fine bristling hairs which deliver the worst of its bite, up and full along the pinkly shining inner length of your opened sex, thoroughly stinging the edges of the waiting inner labia. You mew, kitten-like, forcing yourself to hold still. To move, you know, merely causes the stinging to be worse. Panting, inwardly trembling, you await what comes next.

The end of the bristled stalk touches lightly against the parted opening of your upturned and offered sex and with a gentle insistence is teased between the junction of your inner leaves. Your breath exhales in one long-drawn sigh as slowly the nettle stem is drawn downwards for its full length, dwells a pause, then is drawn upwards again, lavishly stinging the full length of the inside of the highly sensitive flesh. Gasping loudly, you fight to hold your hips steady, to keep your feet held wide apart, although your thighs now tremble visibly as the fiery rite is brought to its climax.

Finally Jasmine's fingers, too, part your flesh, reaching between those of Colette to spread outwards the now bright red lobes of your swiftly swelling inner lips, smoothing them lovingly against the held-apart outer flesh, where they rest, silver-smooth and shining, inner leaves and outer lobes literally stuck together with the glue of your own flooding juices.

The stiff-bristled stalk, glistening now with the same silvery evidence that you cannot prevent appearing when your sex is being worked upon, even with stinging nettles, is laid vertically across the pink mouth, pressed lightly

176

against the soft flesh, then rotated slowly first this way, then that to let the fine stinging hairs prickle and nip and bite at the innermost entrance to your being, setting the very mouth itself of your sex on fire. Your calves, your thighs, the whole length of your stretched and parted legs, quiver and shudder, but you do your best to hold your hips, your opened sex, totally still. You make one long-hissed sibilant of indrawn breath. Later, when the mirror is introduced to your training programme, you will force yourself to keep your eyes open, your face passive, watching yourself betray no sign of emotion even as the fire burns at its fiercest.

The stinging stalk retreats, advances once again, turned endwise this time. The hard end, as thick as a pencil, teases its way into the tight opening. Holding perfectly still, you concentrate on relaxing your lower muscles to accommodate with the minimum discomfort what follows: steadily the stiff stalk, its bite all but spent now, is slid into you until it is firmly held in the tight sleeve itself. Colette and Jasmine step back together – you hear their footsteps behind you – to leave you alone, bent and opened, the single stalk left protruding incongruously, held fast by your flesh. Blushing at the indignity of what is being done, of the picture you must present, you exhale loudly, gripping tight again, crushing what is left of the fine stinging hairs, further reducing their effect. A moment's pause, the sound behind you of a doubled step, and the stalk with tantalising slowness is withdrawn. Knowing your ordeal to be at an end, you reward your smiling tormentors with a low, keening moan.

You know, very well, that this final little ordeal is not of Lady J.'s determination, nor making, but rather a refinement of light-hearted cruelty (light-hearted because, compared with much else you are increasingly required to endure, it is no great burden), thought up and added for their own amusement by your two handmaidens. In your turn, it amuses you ('amuses' may not quite be the word, but it will suffice), to permit this extra licence, to allow the pretence that you think you must endure it also, without question or complaint. You suspect (quite rightly, as I can here confirm to you), that were you indeed to complain, they would themselves be punished. Since you do not complain, the regime which holds them in its sway just as it holds you (though under different circumstances), chooses to make no more of the matter.

When, at the end of each such session, you are given permission to rise to continue with that day's routines you feel your thighs will not properly close, perhaps ever again, so thick do those same lips feel, but the sensation is illusory. Certainly, your flesh is most definitely swollen after each such session – that after all is the intent – but the initial swelling quickly subsides while, true to Lady J.'s promise, the fiery sting is short lived.

None the less you know that, also true to Lady J.'s promise, the cumulative effect of these repeated applications is to begin not so much to thicken but rather to induce a noticeable and, you admit to yourself, succulent fullness of form, a rich plumpness, in those very lips which she initially pronounced 'a little too thin'.

Shopping

One evening, dressed almost in the manner of a bygone era, you are taken by Lady J. to a small shop in a narrow lane close to Covent Garden. Lady J.'s car draws close to the front door so that, when the door of the shop opens, and the car door in its turn is swung open, you follow Lady J. to step from the car almost straight into the shop. The shop door, its central window blanked by a lowered blind which matches in its anonymity the blinds which likewise blank the two small, close-paned bow windows of the shop front, closes immediately behind you.

You see immediately that it is a shoe shop – old-fashioned in its layout, with its neat window displays, a scattering of red leather-upholstered wood-frame chairs, each with arms and a high back and each faced by a low footstool with sloping frontpiece, each topped in red leather upholstery. A heavy green carpet and rows of plain shelves stacked with boxed pairs of shoes completes the Victorian air of a small, successful business which thrives on its reputation and long-established clientele without the need to attract a passing trade.

The woman who opens the door, who leads you both, after a polite but brief greeting to Lady J. which includes the phrase 'the lady of whom you spoke', is perhaps in her late forties, taller than you are with finely moulded features in a handsome face which offers no evidence of make-up. Her greying hair is swept into that heavy, semi-circular roll known as a chignon, she wears glinting patent black shoes, dark stockings (you assume them to be stockings – tights in such an environment would be unthinkable), and a close-fitting tailored black skirt, calf-length, cut to fit close-ly across full, almost too large, buttocks and hips, flaring slightly below the knees to permit, in concert with a deeply cut, double pleat at the back which runs from hem almost to mid-thigh, a stride which bespeaks authority and command while sacrificing nothing in femininity.

Above the skirt is a close-fitted green cardigan over a high-necked white blouse, the blouse with a narrow military collar which might almost be termed a dog-collar were it not for the froth of finely worked lace which softens its harshness. Gold-framed spectacles hang on a thin gold chain upon a high and ample bosom made more noticeable by the obvious narrowness of the back.

Without introduction, this lady leads you through a curtained archway at the back of the shop, into what is obviously a combined workroom and fitting room, its furnishing and furniture rooted even more firmly in the late Victorian era than those front-of-house.

As Lady J. wordlessly seats herself on a low brocade-covered chaise-longue at one side of the narrow room, her arm moving to rest on the single, high-curving arm of the sofa, a small, rotund man, quiffs of greying hair fringing a bald and gleaming pate, swivels himself off a high wooden stool at the far end of the workbench which takes up most of the other side of the room. He is perhaps twenty years older than the woman (her father? you wonder), and wears a three-piece suit with the jacket removed, the front of his waistcoat stuck with large pins (larger and heavier than a tailor might use), a faded yellow tape measure about his neck.

'Ah, Miss Chloe, I presume – and every bit as charming as our good friend Lady J. had intimated. Pray, Miss, be seated.' And with that he indicates a solitary chair immediately to your right, standing where you have stopped, just inside the door, the chair high of back but without arms, three-quarters facing into the workroom.

Still not having spoken since her original greeting, the woman steps behind you to ease from your shoulders the heavy brown velvet cape, revealing beneath a brown velvet, high-necked dress of long tightly fitted sleeves, closely fitted about the torso but with a full skirt beneath a natural waistline. The front of the dress, from neck to hem, is tightly closed by no fewer than sixty-four small pearl buttons, each of which, from hip to throat, have been closed by Madeleine, as she dressed you, by the only means possible, so small are button and button-hole alike: an old-fashioned button-hook.

Beneath the dress and the thin silk chemise of lighter brown than the dress, you have been laced in a well-fitting but not particularly rigorous full-figure corset, pale coffee in colour, which, unusually in the case of the corsets you normally wear, has a conventional bodice which fully supports and partly covers your breasts, leaving only the tops bare but covering your nipples. Beneath the dress, your own bosom is high and pronounced, but, thanks to the cups of the corset, there is no tell-tale sign of your ringed nipples.

The corset is, also unusually in your case, cut low at the back and across the hips. At the front, however, it ends, as do most, just above your navel, leaving your lower belly and pubis uncovered. It is particularly well-boned (but exquisitely so, so that no indication of its presence is apparent from the appearance of your dress), causing you to sit with a particularly straight back.

Sheer brown stockings, with seams, naturally, and high-heeled brown shoes (the heels, again naturally enough, just that fraction higher than is considered conventional), complete your outfit.

'This is Mr and Miss Coldberg, Chloe,' announces Lady J. without preamble. 'It is time you had some interesting footwear. I know of no one better skilled nor equipped to provide it. They already know of my requirements, and will be able to proceed once they have some thorough measurements. Please co-operate with whatever they require.'

The charming, almost cherubic Mr Coldberg, a genial gnome with, you now notice, tiny tufts of grey hair high on his apple cheeks, beams and seats himself on a low stool in front of and to one side of your chair. Drawing across from under the workbench a small worklight which sits on a base with an articulated arm, all levers and springs, he positions the light just between your feet, switching on the lamp which shines warmly on your feet and lower legs.

Daintily, almost reverently, he lifts your ankle, deftly removing your shoe. His: 'Permit me if you will', is at the same time both permission sought and permission taken, and you relax as you feel his sure touch as his hand lightly but firmly sweeps across your foot, testing and feeling.

For some minutes this examination, almost massage, continues, first one foot, then the other, and you relax, enjoying the pleasant sensation. The remarkable Mr Coldberg has so far taken not one single overt measurement, yet you feel he must know your feet intimately. Occasionally he mutters little words and phrases, part observation, part encouragement: 'excellent . . ., exquisite . . ., what a splendid arch you have, my dear . . .'

Finally he rests from his ministrations, as a movement to your left brings you back to clarity, if not alarm. The daughter is bending beside you, proffering to her father what can surely be only an instrument of torture, a heavy wooded boot, made in two halves and hinged along the sole so that it can be fitted over foot and ankle, almost to mid-calf. Mr Coldberg smiles.

'Ah yes, my dear Miss Chloe – you have heard of the Spanish boot, obviously – used by the holy-minded mediaevalists to extract confessions to everything from witchcraft to murder by way of necromancy and devil-worship or, in the case of my own people, to turn good Jews into crippled Christians. But do not be afraid – we are not out for revenge, Gelda and I! And in this establishment feet are clothed in gold – sometimes literally, as well as metaphorically – not crushed and deformed. This is simply to permit me to take the most accurate measurements possible of your exquisite feet and ankles. And you know, we Jews have a saying: "If God wills, from the darkest evil good may come." Observe.'

And gently, tenderly – indeed lovingly – the cherubic Mr

Coldberg takes your left foot and places it with infinite care inside the daunting wooden case, which Gelda softly closes. Soft sponge rubber inner tops lightly grip your calf at the top of the boot, inches above your ankle, as Gelda adjusts the fit, pushing upwards underneath the heel, to ensure your sole is firmly planted.

Now Mr Coldberg swiftly and deftly begins to slide a series of grooved wooden dowels into small holes strategically placed at points around the boot, so that within you feel the dowels lightly touch your foot. Quietly, quickly he murmurs a series of letter and number combinations: 'A three, four; a four, two; a five, two . . .' to Gelda, who in a neat hand writes them into a leather-bound ledger which she holds on her knees as she half kneels, half squats, at your side.

Eventually, after what seem like a hundred such measurements, adjustments, checks, the process is repeated on your right foot, which again Mr Coldberg lifts, reverentially, from the small footstool before you to cradle on the point of his bent knee.

Finally, the re-born Spanish boot is put away, your foot replaced on the footstool.

Mr Coldberg turns to Lady J. 'With your permission, we will take all the measurements this evening.'

'Of course,' says Lady J., who has watched, silently, the process of the past half-hour. She turns to you, by way of explanation which her manner tells you, subtly, is more out of kindness and consideration than any feeling on her part that you are owed any explanation of anything that is done to you, and says, 'we may as well fit you with some boots, as well, Chloe, while we are here.'

The shoemaker turns again to his daughter, a smile lighting his contented countenance, his hands spreading in a gesture part of helplessness, part of surrender. 'Gelda, my dear, if you please . . .' He inclines his head toward you, and you wonder what is coming next.

Gelda rises, standing beside you, level with your hips, straight back and shoulders. 'If you will permit, Miss Chloe . . .?'

And leaning forward she places her hands outside either calf, just below the knee, and draws her hands upwards, bringing with them the hem of your skirt. You sit still – your training by now instinctively tells you this is what is required – your left foot on the floor, your right still on the raised top of the low footstool, your knees slightly parted, as the hem of your dress is raised, the material bunching before it, up your thighs until it stops with the tops of your stockings, darker brown than the sheer nylon itself, just revealed.

If Mr Coldberg considers there to be anything unusual or notable about the sudden disarrangement of your dress, he gives no indication. Rather he busies himself for a moment with the ledger discarded by Gelda and then, as his daughter resumes her half-kneeling position by your side, he returns to her the book and once again daintily takes your right ankle, raising with it the foot and – this time – your parted knee and raised thigh.

His manual examination is as before, but this time begins on and around your upper calf, moving gently to your knee.

Your pulse begins to quicken as your imagination leaps ahead, wondering how long the boots for which you are now to be measured might be.

Raising your foot and drawing it a little to his right, so that as your limb follows your knees and thighs part even further, Mr Coldberg softly passes his firm, testing hands around your thigh, sweeping impersonally higher so that his fingertips stroke lightly around the top of your stocking, stroking fleetingly against the soft inner skin just above the stocking top.

Deftly, so swiftly as almost not to be noticed by anyone other than yourself, his hand passes back across your inner thigh, turned this time so that the extended fingertips brush lightly, imperceptibly, into the crease between the very top of your thigh and the plump fold of your sex lips. You hold yourself absolutely still, your face impassive, your eyes now locked onto Mr Coldberg's smiling face. His own eyes engage your own, holding your gaze. Your lack of withdrawal gives him the signal you will make no objection.

Again the hand sweeps, and this time there is no mistake. As he uses his left hand to draw your foot further to your right, opening your parted thighs yet more, Mr Coldberg's sure, confident fingertips pass back across the top of your thigh, lightly across the tightly trimmed bush of your pubis and then gently, sweetly down the very cleft, parted slightly as it is by the drawing apart of your knees. The fingertips stop momentarily as they encounter the smooth skin of your carefully depilated sex lips, pause again as they discover the hard circlet of a gold lip ring, then sweep lightly but surely into the divide between your buttocks before passing up over the smooth skin of your sex once more, this time tracing the line of both lips, finding the second ring to match the first.

'Ah, how charming,' whispers Mr Coldberg, with a slight inclination of the head.

Blushing, you note Mr Coldberg's gaze drop lightly from your own, his eyes sweeping lower, toward the centre of your person, and you realise that with your foot raised and held thus, your knee bent and parted and your skirt raised high – the heavy material of your full skirt has, with the raising of your foot, fallen further down the reverse slope of your raised thigh, towards your lap, revealing now the bare flesh above the stocking – the shoemaker must have an unrestricted view, illuminated by the lamp behind his shoulder, of all that lies between your parted thighs. And the thought immediately causes your lower belly almost to cramp in a sudden convulsion. You feel yourself melting and cannot help but squirm, only too well aware of what you must be showing.

You squirm not away from, but toward, the seated shoemaker before you, twisting your knee so that you are sure you reveal completely not merely the brown curls at your lower belly but the inner secret that lies between, the secret of your pierced and ringed clitoris.

You close your eyes, suddenly close to orgasm. And the thought of the humiliation you should feel, but do not, at the prospect of the anonymous shoemaker learning the full extent of your willing enslavement, brings you past the point of no return.

Uncaring but not unknowing, you permit yourself a low moan, leaning back, collapsing almost, against the back of your chair while your thighs spread and your sucked-in belly and clenching buttocks tilt your pelvis in open revelation, parting your thighs fully so that the shoemaker may see all.

'Charming, quite charming,' observes the shoemaker again, with a smile. He turns to Lady J. 'A most apt pupil for you, I suspect, madame?'

'Wanton, quite wanton,' replies Lady J. with mock severity. 'I don't know what we shall do with her.'

A week later, you have returned to La Maison Coldberg, to be fitted with the boots which the good shoemaker's examination had presaged. You are attired precisely as before, and once again, Mr Coldberg is seated before you, his eye-level no higher than your knee, and raising your foot to ease you into the long, cream-coloured boot of leather of a softness and texture you did not know could be achieved.

Again, you feel a *frisson* of wantonness begin to come upon you as your knee is raised and you fancy what you might well be showing the shoemaker, but this time there is no sudden rush of sexual feeling, no uncontrollable lubricity. Such moments occur spontaneously, rather than by artifice.

Even so, as the second boot is carefully fitted, involving the shoemaker running his fingers round the very top of the boot, between the leather and the silk-smooth nylon of your stockings, an inch or so below its top you feel stirrings of what you recognise but have no name for. There is no doubt, you well know by now as indeed do those in whose charge you have placed yourself, that there is more than a hint of the exhibitionist in your sexual make-up. The thought of being somehow obliged to show yourself, especially in the process of something unrelated, always gives you this charge, these butterflies.

As the familiar tingle of the first swelling of your sex lips, the first melting of your glands, begins between your legs, you are invited to stand.

'They should come high on the thigh,' Lady J. is saying 'with just an inch of stocking showing. Let me see please.'

With the now familiar: 'Permit me, please, Miss Chloe,' Gelda steps behind you as you face both Lady J. and the curtained far end of the narrow fitting room. With a sweep of his arm, Mr Coldberg, standing beside Lady J., draws back the heavy red velvet to reveal a tall mirror which fills most of the door, formerly concealed, and you see your reflection full face in the mirror, erect, feet together, as Gelda behind you draws the hem of your skirt, parallel with the floor, up your leather clad thighs until the top of your dark stockings show just above the boots. A little further, and above the dark stockings can be seen the white flesh of your thighs. Gelda pauses, holding the hem of your skirt just below the junction of your thighs.

'Perfect, if I may say so myself,' says the shoemaker lightly. 'Exactly the right length, exactly the right fit. Ha! what a picture!'

'Indeed, perfect, Mr Coldberg, as always. Chloe, my dear, as Mr Coldberg says, you look a picture. Gelda, raise her skirt right up, to her waist. The colour should quite match her pubic hair. Let us see her thatch and belly as well.'

And with that, Gelda sweeps the bunched material upwards, over your hips, to reveal not just the neatly trimmed bush which tops the junction of your thighs and the downward slant of the carefully depilated lips which peek between, but the white expanse of the bare flesh below your navel, where the inverted crescent of the lower edge of your corset frames what lies below.

Blushing hotly, you feel yourself lean back against Gelda, closing your eyes, hear Lady J. say sweetly, but so meticulously.

'Feet apart, please, Chloe. A little penance, I think, for the wantonness of a week ago.'

You obey.

'A little wider still, please Chloe.'

You obey again, moving your feet wide apart, full stretched, your hips thrust slightly forward.

'And open your eyes please, my dear. You must watch while you pay.'

Reluctantly, you open your eyes. Lady J. is still seated, more upright now, more attentive, at the end of the chaise-longue, her arm resting, stretched forward, on the single armrest of that distinctive and now neglected example of the furniture-maker's art.

Beside her, facing you, but to one side so that you still see yourself in the mirror, wide-legged, your ringed sex fully displayed, even the ring within displayed, unequivocal, is Mr Coldberg.

You watch yourself, your head now lolling a little to one side, resting against the shoulder of the taller woman who half-supports you.

Mr Coldberg steps toward a small table close by Lady J.'s outstretched arm, picking up what lies on it. Its five or six thongs (you cannot see distinctly how many, precisely), dangling heavily toward the floor, it is a slim whip of the same cream leather as your boots, its handle unmistakably fashioned in the form and shape of an erect phallus, the head and veins faithfully reproduced, thickened with intent. The thongs, some eighteen inches long, are thin leather tendrils of the sort of which leather boot laces are made. Knowing what must come, you make no move or protest.

'Six strokes, I think please Nathan,' Lady J. is saying, and to you, 'Just hold wide open please Chloe, my dear. That's right – how charmingly you obey these days. But bend your knees a little more. That's better – now hold still, my dear, and no moving. Mr Coldberg is extremely accurate, so it is up to you. If you cause him to miss, we shall simply have to begin again. And afterwards, the handle, until you come. It should not take long: Gelda is very skilled.'

And closing your eyes again, you lean once more back against the comforting bulk of the shoemaker's daughter.

Camille

'Ah yes,' reflects Lady J., quietly, 'Camille. Gerard's alter-ego.' She pauses. 'You are sure you wish to ask?'

You nod, dry of mouth. You two have almost finished lunch, the restaurant is quiet, and Lady J. has been especially solicitous of your well-being, and in particular your contentment or otherwise with the regime you have agreed to follow and for which she is largely responsible. It is this solicitous, increasing intimacy between you which has prompted you now to break a hitherto but none the less inviolate rule which, self-imposed, prevents you asking questions regarding anything that lies ahead.

Rather, you prefer to take each day as it comes. Thus, you have waited through the progression of a series of exercises, each increasingly demanding, the object of which has been to lengthen and toughen that part of your person which Lady J., when she brought you first to Monsieur Gerard's curious establishment, declared she wished to be able to see at all times, irrespective of your state of sexual activity or excitement at the moment in question.

Thus you wear for several hours each day a heavy ornamental pendant suspended from the fifth and smallest of your five rings, often wearing it even in the evenings if at home or occasionally out, with Lady J. for example; removing it only when you sleep; replacing it as soon as you return from your morning sessions in the basement gymnasium with Nancy. It is the third such you wear, each having been heavier than that which it replaced, each having been replaced with uncanny perception just when you were beginning no longer to notice its weight upon your flesh as you walked, moved or sat.

And removed again when, tightly corseted in your training outfit for the day, you are required during three ten minute exercise sessions of squat bends and step-ups, evenly spaced throughout your afternoon schedule, instead to bear the weight of a leaden pear-drop suspended from a small articulated steel clamp, the jaws of which are closed, gently but firmly by Colette, over the stalk of your reddened, sensitised nubbin, as near to the tip as possible. Your pleasure bud, reddened and sensitised by having first been lightly brushed with the fiery purple-leaved nettle stems, while you stand unflinchingly still and straddle-legged, in order to induce in your swollen sex lips, the thickening as suggested by Lady J.

Ensuring that only that part which is intended to be touched is touched, Colette, black rubber-gloved for the purpose, holds apart the upper junction of those plump lips, exposing the pink flesh within, to allow the fine stinging hairs on the stiff green stems to reach where they must.

And at the end of each session, with the exercise weight removed but before your jewel-weight is replaced, you must, each week, lift and keep suspended until Colette claps her hands, a larger weight than the week before. The weight being placed on the floor between your parted feet and attached to a slender chain which itself is attached to that cruel clamp. To permit the chain to reach the clamp, you must bend your knees, lowering your torso toward the floor and weight, holding the lewd pose while Colette attaches the chain. At first, you were permitted to effect the lifting of the weight in your own time and manner, accommodating yourself to the inevitable discomfort as best you could.

Recently, Colette has introduced a demanding refinement. Once the weight is attached to the chain, you are required to tension the apparatus by partly straightening your bent knees until the chain is taut, your tip-clamped stem beginning to elongate. This position you must then hold. Bizarrely poised – head up, feet apart, knees bent, hands on hips, back straight so that your corset-supported breasts jut and with your gaze fixed on the wall ahead – you must wait now for Colette's signal.

At the first handclap, you must without hesitation straighten your knees, jerking the weight up off the floor in what Colette laughingly calls 'a snatch lift – just like a real weightlifter'. Gasping, you stand, feet apart, the weight swinging heavily between your parted ankles, your elongated flesh distending elastically, until the second handclap signal, when you may with relief flex your knees to set the weight back on the floor.

Anything between two and five such lifts may be required before Colette is satisfied, by which time sweat glistens between your shoulder blades and in the valley between your jutting, ringed breasts, and your eyes smart with tears. The reddened flesh around the junction of your sex lips aches.

As a stretching exercise, you can attest its effectiveness and have, in truth, begun to observe for yourself, looking into a mirror, that you are indeed being lengthened, noticeably. The tiny gold ring and with it the end of the tender morsel it pierces now peeps coyly from between the thick outer lips of your sex even when you stand with feet and thighs pressed together. When you were first ringed there, the ring was discreetly hidden, when you were relaxed and unaroused, by those same plump folds.

With all these trials you endure, with all these 'improvements', as Lady J. would term them, a nagging doubt remains in your mind, one which will not go away. And as all doubts unaddressed it grows, unbidden; pushing in upon you when least wanted, returning again with even more probing questions each time you push it away, each rebuff serving merely to harden its resolve as if what was once an ephemeral phenomenon, a passing thought, could grow to become a tangible being, to gnaw at you until you must face it and put it away for ever. The doubt now takes the form of Lady J.'s face and – curiously disembodied despite the ghostly presence of the face – her voice. You are standing, in this waking dream, in the Fitting Room, listening to Lady J. and Monsieur Alcard discuss the disposition of your person, before you were admitted to Monsieur Alcard's house for the training you now daily

191

undergo. You remember the words clearly, distinctly, and with total clarity. Lady J. is discussing you:

'You may have a completely free hand with the clitoris,' she says to Alcard. 'The fact she is already ringed will help you – with weights it should be possible to lengthen her considerably, I should think, without even bothering with other methods – but you need not restrict yourself. Use whatever methods you feel appropriate. Indeed you may send her to Camille, if necessary.'

So now you have screwed your courage to the sticking place, and have asked: 'Who is Camille?'

Lady J. continues after a moment more of reflection, silent.

'You have yet to meet Camille. She is Gerard's, how shall I put it? – his companion, his mentor in these matters. You may think Gerard strict, demanding – you have not yet come up against Camille. I sometimes wonder, between the two, just who is the master of whom.

'Gerard and Camille have been associated for as long as I have known them both, which is a long time. If it is decided that you require Camille's attention, her special skills, you will be sent to stay with her, for such time as is necessary to achieve what only she can achieve.' Lady J. pauses again, takes another sip of coffee.

'Camille runs a discreet establishment in the country, in Hampshire: a residential facility for ladies – usually, but by no means always, young ladies.'

'A bordello, you mean,' you quickly suggest, eager now that Lady J. has, by her answer, tacitly agreed to condone your breach of protocol. 'She's a Madame?'

'Good gracious no,' laughs Lady J., 'although she may have been in the past. Camille's is not a brothel – rather the reverse, my dear. More of a sanctuary. Few men ever visit Camille's, and those that do see little of the house or indeed the gardens, and nothing of what goes on there.

'Men, when permitted, are strictly restricted to the drawing room and – in suitable weather – the lawn. And very occasionally, for a special ceremony, for example, the conservatory. But the rest of the house and grounds are strictly for ladies only. And men will only ever come to deliver or collect or very occasionally to visit one of Camille's residents.

'Camille's is a training establishment, if you like. A sort of cross between a finishing school and an academy, with a touch of corrective institution thrown in. If a gentleman has a lady whom he wishes to assume a discreetly low profile for a time, Camille will attend to it. A businessman, for instance, may need to go abroad, and not wish or be able to take his mistress with him. He may not, on the other hand, wish her to remain – how shall we say – on the loose in London while he is away. She will stay with Camille.

'Or a protégé, such as yourself, may require special instruction, or even correction: she will be sent to Camille's, to have the fault corrected or to receive the appropriate instruction.'

'But how,' you ask, 'does it affect me? You mentioned Camille when discussing what you wanted done with – well, with my clitoris. Wanted it lengthened, stretched, made more prominent. Why do I have to go to a corrective institution for that – am I not trying hard enough?' You are clearly distressed, and Lady J. feels for you.

'Of course you are trying, my dear. We are all most gratified with your progress. There is no question of your being sent to Camille for correction – at least not in the punitive sense. Camille's corrective skills are also of an orthopaedic nature, as it were: as a dentist, for example, can correct protruding teeth. Camille has certain skills which she can use to produce a desired effect in an individual's physical features: in your case, your clitoris.'

You raise a quizzical eyebrow, but do not speak. Lady J. continues.

'In the case of the clitoris, she has developed a technique of manipulation – rather rigorous manipulation, I grant – which can effect the most remarkable changes. She can enlarge the little organ to many times its original size, using various devices. For instance, a clear glass tube fitted over the clit and attached to a small vacuum pump can draw the stalk several millimetres into extension. The effect in that

193

case is temporary, of course – but the cumulative effect of all the treatments can be both singular and long lasting.'

'It sounds rather demanding,' you murmur, adding, 'on the patient, I mean. Which I assume would be me.'

'It is something of an ordeal, naturally,' confirms Lady J. 'One of the first techniques she employs is to separate the underside of the hood from the stem itself so the full length of the clitoris is able to emerge, and the stalk can protrude fully. Then the stalk itself can be treated as required. She uses a tiny, padded clamp to hold the clitoral stalk, then with special forceps draws the prepuce back and away, using a fine flexible bladed spatula to stretch the integumen until the hood fits only loosely and retracts automatically as the clitoris itself begins to stiffen in arousal. It cannot be done in one session, of course: it can take many sessions, often several a day, over two or three weeks.'

Lady J. pauses, assessing your face, which has paled visibly at the prospect such information offers.

'Still, you should not worry. It is not something which is appropriate for all of us: in your own case you are already well developed; quite large and readily erect and visible. It may not be necessary – or Gerard may decide you are not up to it. As you can imagine, it is something which takes a certain amount of courage – or bloody-mindedness, depending on one's view of these matters – to submit to voluntarily and go through with. It is not for everyone, and it would certainly not be done to you by force, or against your will. You would have to be willing.'

'But it sounds appalling,' you repeat. 'Not only must it be absolute agony, but surely the clitoris is damaged – what you describe is practically female circumcision.'

'Not at all!' replies Lady J., almost offended by such a suggestion. 'There is no surgery, no mutilation – on the contrary: the clitoris is enhanced, its sensitivity increased – not to mention its versatility, when it comes to lovemaking. The hood remains, it is merely more loose than normal, more easily pulled back to reveal what lies hidden beneath,

194

while the clitoris itself is rendered more prominent, more readily visible and available.

'And as for agony – well, you might call it agony. Orgasm can be agony. Waiting for a phone call can be agony. What is agony? Agony, if you will pardon the descent into cliché, can be ecstasy. It is a vastly overrated state of mind. But in any case, it has yet to be decided whether you should be offered such assistance.'

Your brow wrinkles, puckering your eyebrows. Something in what Lady J. has been saying opens yet another corner of this still unfolding world. Knowing you have already committed an unforgivable breach of the unspoken protocol of your regime, you decide to push ahead, regardless of consequence.

'You said "all of us" a moment ago,' you repeat to Lady J., your voice querulous 'You mean . . .?'

'Oh yes, Chloe, I do!' Lady J. laughs. 'You should not think you are the first to travel – or be taken – down this thorny path.' She pauses again, in reflective recollection, and this time you do not interrupt.

'I was about the same age as you are now, my dear,' continues Lady J., her voice and tone softer now, more consolatory, 'perhaps a little older. Camille and Gerard, but a year or two older than that. My own mentor had already brought me through much of what Gerard now teaches you before he met Gerard, through another connection. Gerard was then a young corsetier, just becoming known in both the general world and in the specialist world. I was sent to him for three months, for rigorous figure training (I was already fully trained in the disciplinary sense of the word, of course).

'Camille had learned her technique from the woman with whom she had first served in Paris, learned it, as it were, at first hand. Her own clitoris was stunning in its protrusion. I often saw her thus, for we were frequently exercised together, and she kept her pubis in the manner of your own, that is to say the mount left covered (but the hair not kept as short as that adopted in your case), but the lips and clitoral junction itself kept bare, the clit itself pushing through like a miniature cockscomb. The corsets she could wear – many of them she made herself – ah, they were magnificent. We both modelled garments occasionally for Gerard and his special clients.

'It was she who suggested I have myself stretched, one day when I was being fitted by Gerard and the woman with whom he then worked, a Madame Feroche, with an outfit for which I had been required first to have my pubis and labia fully depilated, to show the corset I was modelling that evening off to best effect. When he heard the suggestion, my lover of the time agreed that my appearance would benefit from such a modification, and I readily submitted myself to the treatment.

'In my case, so hidden was my little gem, as my lover described it, that it needed many sessions with Camille before I was deemed satisfactorily revealed. Yes, it is uncomfortable of course, at the start. But I quickly became used to it – indeed looked forward to my next session. Camille is highly skilled, and no sadist: I was sometimes in a state of near exhaustion from the orgasms she could induce. After all, there is one very good way to induce the clitoris to swell, my dear – and it does not involve pain. I can assure you it was all worth it in the end, not only for the improved appearance but for the enhanced sensitivity. Even now, all these years later, I can explode like a grenade within seconds if I'm handled just the right way, just there.' She laughs, continuing.

'The whole thing was – is – in the broadest sense part of one's training. In truth,' Lady J. continues after a brief pause, recollecting her own experience yet again, 'it is not nearly as bad as it sounds. The stretching at first feels hot, rather than sharp or painful and of course Camille is careful not to harm the clit itself: the procedure simply stings a bit. It is the thought of the procedure, and the fortitude required to hold still and trust the operator, which provides the sternest test.' Lady J. pauses reflectively, takes another sip of her coffee, before continuing philosophically.

'Still, what is it the French say: "*c'est necessaire soufrir pour la belle*"?'

196

You have been listening spellbound, fascinated now, as Lady J. continues, her eyes distant, her voice strangely quiet as she recalls her own training, long ago. You are at once absorbed and stimulated – you want to interrupt, if only to confirm that what you are being told is not some fantastical tale. But you dare not, lest, having been interrupted, Lady J. elects to bring her reminiscences to an end. You know that this is a moment between you which might never be recreated.

'For my final session,' Lady J. continues, 'when I was already greatly enlarged (I was still being kept with a completely depilated pubis and labia, as well, which I may say I rather disliked), a woman in her mid-forties (I never knew her name, good-looking but quite ferocious in her bearing and manner) was present, to watch, along with another, much younger, who turned out to be her ward.

'The woman – a client of Gerard's – had decided to bring the girl to Camille for the same treatment and Gerard had insisted that the maiden – for she was precisely that – be shown what it would involve. I was chosen for the demonstration.

'For this occasion I was required to be corseted particularly tightly, with a stiff shiny cuirass that covered nearly all my torso, but left my breasts completely bare. It had a high, rigid neck-collar that kept my head up, so that I couldn't look down and watch what Camille would be doing even had I wished to.

'I had to put myself in front of Camille, facing her as she sat on her stool, and place my feet apart and bend my knees then hold myself open and keep my hood retracted myself while they watched. First she drew my stalk out to its full extension, then placed the glass tube over it. Of course, this is why in the first instance the clitoris must be freed from the prepuce. Then she operated the pump. It is of course a very sensitive hand-pump, operated by a rubber bulb, so there is no danger of damage. The feeling is exquisite, in the truest sense of the term. It quickly takes one to the edge of bearability.

'By this time my clit could be drawn to a length of

almost two-and-a-half inches, and Camille took me to full extension, then sealed the pump and bade me bear the test for a full five minutes. Naturally, I was expected to – and of course did – hold completely still for this demonstration, and not betray any discomfort or even excitement I might feel.

'As soon as the pump was released and the vacuum tube removed I was weighted, to preserve the stretching, and exercised especially vigorously: twenty-two full squats, I seem to recall, followed by a brisk step-up session on a low bench and then a work-out on an exercise cycle with the final five minutes full speed. Tightly corseted and heavily weighted, it was a tough call.

'Afterwards, I had to stand in the present position while Camille removed the weights and the woman herself lifted my clit to point out to the ward how the stalk having been peeled was free to swell and protrude, the hood being thus permanently loosened and so completely retractable. By this time my clit was so sensitised I nearly orgasmed on the spot – but happily the woman pre-empted such an embarrassment by the simple if somewhat uncomfortable expedient of rather roughly pulling my hood back herself as far as it would go, to leave the stalk completely revealed. The rough handling served to delay the onset of orgasm – but left the clit itself positively pulsing. The woman then rather exceeded her permission, granted by Camille, and pulled and twisted my poor stem until I could, indeed, no longer bear the test in stoic silence, and was induced to gasp. It was what she wanted of course – but the young lady went distinctly pale.

'She did agree to her guardian's wish, though. She was somewhat under the other's somewhat dominant thumb, I fancy, and – Camille told me later – about to be sent to a finishing school in Germany known for its fairly Prussian discipline. In addition to a known addiction to the rod, the headmistress of the school, a ferocious disciplinarian, was said to endorse clitoral extension, and to favour the use of the same technique to see it produced. Indeed it was rumoured to be a requirement for new junior teachers to have themselves extended before arrival, or visit the matron for the purpose during their first term.

'I believe the woman wished to demonstrate that anything the Prussians could do, the English could do better. There was a supposed tradition, much spoken of but never confirmed, that when a girl was selected to be head girl, she was first required to pass an intimate and rather special, not to say embarrassing, test. On the night before the formal announcement to the school of her appointment she was required to submit herself, stretched backwards and naked over a special goatskin-covered bench – only ever used for this particular annual ceremony – in the staff room and in front of all the members of staff both junior and senior, to having her pubis shaved completely bare and then have her clitoris measured. The rule, if you'll pardon the pun,' (Lady J. gives an endearing giggle at the unintended humour of her own joke), 'was that the clit had to be more than 25 mm long, measured from its base. There was a small silver gauge specially commissioned in the early part of this century for the ceremony. It was placed against the clit-root, underneath, and the stalk was drawn forward until the clit-tip passed an appropriate mark on the gauge.

'Needless to say having gone that far no girl wished to fail the test, and little feeling for the girl's discomfort would be shown should she not in the first instance measure-up. By the end of the evening the clit-tip would have been coaxed past the mark, no matter how much pulling and tugging the unfortunate candidate had to endure. It was a sort of initiation rite, to demonstrate her stoicism – much admired, of course, by the Prussian mentality – and willingness to conform. Naturally, given the culture of the place, protocol dictated she neither flinch nor make any sound during any part of the rite, since to do so would be seen at once as evidence of unworthiness for the position. Head girls of the place were thus said to have "ridden the goat". The woman had ambitions for her ward in that direction – ambitions which, I understand, were fully realised.'

Lady J. again pauses, and then takes your silence as the signal to round off the tale.

'Camille admitted her that evening, and later told me the young woman was already most remarkably developed, with a most unusual, heavy-set sex with thick outer labia through which the unusually large inner lips protruded, hanging down in two fleshy lobes almost an inch long. She also possessed the thickest, blackest bush Camille had ever seen, and which completely concealed this curious labial configuration even when the girl stood with legs apart.

'The woman was quite insistent that the girl should not be trimmed or shaved, even around the lips and clitoral junction, to facilitate what was to be done. Great hairiness, she told Camille, was much admired at the Prussian college – which was why to submit to the ritual depilation which preceded the goat ordeal had such special significance.

'According to Camille, the girl took it all without so much as a murmur, carefully parting the veil of black hair before presenting and holding apart the outer labia like a seasoned campaigner – she was obviously well used to the strictest possible discipline, even then. The woman told Camille that she used urtication as a punishment and would require the girl to hold her quim lips – as she termed them – open first for the inner labia to be thoroughly treated, then have her grasp and pull even those apart to allow the nettles to be applied right inside, since according to the woman the girl's great hairiness tended to reduce the effectiveness of nettling on the outside. The young woman's clit was already heavily engorged as a result. You yourself will know from your own experience under the nettles the degree to which her powers of self-restraint were, even by then, developed.

'When the woman came ten days later to collect her ward she showed Camille her own clit, which was apparently enormous, and which she said had been elongated at the behest of her own guardian when she – the woman – had been nineteen. She had been living in Paris at the time, and had been taken to a Turkish madam whose establishment had a reputation for having girls with unusual development – much of it artificially, if somewhat ruthlessly, induced. Like the younger, the older woman also was possessed of unusually extended labia minora, and these had been ringed. The clit itself had also been pierced, rather like your own – but in her case she wore not a clitoral ring but a small gold cap, rather like a miniature ferrule, kept in place by a horizontal pin thrust through the clitoral piercing. A formidable duo.'

Lady J. pauses again in her narrative. And again you remain silent, waiting for her to continue.

'As for myself,' she resumes, 'it took four full weeks to achieve the desired effect, but in the end my clitoris was lengthened by over an inch, as well as being fully exposed, and I have not regretted it at all.'

To hear Lady J. speak so candidly thus, particularly of herself, intrigues you almost as much as the idea of what she has just described, but with the shock there has come also an absorbing fascination.

In your mind's eye you see not Lady J. but yourself submitting to Camille and her rigorous ministrations: see yourself leaning, wide-thighed, before a Camille already seated on her ominous little stool, her jet black hair (she would have to have black hair, your imagination immediately tells you), pulled back in a severe bun.

Your mind's eye sees you as one detached, outside yourself, gazing down as you put yourself through this new ordeal, this new self-imposed test of resolve. Lady J. and Gerard watch as Camille begins her work. Your back arches, head lolling back, eyes closed, teeth bared as the stretching of your prepuce is begun. Your buttocks clench, the muscles on the front of your thighs stand out as knotted cords, sweat begins to glisten on your skin, your knees tremble – but otherwise you remain unmoving, groaning lowly, as Camille works painstakingly on, enhancing your womanhood as you submit to the intimate rite.

Could you stand it? you ask yourself. Suddenly, you know that you want to know the answer to such a bizarre question – and that there is only one way to find out.

How odd that your churning emotions, deep down in the pit of your belly, should churn most strongly with the thought – casually planted by Lady J. – that you might be excused this extraordinary ritual. Worse, that you might be thought unfit.

And you know, from that unmistakable *frisson* of disappointment that such a thought produces, that some day, even if at your own initiative, you too will visit Camille.

Punished

You knew of course that your deliberate breach of protocol in asking Lady J. to tell you about Camille would bring inevitable retribution. It does.

As with any punishment, you are told beforehand what it will be, and given the opportunity to accept or decline. It is, has been since you began your specialised training regime, your personal promise to yourself that you will never decline whatever punishment is suggested: not so much 'you will never decline', rather that should you find yourself unable to face whatever has been suggested, and thus exercise your option to decline, then you will also, you have vowed to yourself, quit the entire programme. The punishment which Lady J. suggests on this occasion gives you cause to pause, to ponder carefully, before you accept. But accept you do.

You are to be caned (that much you expected). It is the nature of the caning, and the circumstances in which it is to be carried out, which give you pause for thought. You will be caned before an audience, an audience composed not of people you know, not even part of the eclectic circle of friends of Lady J. and of Stephen to whom, gradually and over the weeks of your training, you have been introduced, but rather of complete strangers. You are, in fact, simply to be part of an entertainment. An act, as it were, in a doubtless expensive, clandestine cabaret.

Your anonymity will be wholly preserved by the mask you will wear; your body displayed by the costume into which you will be put – a costume as bizarre as any you have been fitted with during your figure training sessions at Monsieur Gerard's. Much will be made, by the costume and by the way in which you will be presented, of your ringed state, including the most intimate 'fifth ring', the ring of your inner self, from which will be suspended, during your punishment, not only a small weight (lighter, you learn with relief, than the training weights so regularly used on you by Colette), to which will be attached a bell. If the bell rings during your punishment, Lady J. assures you, each ring will earn you one extra stripe.

You will be secured over a whipping frame, your thighs widely parted, your inner lips revealed, your buttocks, of course, bared. You will be given twelve strokes. All this you learn beforehand, from Lady J., before you agree to accept the punishment.

It is probable the club itself is elegant, exclusive, its interior plush and well-kept: the same cannot be said of the dingy waiting room where you have been kept since your arrival, nor of the immediate backstage area where, with Madeleine, you now stand, so bizarrely and uncomfortably clad, for your show-business debut. But then even the backstage of the most elegant theatre is a mess of wires, bare walls, and the paraphernalia of illusion. This is no exception – only it is smaller, so small that as you stand, placed thus intentionally by Madeleine, as one might dispose a naughty child for punishment, facing the wall you must stand so close that the stiffened nipples of your artificially jutting breasts actually brush against the bare plaster.

The nipples themselves are not merely rigid, but sore, while your breasts ache. The soreness is induced by that procedure recently carried out by Madeleine to ensure the stiffness, the ache caused by the garment, in particular the bustiere of the garment, you are wearing for this your peculiar punishment.

The costume is an advanced version of that first produced for you the day Monsieur Alcard introduced you to the itching powder test: a tight fitting cuirass in soft but brightly shining black patent leather, moulded over your hips and torso, skilfully boned and tightly laced to hold your torso rigid, your waist impossibly small. Like the first such garment you wore, this one has twin circular apertures where the cups of a normal corset should be. Through these apertures your breasts protrude, their natural firmness artificially, indeed outrageously, enhanced by the use of metal hoops which ring each aperture, each hoop being individually tightened by a discreet but effective screw mechanism. With the garment fitted loosely, you have first been tightly laced, then the breast-hoops tightened so that, tightening round the base of each in turn, they cause the breast to swell and jut forward, the skin at the same time stretching into a smooth sheen. In time this constriction of your breasts causes each first to redden, then grow flushed while the skin appears to shine ever more sleekly, seal-like.

The broad, full areolae at the tip of each of these purple cones have also swollen, thanks to the engorgement of the whole gland, while to stiffen the nipples themselves, Madeleine first merely tweaked and twisted each in turn, pulling them into erectness, before coating each with that mixture of glycerine, sugar and water which all confectioners use to harden icing and which, applied to your nipples, causes them both to itch fiercely and to remain in a rigid state.

All this was done before you left Lady J.'s, to be brought here. Moments ago, Madeleine indulged in a minor cruelty which surprised you, for Madeleine herself is rarely employed in the trials inflicted upon you, rather tending you as your intimate maid and indeed ministering with sympathy to your occasionally tested flesh.

Taking from her handbag a simple emery board, of the sort you might use to file your nails, she carefully rubbed off the hardened sugar coating – but continued to apply the board to the thus-revealed flesh of each tender breast-tip long after the protective coating had gone. You had gasped, eyes watering, struggling to hold yourself still for this treatment, as Madeleine had used each golden nipple ring in turn to hold the teat, pulling it outward to elongate the flesh and facilitate her cruel little task.

Your nipples now are brightly inflamed, infused with a deep, hectic crimson – and hurt not a little. You smoulder with resentment at Madeleine's treachery, her unexpected cruelty. (You do not stop to think now, but will later, that the cruelty is not Madeleine's but that of someone else, under whose instruction Madeleine, like yourself, presently leads her entire life.)

Under the lights of the tiny stage onto which you are led, you can see nothing of your audience, but sense its presence from the low hubbub of conversation which stops, momentarily, as you appear with Madeleine at your side, then recommences, quickened but quietened, almost immediately.

The stage is small, semi-circular. At its centre, but upstage, is the padded frame over which your punishment will be carried out. All around the stage are full length mirrors, arranged so that the subject on stage – that is, you – can be viewed by the audience from virtually every aspect.

Madeleine leads you first to the centre of the stage, downstage, where the footlights and the overhead spots reveal you in all your glory. Through the narrow eye-slits of your helmet – you have become used to its heat, now, and to the pressure it exerts on your face – you can just make out the individual shapes, though not the features, of your small audience: it cannot number more than two dozen, men and women, all formally dressed, as if for dinner. Clearly, while you are being put on show, your punishment made spectacle, this is no sleazy skin-show. You might wonder more about your audience, but now that your ordeal is truly upon you, your mind is wholly taken up with, on the one hand a growing apprehension of what you must endure, and on the other summoning the willpower, now the moment is at hand, to submit yourself with total indifference. No matter what they do, they shall not break you.

Madeleine turns you, displaying your charms – or such of those as are revealed by your bizarre costume. She caresses her hands over your swollen, jutting breasts, cupping them and pushing upwards, then downwards, her hands cupped first underneath each breast, then over their upper slopes, to reveal their tautness, and the rigidity that tautness induces. As she pushes, first up, then down, the deep crimson cones barely move. Rather, they quiver like stiff rubber, the nipples thick, like purple berries, the bright gold of the rings glinting in the lights, the drum-taut skin shining. Each touch of Madeleine's hands on your breasts burns the drum-taut skin: you moan inwardly. Outwardly, you are passivity personified.

Madeleine drops to one knee to unlatch the two popper studs which hold the crotch piece of your costume at the front, deftly with her other hand undoing the single stud which holds the thin rear strap where it emerges from the cleft of your buttocks at the base of your spine. Swiftly, she allows the underpiece to fall away in front, tugging it out from where it is held by the swell of your buttocks and casts it aside, so that you are revealed below the stiffened lower edge of the garment, just below your navel, to the top of the pliant thigh boots. Your cream-white belly swells femininely, beneath which is revealed the trimmed thatch of your hair and the outline of the beginning of your depilated sex lips and slit.

Madeleine stands beside you, to your right, then bends forward, bending round you, so that (for she, too, is part of the display) the low décolletage of her black dress reveals the widely divided cleavage between her own firm breasts, offering, incidentally as it were, to the audience an extra treat. Gazing ahead through the eye-slits of your helmet you cannot see, but those who gaze upon you, on the stage, can see the deep valley between, the enticing inner swell of Madeleine's breasts. Her left arm encircles your left hip. She uses both hands to brush downwards on the front of your thighs – instinctively, knowing what to reveal, you move your feet apart to open your thighs – and she draws her hands upwards, allowing her extended fingers to sweep up your inner thighs and outwards, from between your buttocks outwards and upwards to your mons, along the length of your sex. The index finger of each hand catches and lifts b.iefly the gold rings which pierce each lip.

Her fingers return to the rings. She takes each, simultaneously, between index finger and thumb, draws it outwards, downwards then upwards, stretching each lip, pulling hard, to show that the rings are for real, that your sex lips are truly pierced, that the gold wire has indeed punctured your flesh.

She releases the lip rings, uses the first finger of each hand to trace the line of each lip upwards towards the junction below your close-trimmed mound, pulling apart as she does the plump folded flesh to reveal the inner pinkness, the stiff stalk and its smaller ring. There is complete silence now from the audience, as they see the reality of your inner secret. Madeleine deftly causes the fingernail of each index finger to score, lightly, along the sides of your stalk, highlighting its length and rigidity even while making you wince.

Next, using her left hand pressed flat against your mound, pressing upwards so that your sex lips and slit are pulled upwards, rendered more visible, she takes your clitoral ring between finger and thumb of her right hand, draws it outwards, drawing with it the stalk of your clitoris, pulling it out from its secret nest between your sex lips, stretching it until again you gasp and your hips writhe. Yet she continues to pull, as if – or so it seems to you, struggling with your inner self to retain your composure, to hold your hips steady, as if unconcerned and uncaring at this pulling about of your most sensitive flesh. You push your hips forwards and upwards, following her leading fingers. Your clitoris is pulled fully two inches out from its natural position, the tiny stalk suspended from the ring which pierces its outer end.

Abruptly, Madeleine releases the ring. Your stalk springs back a little – but remains revealed, pulled out through your sex lips, unusually prominent.

Next, Madeleine takes from a small circular table set on one corner of the stage, almost hidden in the drawn curtains and thus invisible to the audience, a bright red ball, halfway in size between a golf and tennis ball. Through its centre is a black leather strap with a buckle. She gently places a finger on the point of your chin, the pressure indicating to you that you must open your mouth, and inserts the ball fully between your parted teeth, carefully setting it so that it presses down on your tongue, and then closes your jaw again on the ball. You are effectively gagged, your jaws held open but your tongue and voice silenced so that, should you wish to make any sound, that sound could be no more than a muffled, unintelligible grunt.

Such a gag is new to you: it has never been needed in any of your training sessions, no matter how sharp the lesson to be learned. Occasionally, of course, you have cried out – but screams, until now, have never been any part of your existence. You shudder with foreboding at what this new development may portend: but you have set your hand to the plough. The thought of turning back, of reneging, never enters your mind. Instead, another Rubicon is crossed.

Now Madeleine turns you and leads toward the heavy-set, padded trestle which holds centre stage, and upon which your sacrifice is to be accomplished. Compliantly, you stand before it, your back to the audience, your hips pressed against the padded upper rail. You bend forward and down, leaning over the bar, and reach to grasp the lower rail, spreading your hands apart as you do. You need no instruction. You are the willing accomplice of your own denouement: there is no struggling, no feigned reluctance, no coercion, theatrical or otherwise.

Elaborately, and for the benefit of the audience, Madeleine fastens your wrists to the lower bar, using broad leather cuffs with buckles. She moves to your ankles, which she parts even more widely than your initial stance had assumed, offering as she does so to the audience an even fuller view of your intimate anatomy, wide-spread and open, and fastens your ankles with similar cuffs. The further spreading of your already wide-spread feet settles your hips more firmly against the padded bar of the whipping horse.

You feel your inner flesh being opened and tugged: Madeleine has produced the weight and bell of which Lady

J. warned you. You feel its weight attached to your clitoral ring, feel Madeleine let the weight go, so that it hangs between your spread thighs, feel the stretching of your flesh. Madeleine, and the audience, can see how the weight pulls the pink stalk of your clitoris downwards, hanging vertically towards the floor, apparently lengthening the divided cleft of your sex.

You feel Madeleine's hand brush against your inner thigh, feel your stretched flesh stretched even more, a rhythmic tugging: you sense that Madeleine has caused the weight to swing. You feel Madeleine's hand again, the tugging increases sharply: there is the sound of a tinkling bell. Madeleine is demonstrating to the audience the limits of movement permitted to you. Under your tight-fitting helmet, you blush deeply.

You hear, but do not see, the apparition which materialises on stage beside you – see her only when deliberately, she moves in front of you. You see first the black boots with the extraordinarily high heels; you raise your head, see the rest of the leather-clad figure, encased entirely in a tight fitting suit which moulds exactly, exaggeratedly, to the contours of the body: the legs long, the waist as tightly encircled as your own, the breast-cups of the suit jutting grotesquely.

Like your own, her head is completely enclosed in a close-fitting helmet, with only the eyes visible through slitted eye-holes. You recognise the eyes at once. It is Colette.

Atop the helmet, a bizarre affectation: a long blonde pony-tail, emerging vertically from the helmet to cascade down the back, reminiscent of a Life Guard trooper's plume, reaching almost to shoulder level. It is, of course, an artifice, a hairpiece: but no less striking, compellingly erotic in its contrast – the soft feminine hair against the asexual, androgynous leather.

Colette carries in one gloved hand a long, thin cane: four feet, by your estimation, as thick, perhaps, as a pencil. She bends it, almost double, before your eyes, and those of the audience who have again fallen wholly silent. You allow your head to drop, staring blankly at the floor between your outstretched, shackled wrists.

One cruel refinement remains. Madeleine takes your chin, tilts it upwards, causing you to raise your head. In the mirror ahead of you, you see her affix a silver chain to a ring on the top of your helmet, feel your head pulled back, sense rather than see the other end of the chain clipped to a ring on the waistband of your tight-fitting cuirass, somewhere in the small of your back. The effect is to pull, and keep pulled, your head, tilted back unnaturally, but causing you, despite your bent posture, to stare straight ahead, at the mirror in front of you.

Thus you see yourself, bent as you are over the whipping frame: head low and bent back, arms akimbo and – visible in what to you is the far side of the frame – your wide-parted legs and feet. And you can discern, above the abrupt line of black leather where your cuirass ends, the white, rounded tops of your no-less wide-parted buttocks.

You can also see the black-clad figure of Colette. She stands behind and to one side of you, further from you than the length of the cane would suggest would allow her to reach. Without further ado, she raises the long yellow cane first to shoulder height, pauses – then, half-turning away from you, swings it up and back, her elbow crooked, her arm raised high.

She pauses for long seconds then, in an explosion of released tension, moves her half-twisted body, uncoiling like a highly tensioned steel spring as, with two short, hopping steps towards you, she swings the cane down in a blur of movement.

The pain is acute, but bearable. The cane lands across your bare buttocks like a red-hot firebrand: the first sensation a stinging slash, then a slow-rolling thunder as the heat and hurt flame outwards. Involuntarily your buttocks jerk and clench in response, your heels rise from the floor to tattoo down again in a rapid, nervous reaction. One.

By the end, your grunts at each stroke (you remain stoically silent until the seventh), are loud enough to be heard off-stage. After each, your legs, despite the binding at your ankles, jerk upwards, your buttocks fluttering involuntarily. At the tenth, the tattoo of your heels on the floor, the

211

backs of your wide-parted thighs juddering, cannot be contained: you feel the weight suspended from your clitoris swinging as your hips writhe, tugging out its warning to you, but even as you struggle to control its swing, to press your heels flat on to the floor, keep them there, you hear, like the betraying voice of Judas, the tinkle of the traitorous bell.

Colette, as promised, adds the extra stroke to the twelve prescribed: but you have rung your bell only once.

The picture you present, afterwards, is powerful: from in front of the stage, every aspect of you can be seen, thanks to the carefully positioned mirrors – but it is the unreflected view which is most striking. Your tall black boots stretch outwards and downwards to your pinioned feet. Above them the white columns of your wide-stretched thighs, between which, at their upper junction, glistens the pale pink of the split orb of your sex, the peach-smooth lips with their gold rings slightly parted by your stance, the cleft between lengthened by the unnatural distension of your weighted clitoris, pulling downwards (though in fact, anatomically speaking, upwards, because of your inverted stance), the weight of the gold pendant and bell attached to your distended stem apparent from the way in which your flesh and inner labia are pulled into extension.

And above, the twin globes of your buttocks, creamy-white to begin with, now glow hectically, the thirteen closely spaced horizontal stripes a bright red grille spaced neatly, geometrically, from the crown of the pale sphere to the base, the lowest stripe – the thirteenth and last – broken in its centre by the split peach of the swollen, glistening sex.

Through misted eyes you watch, your strained neck muscles aching from the enforced stretching as your head stares fixedly ahead in its chained constraint, in the mirror ahead of you as Colette turns to face the audience you cannot see. Stepping to one side, she gestures, impresario-like, with her arm towards your bent form as the curtains of the stage swish closed. To your amazement, you hear the incongruous sound of applause before the heavy curtains muffle all.

By the time you are released by Madeleine and walk, stiff-limbed, from the stage Colette, if indeed it was she, has disappeared. Just before you leave, wrapped in a heavy cloak to be ushered to Lady J.'s waiting car, Madeleine pulls the imprisoning leather face-helmet over and off your head, freeing your own short hair before planting a gentle kiss on your cheek.

'There now, Mademoiselle, it was not so bad, *n'est-ce pas?*'

The night air as you step gingerly across the pavement to the waiting car, its door already held open by the impassive Leopold, Lady J.'s faithful driver of whose precise knowledge of your predicament you often wonder but are never told, cools your cheeks, drying the incipient tears while making your eyes water yet again. You do not trust yourself to reply.

A Trial Offer

There is to be no training session, either with your physical
fitness coach Nancy in the basement gymnasium nor with
Monsieur Alcard at the corsetier. Madeleine, who with
your breakfast has brought this letter with the express instruction that you read it through before rising, will report
this evening on your state of health and general feeling,
and it will be decided when your programme is to resume,
if indeed it is to resume at all. For the moment, you are
simply to rest, and recover.

Yesterday was perhaps the most difficult day so far of
the specialised training you have agreed to undergo at
Monsieur Alcard's establishment, and although you have
agreed to accept, to submit yourself to, anything that Monsieur Alcard or Lady J. decrees should be done to you,
yesterday was as extreme as anything you have undergone
to date.

Yesterday you discovered what Lady J. meant when she
spoke of you, to Monsieur Alcard on the day on which you
were first taken to him, while you stood for your inspection, hearing yourself discussed so academically, as if you
were not flesh and blood standing not just within earshot
but where the heat of your body, the rhythm of your
breathing, the glow of your being could be seen and felt by
those discussing so casually the disposition of your flesh.
Lady J. said, 'I repeat that you should know what it is to
be mastered.'

Madeleine, as she had dressed you, had given you your
first hint of what lay in store. Instead of one of your usual
high-topped corsets, those which reach almost to your

breasts, or those which have even some small support for your breasts, lifting and presenting them more formally than even their natural firmness might offer, instead, as I say, of such a corset she laced you instead into what is sometimes known as a 'waspie': tight, of course, as now are all your corsets, but narrow, reaching not even above the lowest ribs, ending high on the hips.

While that in itself was unusual but not unknown, Madeleine had also touched your breasts more than the strict requirement of her dresser's duties entail – a liberty she permitted herself anywhere upon your person only when she knew you were to undergo some particularly stern trial.

'Pauvre Mademoiselle,' she had said, her long fingers gently sweeping over, barely touching, the curve of one of your breasts, touching the nipple lightly, 'it will go hard for you here today, I think.'

'Why? What have they in mind for me today?' you had asked.

'Forgive me, Mademoiselle – I have said too much already. You are not to know the schedule for the day, and what is planned for you, until you arrive at Monsieur Alcard's.' And your maid, confidante and now, as one knows she has become, your close companion and friend, would say no more.

She merely bent her head, the long black hair, potentially so lustrous which, when on duty with you, she wears pulled back into an old-fashioned chignon, glinting glossily in the light. And she had lightly kissed your breasts, first one, then the other.

While you are aware of the affection that has grown between you, such an overt display has hitherto been unheard of. Yet you were touched (metaphorically, as well as literally), by your maid's concern, rather than affronted – very much so, should the truth be told – and your own hand briefly touched the strong, tight roll of rich black hair, your fingertips lingering momentarily – not long enough to offer further invitation, long enough merely to offer a return of fellow-feeling – in the nape of the white

215

and beautiful neck, suddenly rendered so vulnerable by the lowering of the maid's head to your bare bosom.

How vulnerable are we all, you thought.

And we are. All, although you do not realise it.

You, vulnerable in the way in which you have given yourself without reservation to the decisions of others made on your behalf, decisions of which you alone must face the consequences, both immediate and sometimes physical, even briefly – or, as yesterday, acutely – so; and long term, in the yet unanswered question of 'where will this all end?'

And Madeleine, vulnerable to your affection, and your wrath: for while you have not been given any authority to punish Madeleine (you would be, have you realised, were you to ask for such?), any adverse comment on your part regarding your maid, either in her service or in her demeanour toward you, would – as Madeleine well knows, even if you, until this moment, do not – result in Madeleine being punished.

Madeleine, vulnerable also to her own affection. Did you know of the nervousness she herself felt, in bending to bestow the sympathy of her lips upon your flesh? The risk, real or imagined, she felt herself to be running, risk in that you might react negatively to her action: risk of the rejection of the proffered gift of her more intimate affection, risk of the consequences of any objection you might raise, whether in the hurt of a direct rebuke, or in the more palpable hurt of a complaint on your part objecting to her importunity.

And we, who have set you upon this path and are responsible not simply for your tuition – training if you, as do we, prefer – but for your well-being, both from day-to-day while you have given yourself over to our charge, and for the future, whatever it might hold, whatever you might choose, when this training is over. (I almost said 'complete', but can training in such phenomena as you now explore ever be complete?) And even though it will be you who will eventually choose your future, will you not be making that choice under the influence of that which has been placed in your path? We too are therefore vulnerable.

And Madeleine is not alone in her vulnerability to your spell; there are those in whose apparent charge you now rest whose feelings towards you warm with every passing day, with every trial successfully borne, with every complaint left unspoken, with every minor victory. For whose victory is it when your waist is reduced by one more millimetre; when you accept one more demand for effort, or upon your fortitude, and respond; when the strokes you are expected to bear without cry or tear are increased yet again?

We are all vulnerable.

Your sense of apprehension increased when you learned that, unusually, Lady J. would not call for you herself, to take you to lunch before delivering you over to Monsieur Alcard's ministrations for the afternoon. Instead, her car and driver only came to fetch you, later than normal, to take you, after a short drive to kill time, direct to Monsieur Alcard.

When you arrived, you were greeted as usual by the staff, discreetly but with that exquisite mixture of deference and familiarity which is the mark of the best of any establishment, of whatever type, but which is surely nowhere more in keeping, nowhere more appropriate, than in the enforced intimacy of a ladies' corsetier.

It was unusual, too, for Colette, who now attends you so regularly in your sessions with Monsieur Alcard and from whom there can be no possibility of secret concerning you, to accompany you through the discreetly placed and scarcely visible door which leads downstairs to the suite of basement rooms in which your daily trials are accomplished and down the stairs, but not take you through into the changing room where daily those trials begin, with your disrobing.

Instead, you went through the door yourself, to find – most unusually, so unusual in fact that you cannot remember it happening before – Monsieur Gerard Alcard himself waiting for you in person. Normally, of course, Monsieur Alcard does not see you until you have undressed, and have presented yourself for his inspection.

217

This day, however, Monsieur Alcard was waiting for you, in the ante-room.

'Chloe,' he began, having briefly exchanged with you the courtesies of the day, 'before we begin today, it is necessary for you and I to have the small discussion.' And you had learned what lay ahead.

'You know that you have always the right – and indeed the duty – to object to any part of the programme that has been ordained for you but which you do not feel willing to undergo?' It was as much a statement as a question, none the less you nodded silently, suddenly and acutely apprehensive.

'Today, a somewhat special trial has been ordained. It was in fact ordained on the day you first came to me, with Lady J., but it was left to me to decide upon the precise timing, and indeed upon the precise manner, of when and how to proceed.

'I have decided that now is an appropriate time, and have informed Lady J. of my decision. She has accepted my recommendation, but has in addition laid down certain conditions with which, I am bound to say, I entirely and wholly agree.

'Today, I propose to suspend your normal routine of training, dispensing with the usual exercises, and concentrate instead simply upon one area.

'You may recall I asked Lady J., when first you came here, if you had ever felt the crop upon your breasts, and she replied in the negative, adding the suggestion that perhaps it would be a beneficial general adjunct to the more specific aspects of your training if, once at least, you were to have such an experience. That you should learn – if you recall her words precisely – what it is to be mastered. Well, today I propose to offer you this lesson; to remedy, as it were, this defect in your education.

'However,' continued Monsieur Alcard urbanely, as if offering you a choice of cream or milk in your afternoon tea, 'before doing so – and this is the condition upon which Lady J. insists, and about which I agree – I must offer you the opportunity to decline. Unlike other exercises you

218

undertake at my request,' (a quaint way of phrasing things, you thought idly), 'this exercise serves no specific purpose, other than that of broadening your experience, and will surely be an ordeal you are unlikely to enjoy.

'In that circumstance, of course, you as always have the facility to stop the matter in hand immediately, simply by uttering the one word: "enough". And I remind you that no other word, however beseechingly offered, will have such an effect, since in some circumstances the mere act of pleading is itself sufficient palliative to allow the procedure being undergone to be borne, and hence to be continued. Although you have not yet felt the need to make use of this device, if we proceed with what I have planned for you to-day it seems quite likely that at some stage you will need to seek some sort of relief, however temporary.

'You may, therefore, in addition to your safety word use another: you may seek temporary relief by asking to be given a rest. Should you do so, I shall immediately stop, and shall not begin again until you have spoken to me the wordy "Ready". None the less, these precautions notwith-standing, what is proposed for you today demands that you be acquainted with what lies ahead, and given the op-portunity to "walk away", as the Americans would say. There will of course be no recriminations should you so de-cide; our conversation, nor indeed the matter at all, will not be referred to again, and your normal programme will be resumed tomorrow, as if today had never been.'

He paused and, not unkindly, smiled at you.

'I shall leave you for a few moments to decide. If you are still here when I return, I shall take your presence for per-mission to proceed.'

At this Monsieur Alcard made to leave, and would have done so had not your voice immediately arrested him.

'Wait, please. There is no need for you to leave. I am nei-ther deaf, Monsieur, nor devoid of imagination. I well recall the conversation you refer to, and have on several occasions since tried to imagine its realisation. Now, it ap-pears, it is time for me to try reality against imagination. I am already – to use your own catchword – ready.'

Monsieur Alcard's voice was low, kind – almost fatherly. Clearly, he was under instruction, presumably from Lady J., to leave you under no illusions about that to which you were being invited to submit. 'Chloe,' he said, 'I must tell you again. You have occasionally been lightly smacked upon your breasts – but to take the crop is most acute. I wish you to be well aware.'

'Please,' you repeated, 'you have already told me I am not going to enjoy it, and I well believe you – do not frighten me to death before we begin. But I also know that Lady J., if the truth be told, wishes to have me undergo this. And I have no wish to disappoint her, having promised myself to shy from nothing that Lady J. proposes until I have tried it at least once, however uninviting the initial prospect.

'I will not say, for it is simply not true, that I want you to crop my bare breasts. I am not looking forward to this at all, and indeed am more than a little scared, although I confess I am not sure what I am more scared of – the fact that it will quite possibly hurt, or the prospect that I might not be able to take all that you demand. But I suppose,' and here you permitted yourself a small smile of self-admission, 'that I do want to have you be able to tell Lady J., when it is over, that my poor breasts have learned their lesson – and have survived their education.'

'*Vraiment*,' said Monsieur Alcard quietly, '*Chloe tu es une femme très forte*. Very well then. Let us proceed. Please be so kind, Chloe, as to disrobe in your usual and invariably delicious manner.'

And so, your Rubicon was crossed.

The room, the one you always entered first, for it adjoins the small dressing room which you daily occupy, is on this day furnished differently from usual. The straddling frame, the leather-topped trestle and the other accoutrements of your curious schedule have been removed, to be replaced by two items of furniture, one of which is a low, slope-topped kneeling stool, some four-feet long with padded leather top, of the type often found in the confessionals of churches of an Anglican or Roman persuasion.

220

The other is a stoutly built wooden chair, with four square, squat and heavy legs, a low back (the top, like the kneeling stool, padded with plush-red leather and, to judge by the incongruous chrome levers at its base, adjustable for rake and height), and with heavy arms, fashioned in keeping with the powerful legs. At the ends of the arms, opened and waiting, are affixed leather wrist straps, each with a solid brass buckle. You swallow. Nothing yet undergone has required that you be restrained in such a manner. ⌐│

There is also, against one wall, a small Georgian cabinet, incongruous in its drawing room elegance beside the ecclesiastical, almost penitential, kneeling stool and the farmhouse solidity of the chair. The doors of the cabinet are closed.

You undress in the manner and to the degree that is usual for the opening moments of one of your training sessions, that is to say removing all save for shoes, stockings and the corset of the day, and you are thus effectively naked, yet enticingly not quite so, your fair pubic fleece and lush, heavy breasts with their prominent nipples, are fully revealed. Today, instead of the usual routine of display that is now the norm, you simply advance toward the already waiting Monsieur Alcard. Your mentor has been joined by your by now regular attendant at these sessions, Colette, dressed as always on such occasions in old-fashioned black bombazine dress and starched white apron.

You stand, feet together and arms at your sides, waiting now yourself. You are by now used to Monsieur Alcard's intimate knowledge of your body, and stand unconcerned with the fact that your breasts and pubic fleece are on view. Both Monsieur Alcard and Colette have seen it all before.

Monsieur Alcard makes a small gesture towards Colette. 'The rings, if you please, Colette.'

Unspeaking, the maid steps towards you and, carefully, gently, causing you to wince but once, removes the gold rings from your nipples, the tiny twisting movement necessary to open them causing you to purse your lips. The rings opened, you feel them being lightly withdrawn through your nipples.

'Please, kneel on the stool, Chloe, with your knees together and your hands by your sides.'

You obey, kneeling as one would submissively, legs bent double, the backs of your upper thighs resting on the backs of your calves and lower legs, your heels tucked under your buttocks, your arms, as instructed, held loosely by your sides.

'Normally, if one is using a cane or crop to bring a degree of pleasure along with its more obvious attendant sensations, one begins lightly, working ever more forcibly towards severity.

'In view of the singularity of what is required today, I intend to be brusque from the outset. That way, when you realise fully the implications of what Lady J. wishes you to endure, you may find the initial excoriation sufficient for your purpose and hers, and we need delay ourselves no longer.'

Alcard produces, as if from thin air, a slim, black, leather-bound riding crop, no thicker at its thickest than a pencil, tapering even thinner.

'I shall begin with this, and while you hold a simple position of supplication which will allow ready access, I shall strike swiftly across the top of each breast, three strokes. I shall then strike each nipple twice.

'We shall then, I think, stop and re-assess the situation. Assuming you have not by that time experienced enough for one day I shall, with Colette's assistance, then continue your trial. Are you ready?'

'Ready,' is your simple reply, quietly uttered, your throat drying rapidly in nervous anticipation of what lies ahead.

Smiling faintly, Monsieur Alcard momentarily inclines his head in acknowledgement. It is almost a bow in your direction, an executioner paying his respects, perhaps, or the sensei acknowledging the courage of a pupil. Holding the menacing switch in both hands, horizontal before his own torso, he sets about the chastisement of your own.

'Very well, Chloe. We shall begin without further delay. Be so good, please my dear, as to make your nipples erect.'

Unselfconsciously you comply. In the intimacy of your training sessions you have no inhibitions regarding the re-active mechanisms of your body, and teasing your nipples into rigidity – even being required publicly to produce, by your own ministrations, the silver secretions of your sex lips – is now almost commonplace. Reaching with both hands simultaneously you begin to pluck lightly at your nipples, which – already partly aroused by Colette's ma-nipulations while removing your rings – instantly respond, stiffening quickly.

Your breath comes in an increasingly shortened pattern and your nervousness increases, nerves in your stomach tingling and fluttering. This is the sacrificial lamb preparing herself for the slaughter: while the sensation of your nipples stiffening is pleasant, you well know that your erect nipples will now merely be more protrusive, more sensitive, more likely to sting and hurt, when their turn comes.

With your nipples fully erect, stiffened into hard points of sensitivity, blatant in their invitation, you drop your hands again to your sides, waiting passively.

'Kneel upright,' continues Monsieur Alcard, ever the patient instructor, in quiet tones which serve merely to heighten the almost electric tension in the small, suddenly airless room. Beads of perspiration begin to appear upon your brow, you feel a trickle of sweat tickle its way from your armpit. 'Move your arms a little to the rear, to pull your shoulders back and present your breasts properly.'

He moves to a position just behind your left shoulder.

'I shall begin from here. You may prefer to turn your head away.'

Your breath now comes in short, sharp pants, causing your breasts to quiver lightly. You turn your head away, close your eyes, concentrate only on trying to hold your torso steady, your breast thrust outward. The silence, the tension, in the room, is palpable.

'Please,' you plead inwardly, 'just get it over with: let it begin, then at least I shall know. And please, let me be able to show I can take this, too.'

A faint whistling noise answers your unspoken prayer, a

223

crack the loudness of which surprises you, and your breast bounces under the impact of the thin switch.

One.

You gasp, loudly – but hold still. The second stroke, then the third, follow swiftly.

You keep your head turned to the right as Monsieur Alcard briskly steps across to that side, and prepares to repeat the treatment.

'Turn your head the other way, and twist your torso slightly to the left, Chloe: thrust your right breast out more obviously. The invitation thus implied is most important.'

The right breast, offered so eagerly, receives its due, and smarts therefrom.

'Now square your shoulders: offer both breasts together.'

Still working swiftly, Monsieur Alcard steps a little to your front and, swivelling your eyes as far to the right as you can while still turning your head away from the crop you see, from the side of your eye, Monsieur Alcard's elbow rise and then blur downwards, and feel your left nipple sting in a sensation of such acute sharpness that you almost say, as you may and as indeed Monsieur Alcard appears to expect that you will, 'Enough' there and then. But you do not.

Again you nipple is flicked, then two are applied to the right.

Monsieur Alcard pauses. You are breathing hard, head still turned sharply to your left, panting loudly through parted lips, and trembling not a little – but you neither speak nor move. Light red lines traverse the milk-white skin of your breasts, your nipples have reddened perceptibly.

You remain as you are, kneeling upright, but swaying back and forth, your hands grasping your buttocks to give something onto which you might hold, your breath coming in rapid pants. Nothing you have put yourself through until now has been quite like this, quite so – explicit.

You press your upper teeth into your lower lip, sucking in your breath, trying to be quiet but you are heard none the less by Alcard and by Colette. The two watch silently, neither offering aid nor evincing impatience, as you regain your composure. Perhaps three minutes pass before you open your tightly closed eyes.

You wait a moment or two more, before you speak, unsure of your voice.

'Ah, Monsieur Alcard. What can I say? I had no idea . . . If that was merely the opener, what will the rest of the afternoon be like.'

And you resume your high-kneeling position, breasts thrust forward.

'Go on, just go on, please, and let me get it over with.' You pause, drawing deep breaths. Your breathing begins to settle. You look up at Alcard, still standing over you, the crop still dangling loosely from his right hand.

You draw a deep breath, pull your shoulders back, speak but one word.

'Ready.'

But instead of beginning again, Monsieur Alcard assists you to rise. His voice is soft, even affectionate. 'Now that you have that behind you, my dear Chloe, I think we can take a little more time. Please . . .' and he indicates the chair.

You had not seen, having moved straight to kneel on the confessional stool which left you facing the wall, the chair from the front, and your 'Oh no – not that as well' is no charade.

'It will help you hold position, Chloe – and who knows, perhaps even give a little respite when we pause for breath.'

'That' is a thick vertical dowel, an inch-and-a-half in diameter, six inches high and carved into the life-like and realistic shape of an artificial phallus, suitably erect and appropriately positioned in the centre of the chair seat. Of dark, polished wood, it rears compellingly from the centre of the chair seat, its purpose and intent unequivocal. You see that it is not completely straight, but rather it is lightly curved, the head above the base but the stem slightly curved back towards the back of the chair, so that when you have, as you realise you must, lowered yourself onto it, it will hold you fast. To accommodate the dong in comfort, you will have to sit with not only your pelvis tilted forward but your torso also, matching as it were the curve of the rearing monster, and this position will once more thrust your breasts into prominence.

'Set yourself over the upper end of the central dowel, if you please Chloe, and lower yourself down onto it. Colette will open you to assist entry. It has already been lubricated for you – slide yourself down so that the rod is properly embedded. It will make a most secure means of keeping you in position, and may even afford a little pleasure. Once you are firmly down and the rod fully nested, Colette will secure your wrists to the arms of the chair and adjust the chair back to display your breasts to best advantage. Then we can get to work.'

At last, Monsieur Alcard indicates to Colette to release you from your intrusive seat, and bids you to stand, guiding you to move a few feet away from the chair so that you stand alone, uncluttered by furniture. You are weary now of this trial. Your breasts, though in truth not treated as testingly with the light lath or the tease whip as with the initial crop, are now glowing a bright pink, the skin tingling hotly. The brush with which your front was stroked between sessions with the light lath was almost harder to take than the lath itself, the light-as-a-feather drag of the bristles was fiery where the light smacking of the lath had merely smarted, somewhere between heat and hurt.

The implements Monsieur Alcard produced from the elegant Georgian cabinet were all light of weight, designed to tease rather than hurt, but varied and indeed ingenious in their innocuous ability to test your resolve. Once after Colette had introduced you to what she called 'the propeller' – a multi-thonged fly-whisk of vaguely African design, the tails perhaps nine inches long, whirled briskly above your breasts in such a manner that only the tips of the rubber tails smack, lightly but incessantly, against your skin – you are forced to ask for a rest. Colette had followed the propeller with the stiff bristled brush and, halfway through what was the fourth (or was it the fifth?) combing of your breasts you had to beg for a moment's peace. You wondered if that would cause you to fail your test. It did not. Not being prepared to resume would have caused you to fail.

'You have done well, Chloe – but that was really only to be expected,' says Monsieur Alcard as Colette now guides you to a spot in the centre of the room. 'But now we reach the *dénouement*, as we French say. Feet together my dear, stand up straight and clasp your hands behind your neck: it is a familiar and indeed classic pose for you, but one which, for our purpose, cannot be improved upon. It raises and presents your breasts perfectly.'

There cannot, surely, be more. You wonder both how much more you can take and how much more they will ask you to take. You do not wish to fail – cannot, after all this time, fail. But now you do not want to go on. You contemplate rebellion. You have only to say 'Enough', and whatever more is in store for you will stop, at once. The temptation is great. But you go on.

You draw a deep breath, of itself swelling your rib cage and raising your reddened breasts. You close your eyes, slowly roll your head back until your unseeing eyes stare at the ceiling and your head rests, comfortably cushioned, in the clasp of your joined fingers behind your neck. Your elbows come forward, moving together alongside your head, a movement which causes your breasts, still raised, to come closer together on your rib cage, presented even more uniquely and roundly for Monsieur Alcard's and for Lady J.'s final test of your will.

Your breath exhales deeply, draws in again, exhales again, settles. Wearily, not moving your head nor opening your eyes, you say quietly,

'Ready.'

Monsieur Alcard motions once more to your maid for the day, the tall and impassive Colette.

'My dear, if you please.'

Colette moves behind you, the tips of her high-heels clicking on the dark-stained boards of the low dais as she steps up close to your bared back and raised shoulders. You can smell her perfume, sense the warmth of her body on your own bared body, feel her breath on the side of your neck. You feel, briefly, the starch-stiffened front of her uniform, the breasts soft beneath, touch momentarily between your shoulder blades. She reaches, under your raised arms, round in front of you. You lower your gaze, follow the movement of her hands with your eyes, looking down at your pinkly shining breasts.

You see Colette's hands reach for the ends of your breasts to grasp each nipple between finger and thumb, wringing from you a small cry. Squeezing for a better grip, she draws both cones upwards, exposing and stretching the sensitive undersides. Alcard, before you, appears not to move yet the crop flicks lightly, smarting none the less, across the undersides of your breasts, first the left, then the right. Three fast flicks.

'And down, Colette.' Colette releases your nipples, letting your breasts fall again to quiver in the natural position.

'Now face the front, Chloe; present your nipples once more.' You turn your head, your eyes shut tight, the last vestiges of self-control beginning to slip from you, a red sea swimming now beneath your tightly clamped eyelids.

The crop sings, four times, as with teeth bared your breath is drawn in sharply. You clench your jaws together, grinding your teeth to avoid crying aloud.

As quickly as it has begun this, the final stage of your ordeal, stops.

And still you do not weep.

So now you must rest. Madeleine will attend you, as she did last night when you were finally brought home, pale and chastened, your eyes now a little red. Had you wept, unseen, alone in the Lady J.'s car?

'You knew, didn't you?' you asked of Madeleine as she helped you off, gingerly, with your dress. Madeleine knelt to remove your shoes, corset and stockings, the sound of your already running bath loud from the bathroom which adjoins your bedroom. 'You knew.'

'Oui, Mademoiselle, I knew. But Lady J. forbade me to say. And I too have been mastered as you, Mademoiselle. It need not be forever. But Lady J., and Monsieur Stephen, they say of me, when I too was given my Trial, that it is necessary once, at least, for us to know the truth about ourselves and the games we play. Lady J., she told me yesterday that they would do it for you today – but as I say, Mademoiselle – it need not be forever.'

No, Chloe, it need not be forever. But only you can now decide.

Prepared

So you have decided to continue. I am pleased, greatly pleased – indeed relieved. I have become very fond of you these past months, and am loathe to let you go just yet.

Yet let you go I must, and soon. Your training is almost at an end, both in what you have achieved and in that the time to which you agreed is almost up. It is time now to put into practice all that you have learned, to be all that you have become.

You will discontinue your visits to Monsieur Alcard straightaway. Likewise your visits to Nancy, and the gymnasium. Should you wish to continue with your fitness routines, another venue – a regular health centre – can be found but in view of the programme now ordained for you that would appear pointless at the moment.

Instead, you are to be prepared straightaway for presentation – look upon it as your final examination, your graduation ceremony, all rolled into one final evening – at a party I shall arrange where you will be the principal, although not the sole, attraction.

There is little you need to know beforehand. Know only that on that evening you will be dressed as rigorously as you have ever been dressed. Gerard is even now supervising the making of your costume by Colette. Never have you been held more rigidly, never will your waist have been narrower, never will your heels have been higher.

You have grown to enjoy the sight of yourself in such costumes, costumes the outside world might call bizarre. You may imagine yourself now, dressed as you will be on that night.

Tightly masked, your face will be hidden from view, making you both visible and invisible at one and the same time: visible since all can see you, invisible since none can know or recognise you. You will be there, and not there.

Your breasts will not be hidden, but displayed in a way both familiar and as never before. You must bear their decoration with patience, as I know you will, so you may present them with pride. It will, estimates Colette, take some two hundred and fifty tiny jewels, each no bigger than a large bread-crumb, each set in a special varnish which must first be painted on to your gleaming skin, to achieve the illusion desired. She estimates also that it will take some twenty minutes to arrange them neatly in place. They are too fine to be handled by hand, and must therefore be set upon your flesh using fine tweezers, once your nipples and the greater haloes of your breasts have been coated. The intention is to encrust, entirely and so that the natural areola be covered, be be-jewelled, completely, the whole of the halo which crowns each proud orb. I am sure you will show the fortitude you have come to learn and I – we – have come to expect while you are thus jewelled.

In regard to the new rings to which I have just alluded, Madeleine will take you to the jewellers tomorrow at ten am. Your present rings will be removed and the new rings of which I speak fitted. At the same time, your nipples will be re-pierced and a second set of rings fitted, behind the original set which are, now that your nipples have lengthened and thickened, nearer the tip of your nipple than its base. The final effect will be for you to be double-ringed: the rings in the new piercings will be larger in diameter, though no thicker, than your existing rings.

Your breasts thus displayed and decorated, you will be put on show. But you are to be more than a mere object of display, of visual delight. Your final examination will have its rigorous moments – but already, I reveal too much.

Know then only this more: You will be given to and taken by strangers, whipped at least once.

Afterwards, you will be free to go.

231

This final act in your training will be held in ten days time, a week on Saturday, at Lady J.'s residence, in the country. This afternoon, Wednesday, you will go shopping. This evening dine with Lady J. and with Stephen.

Tomorrow, Thursday, Lady J. will come for you at lunch time. Before that, when you return from the jewellers, Madeleine will prepare you for one more nuance of enhancement. Using a small pair of jewellers' pliers, she will snip the gold wire and remove the small gold ring which was originally fitted through your clitoris and which, at your request, cannot be opened. It has served its purpose.

Lady J. will deliver you to a discreet and highly specialised jeweller. You will be left there. When you are at the jewellers you will be required, in addition to baring your breasts and nipples, to bare also your most intimate self. In the piercing just vacated by your clitoral ring will be fitted instead an emerald stud, thicker in its diameter than the rod from which your original ring was made. To fit your jewel it may be necessary for the jeweller to manipulate your clitoris first into considerable extension. You should know that he has both the permission and the trust of Lady J. – and indeed of myself. You are to permit whatever is required.

The emerald stud can be removed at will. This is intentional. When you have finished at the jewellers you will have just ten days until your final ordeal. Lady J.'s car will collect you direct from the jewellers, your cases and other luggage will have already been packed. From the jewellers, you will be driven to the country, to Hampshire.

There, you will spend your final ten days of training with Camille.

232

Circles

The control you exercise is now complete. At the house party which was, in effect, your final examination, your mastery of the situation was total. All the guests speak of none but you: who are you, where did you come from, where are you going?

Your appearance was electric: from the high plume atop your helmeted, high-collared head to the heels of your shining patent boots. Your breasts, jewelled and gleaming in their taut constraint through the breast-holes of your cuirass, jutted more magnificently than ever before. You bore with stoicism and pride the necessary discomfort of their display, from your solidity as Colette tightened to new levels of constriction the hoops binding their base, forcing them outwards in numbed erection, causing the skin to shine pinkly, the tips and nipples to purple in royal richness, to your fortitude as she applied first the varnish, then the jewelled crumbs themselves.

The varnish, with its soft camel-hair brush, had seemed innocuous to start – so much so that you wondered as to the weight of foreboding placed upon you by my earlier warning. It was only as the first coat began to dry and harden that you realised what was then in store: it re-minded you of Monsieur Alcard's itching powder, seemingly so long ago. You see, my dear Chloe, how all is come together. There is nothing, as the American writer Melville once expressed it, that we do in this life nor that is done to us but that it prepares us for something else. All, in the end, is benefit. Thus with Monsieur Alcard's silly little itching powder games. How else could you have endured the ever tightening grip of the hardening crystal around the sensitive tips of your enforcedly engorged cones. An itch to end all itches – repeated not once, but twice: once for the initial coating, a second time for the coat required to soften the varnish again so that the jewel-crust could be applied. The heat – how like your candle wax sheath – was generated by what is known as thermo-plastic reaction: it is a phenomenon well known to all who work with epoxy varnish. And now to you, also.

The matching emerald stud fitted earlier through your clitoris was perfect, and how your stalk itself, reddened and swollen still from Camille's constant and rigorous ministrations, stood proud and protrusive, freed now from the constraining shroud of its enveloping hood.

Fine gold chains ran from the rings of your sex, through small rings on the front of your rigid corset at your waist, to the rings of your nipples, a final loop of chain joining each and hanging in a glinting loop below your shining breasts.

So for almost an hour you stood, immobile, a magnificent living statue, as the guests admired you. Your rigid breasts, reddened by the pressure of their constraint, literally shone and glistened with the fine oil Madeleine had lightly massaged into them to ease their throbbing once the breast hoops of your costume had been wound tight. The plentiful candlelight – you noticed, of course, how you had been placed so carefully between two laden free-standing candelabra? It was a refinement of which I was particularly proud – the plentiful candlelight, as I say, danced in myriad beams and flashes from the close-packed jewels clustered so heavily at the tips of your breasts and even on your thickened nipples.

The fine gold chains linking these double-ringed berries and your double-ringed sex glinted below in the glow of the single candle, tall on its long candlestick, placed between your parted feet, its heat gradually warming the bare and carefully depilated lips of your sex, its reflection flickering off the jewel of your distended stem.

After the long period of immobility – how splendid you

looked – perhaps the most severe test, if only because so unfamiliar, never introduced in your training. But your training saw you through. You trusted Lady J.'s instruction that, if you did exactly as she told you, you would not be burned: a mild stinging sensation, not wholly unpleasant, was what she promised – provided you did not falter. Carefully, at her instruction, you moved your feet wider apart, easing open the lips of your sex, until you could feel the candle-heat rise directly into your pink and glistening core. Catching the dangling loops of chain at your finger-ends, you as instructed placed a hand on each hip, feeling the tugging underneath as the action drew wide with each hand the chain looped in the fingers, the chains in turn pulling on the rings, opening wider that part of you to which they were attached. You felt the candle flame's heat rise within you, within the centre of your pink opened being.

The long mirror placed before you enabled you to see yourself full-length, know exactly what to do when Lady J. gave you the command, before so many, to snuff the candle. You paused but briefly, steeling yourself: then you flexed and opened your thighs, opening wider yet the mouth of your sex as, your torso held still erect, you dipped your hips in one sudden, deep movement, plunging straight downwards, taking as it seemed the tiny flame within you even as it died in your moment of self-immolation.

You paused, the snuffed candle-end held fast, embedded within you.

From the watching guests, summoned by Lady J. as witnesses to a demonstration, there came, incongruous, a tiny ripple of applause. Inwardly, you glowed with satisfaction. You had clearly passed.

Then you yourself were taken, to be bent forward over your trestle, feet wide planted, your upper body rigid and horizontal, your arms pulled forward to the pillar to which they had been bound, so that you might be, and were, taken by any who wished it. Eight male guests, one following upon the other, took you thus, to leave your sex gaping, glistening, thickened.

After, your whipping, still bent over the trestle, witnessed by all: the final strokes fell across the plump and opened sex as the plume atop your helmet tossed. You were glad then of the gag which you gripped between your teeth, held fast by the silver buckles at each side of the soft face mask of your helmet.

That should have been all your trial. It was not I who ordained, but you who permitted, this your final test to be extended.

Senõr Alvarez who, once you had been released and cleaned by Madeleine, asked for, and to whom you gave, permission to use the switch upon your breasts, in private, is now your devoted slave and wishes to purchase you at whatever cost. I have taken the liberty of assuring him that you are not for sale.

Your ordeal with Senõr Alvarez was not entirely private. I, who have watched and watched over you, also took the precaution of being present, if discreetly and unknown to either of you, to ensure that no harm befall you. I saw all. Saw you present as instructed by the Spaniard, hands behind your neck, as first the slim gold chains clipped to your nipple rings were unhooked, to dangle loosely from your ringed sex. Saw you, at his murmured command, lean forwards, arching your spine and craning back your neck and head to leave the way clear for the slim but wicked little lightweight switch. *La cravache petite* as the French call it. The Lady Whip. Saw you calmly, unflinchingly, receive its caress across your stiffened bosom.

And saw, too, your riposte, your final posture, assumed not at any instruction or request from your catechist, but by your own volition. Dumb within your face mask, you gestured for a moment's respite; he thought he had humbled you.

Instead you knelt, thighs straight, then leant back, your back arched, hands on heels, so that your gleaming breasts – held so rigid and conical by the constraint of the hoops which bound so tight around the base of each, encrusted with their tiny jewels at each tip – thrust directly upwards so that their tenderest underside might in turn receive and accept their trial.

236

The tight helmet of your costume prevented speech, but not communication. You raised your hands, three fingers of each extended, splayed, then with one scarlet, painted fingernail, its sharpened point leaving a faint white line across your tautened skin, you drew three times across your flesh, below the jewelled nipple, where the rod was to strike. Reaching again once more for your heels, you arched your back further, and waited. And as your amazed preceptor prepared to offer his homage to your beauty, you moved your knees wide apart, revealing all within.

Afterwards you rose, the lines pink and bright across and under your smooth and shining bosom, and turned and left, to leave our grandee humbled, and enthralled. Only Madeleine, as she removed your helmet, saw the tears that glistened still in your eyes.

And none is more totally in your thrall than I, in whose house you first felt your waist encircled by a corset, in whose house you first tasted the crop, in whose house your gift to your lover was accomplished, in whose house your first tentative steps in training and self-control were taken.

Lady J. and I have nothing more to teach you. You have mastered all. The next step is yours, and yours alone: you may, of course, simply bring this small experiment to an end, a diversion now to be done with. The arrangements originally made for you still stand.

Or you may, if you wish, come back to the house, my house, its wished-for mistress. In complete control.

Madeleine, who is both your maid and servant, will convey your decision to me.

In the meantime, I remain, Chloe,

Your architect, your mentor,

Your Obedient Servant,

Stephen.

NEW BOOKS

Coming up from Nexus and Black Lace

Different Strokes by Sarah Veitch
August 1995   Price: £4.99   ISBN: 0 352 33020 1
What do an impudent secretary, a careless maid and a negligent slimmer have in common? Answer: a sore bottom. And they're not alone. This collection features twenty-two stories of submission and discipline from the undisputed mistress of CP.

Letters to Chloe by Stefan Gerrard
August 1995   Price: £4.99   ISBN: 0 352 33021 X
Found in a briefcase in an old London mansion, the letters document an extraordinary and passionate relationship: a relationship that stretches the boundaries of trust, obedience and power. Each letter persuades Chloe to break a new taboo, and each taboo takes her to previously unimagined heights of arousal.

A Matter of Possession by G. C. Scott
September 1995   Price: £4.99   ISBN: 0 352 33027 9
Barbara Hilson is looking for a special kind of man; a man who can impose himself upon her so strongly that her will dissolves into his. In the meantime, she has other options – like an extensive collection of bondage equipment, and her glamorous and obliging friend Sarah.

The Island of Maldona by Yolanda Celbridge
September 1995   Price: £4.99   ISBN: 0 352 33028 7
Jana, imperious leader of the female order of Maldona, is restless. A rapturous dream inspires her to take a party of her most nubile and obedient followers on a grand erotic adventure to the Aegean. But soon her position as Supreme Mistress comes under threat from a gorgeous woman claiming to be Aphrodite.

The Intimate Eye by Georgia Angelis
August 1995   Price: £4.99   ISBN: 0 352 33004 X
The construction of Sir Horace Balfour's country estate is driving his wife to distraction – though not as much as the sweaty, muscular torsos of the labourers. With the arrival of Joshua Foxe, the rakishly handsome artist commissioned to paint the family portrait, it seems her brimming desires are destined to spill over into full-blown indiscretion.

The Amulet by Lisette Allen
August 1995   Price: £4.99   ISBN: 0 352 33019 8
In a Celtic tribe near York, Catrina is training to become a priestess when a captured Roman legionary brings a new dimension to her life. But no sooner has she fallen in love with him than he steals her mystical amulet and escapes to Rome. Catrina sets out for the city of decadence prepared to do anything to retrieve her precious charm.

Conquered by Fleur Reynolds
September 1995   Price: £4.99   ISBN: 0 352 33025 2
16th-century Peru, and the Inca women are at the mercy of the marauding conquistadors. Princess Inez eludes their clutches and sets out to find her missing lover, only to be taken prisoner by an Amazonian tribe. But her quest is soon forgotten when she is initiated into some very strange and very sensual rites.

Dark Obsession by Fredrica Alleyn
September 1995   Price: £4.99   ISBN: 0 352 33026 0
Annabel Moss had never thought interior design a particularly raunchy profession – until she was engaged at Leyton Hall. The Lord and Lady, their eccentric family and the highly disciplined staff all behave impeccably in company, but at night, the oaken doors conceal some decidedly kinky activities.

NEXUS BACKLIST

All books are priced £4.99 unless another price is given. If a date is supplied, the book in question will not be available until that month in 1995.

CONTEMPORARY EROTICA

THE ACADEMY	Arabella Knight	
CONDUCT UNBECOMING	Arabella Knight	Jul
CONTOURS OF DARKNESS	Marco Vassi	
THE DEVIL'S ADVOCATE	Anonymous	
DIFFERENT STROKES	Sarah Veitch	Aug
THE DOMINO TATTOO	Cyrian Amberlake	
THE DOMINO ENIGMA	Cyrian Amberlake	
THE DOMINO QUEEN	Cyrian Amberlake	
ELAINE	Stephen Ferris	
EMMA'S SECRET WORLD	Hilary James	
EMMA ENSLAVED	Hilary James	
EMMA'S SECRET DIARIES	Hilary James	
FALLEN ANGELS	Kendal Grahame	
THE FANTASIES OF JOSEPHINE SCOTT	Josephine Scott	
THE GENTLE DEGENERATES	Marco Vassi	
HEART OF DESIRE	Maria del Rey	
HELEN – A MODERN ODALISQUE	Larry Stern	
HIS MISTRESS'S VOICE	G. C. Scott	
HOUSE OF ANGELS	Yvonne Strickland	May
THE HOUSE OF MALDONA	Yolanda Celbridge	
THE IMAGE	Jean de Berg	Jul
THE INSTITUTE	Maria del Rey	
SISTERHOOD OF THE INSTITUTE	Maria del Rey	

JENNIFER'S INSTRUCTION	Cyrian Amberlake	
LETTERS TO CHLOE	Stefan Gerrard	Aug
LINGERING LESSONS	Sarah Veitch	Apr
A MATTER OF POSSESSION	G. C. Scott	Sep
MELINDA AND THE MASTER	Susanna Hughes	
MELINDA AND ESMERALDA	Susanna Hughes	
MELINDA AND THE COUNTESS	Susanna Hughes	
MELINDA AND THE ROMAN	Susanna Hughes	
MIND BLOWER	Marco Vassi	
MS DEEDES ON PARADISE ISLAND	Carole Andrews	
THE NEW STORY OF O	Anonymous	
OBSESSION	Maria del Rey	
ONE WEEK IN THE PRIVATE HOUSE	Esme Ombreux	Jun
THE PALACE OF SWEETHEARTS	Delver Maddingley	
THE PALACE OF FANTASIES	Delver Maddingley	
THE PALACE OF HONEYMOONS	Delver Maddingley	
THE PALACE OF EROS	Delver Maddingley	
PARADISE BAY	Maria del Rey	
THE PASSIVE VOICE	G. C. Scott	
THE SALINE SOLUTION	Marco Vassi	
SHERRIE	Evelyn Culber	May
STEPHANIE	Susanna Hughes	
STEPHANIE'S CASTLE	Susanna Hughes	
STEPHANIE'S REVENGE	Susanna Hughes	
STEPHANIE'S DOMAIN	Susanna Hughes	
STEPHANIE'S TRIAL	Susanna Hughes	
STEPHANIE'S PLEASURE	Susanna Hughes	
THE TEACHING OF FAITH	Elizabeth Bruce	
THE TRAINING GROUNDS	Sarah Veitch	
UNDERWORLD	Maria del Rey	

EROTIC SCIENCE FICTION

ADVENTURES IN THE PLEASUREZONE	Delaney Silver	
RETURN TO THE PLEASUREZONE	Delaney Silver	

FANTASYWORLD	Larry Stern	
WANTON	Andrea Arven	

ANCIENT & FANTASY SETTINGS

CHAMPIONS OF LOVE	Anonymous	
CHAMPIONS OF PLEASURE	Anonymous	
CHAMPIONS OF DESIRE	Anonymous	
THE CLOAK OF APHRODITE	Kendal Grahame	
THE HANDMAIDENS	Aran Ashe	
THE SLAVE OF LIDIR	Aran Ashe	
THE DUNGEONS OF LIDIR	Aran Ashe	
THE FOREST OF BONDAGE	Aran Ashe	
PLEASURE ISLAND	Aran Ashe	
WITCH QUEEN OF VIXANIA	Morgana Baron	

EDWARDIAN, VICTORIAN & OLDER EROTICA

ANNIE	Evelyn Culber	
ANNIE AND THE SOCIETY	Evelyn Culber	
THE AWAKENING OF LYDIA	Philippa Masters	Apr
BEATRICE	Anonymous	
CHOOSING LOVERS FOR JUSTINE	Aran Ashe	
GARDENS OF DESIRE	Roger Rougiere	
THE LASCIVIOUS MONK	Anonymous	
LURE OF THE MANOR	Barbra Baron	
RETURN TO THE MANOR	Barbra Baron	Jun
MAN WITH A MAID 1	Anonymous	
MAN WITH A MAID 2	Anonymous	
MAN WITH A MAID 3	Anonymous	
MEMOIRS OF A CORNISH GOVERNESS	Yolanda Celbridge	
THE GOVERNESS AT ST AGATHA'S	Yolanda Celbridge	
TIME OF HER LIFE	Josephine Scott	
VIOLETTE	Anonymous	

THE JAZZ AGE

BLUE ANGEL NIGHTS	Margarete von Falkensee	
BLUE ANGEL DAYS	Margarete von Falkensee	

BLUE ANGEL SECRETS	Margarete von Falkensee	
CONFESSIONS OF AN ENGLISH MAID	Anonymous	
PLAISIR D'AMOUR	Anne-Marie Villefranche	
FOLIES D'AMOUR	Anne-Marie Villefranche	
JOIE D'AMOUR	Anne-Marie Villefranche	
MYSTERE D'AMOUR	Anne-Marie Villefranche	
SECRETS D'AMOUR	Anne-Marie Villefranche	
SOUVENIR D'AMOUR	Anne-Marie Villefranche	

SAMPLERS & COLLECTIONS

EROTICON 1	ed. J-P Spencer	
EROTICON 2	ed. J-P Spencer	
EROTICON 3	ed. J-P Spencer	
EROTICON 4	ed. J-P Spencer	
NEW EROTICA 1	ed. Esme Ombreux	
NEW EROTICA 2	ed. Esme Ombreux	
THE FIESTA LETTERS	ed. Chris Lloyd	£4.50

NON-FICTION

HOW TO DRIVE YOUR MAN WILD IN BED	Graham Masterton	
HOW TO DRIVE YOUR WOMAN WILD IN BED	Graham Masterton	
LETTERS TO LINZI	Linzi Drew	
LINZI DREW'S PLEASURE GUIDE	Linzi Drew	

Please send me the books I have ticked above.

Name ....

Address ....

....

....

..................Post code ....

Send to: **Cash Sales, Nexus Books, 332 Ladbroke Grove, London W10 5AH.**

Please enclose a cheque or postal order, made payable to **Nexus Books,** to the value of the books you have ordered plus postage and packing costs as follows:

UK and BFPO – £1.00 for the first book, 50p for each subsequent book.

Overseas (including Republic of Ireland) – £2.00 for the first book, £1.00 for the second book, and 50p for each subsequent book.

If you would prefer to pay by VISA or ACCESS/MASTER-CARD, please write your card number and expiry date here:

....

Please allow up to 28 days for delivery.

Signature ....
